# GODDESS FORSAKEN

---

## RISE OF THE LOST GODS - BOOK 1

### NICOLE HALL

*To everyone, you are worthy of love*

**1**

---

*Lindsey*

HOW HAD she lived so long without a hot tub? Lindsey Haven inched lower until the water covered her head, allowing the jet to hit her sore shoulder muscle. A meathead in Detroit had come after her with a metal pipe, and she'd taken a hit before she'd subdued him. The bruising had finally faded, but the muscles were still pissed.

Thanks to Sabine and Alex's offer of their house, Lindsey could take a break for the summer. Avoid any more meatheads while she figured out what the hell had been happening to her. Strange lights no one else saw, faint voices no one else heard, and worst of all, random fires that no one else could have caused. Technically, she couldn't have caused them either, but seeing flames erupt from literally nothing—more than once—had made her a quick believer.

Lindsey pushed the memories away. She had a summer of solitude, starting now, to figure out what was happening. The pressure and the hum of the vibrating jets against her skin allowed her to focus on something besides the turmoil of her thoughts.

As long as she could hold her breath, the world—and all her problems—would cease to exist. Though Lindsey had never been one to hide from the hard stuff, she stayed right there under the water until her lungs burned for air.

When she surfaced with a gasp, the last thing she expected to see was another person watching her from the deck. A tall, good-looking man wearing black swim trunks and nothing else. Her gaze tripped up the sleek muscles on display to his face where it stopped on high cheekbones and piercing hazel eyes.

Adrenaline zipped through her system as she took stock of her situation. No weapons in her bikini or the hot tub, but she'd taken down bigger guys on her own. He stood at the far edge of the patio with his arms loose at his sides, but his artful nonchalance belied an alertness that made her nervous. The water would offer a certain amount of slippery protection, but she'd move better on land.

Lindsey stood, then gingerly stepped onto the deck. His focus stayed firmly on her face, points for that, and the appreciation there triggered an answering fire in her belly. She didn't have a problem with the attraction, especially when it seemed to be mutual, but trespassing was a solid no-no, even for sexy criminals.

He smiled slowly and lifted his hands in surrender. "I come in peace."

"That's reassuring. This is private property. Who are you, and what are you doing here?"

"I'm Dax, and I live here. At least for the next couple of months. Who are you?"

Lindsey's eyes narrowed. Granted, she'd been tired when she'd fielded the call from Sabine a few days before asking her to house-sit, but she'd have remembered any mention of a dangerously attractive man staying there with her. He definitely hadn't been around when she'd arrived earlier after driving south for almost twenty hours.

"Lindsey. Got any proof you're supposed to be here?"

He jerked his head at her phone, sitting on a chaise next to her. "Call Alex. I assume you have his number since I found you relaxing in his hot tub."

Lindsey watched him while she scooped up the phone and speed dialed Sabine.

"Hey Lindsey, did you make it in all right?"

"Do you know a Dax?"

The pause on the other end of the line told her Sabine had definitely kept some information to herself. "Yes."

"Can you describe him please?"

Sabine chuckled. "His last name is Russell. Tall, dark hair, hazel eyes. Wicked grin. Even more wicked sense of humor. Looks like he belongs on the cover of a romance novel. I think he—"

A shuffle and a thud in the background interrupted her, then Alex came on the line. "Dax is doing a job for me, and I insisted he stay at the house."

Lindsey didn't talk to Alex often, but there was no mistaking the command in his voice. "Sabine asked me to house-sit while you guys were gone for the summer."

He sighed. "I'm aware. I forgot to warn Dax."

Irritation tightened her grip on the phone. She had other places she could go, but none immediately. And none where she wouldn't be putting people in danger. "If Dax will be here, it doesn't sound like you need a house-sitter."

"Maybe not, but Sabine had her reasons for asking you. If you'd rather not stick around—"

Another jostle as Sabine shouted something that

sounded suspiciously like *traitor*. Suddenly, she was back, breathless.

"This was all last minute when Alex accepted the contract with this new company, and the assholes insisted we had to work in their office. We couldn't pass up the chance for the business. It's only for the summer. I'm sorry for springing Dax on you, but we have plenty of space in the house. You won't even notice him. Please stay."

Lindsey watched heat flare in Dax's eyes as he stared back at her, waiting for judgement. Sabine was wrong. The house could have separate wings and she'd notice him.

She was on the verge of a polite refusal when a flash of light near the back door behind him caught her attention. It was there and gone in an instant, so Lindsey couldn't be sure she'd even seen it, just like all the other times. But unlike before, the quiet female voice in her mind came through crystal clear.

*You need to stay.*

She didn't react. Lindsey *knew* she didn't react, but when her attention returned to him, Dax's smile had disappeared. His brow furrowed, and he took a step forward. When Lindsey held up a hand, he stopped immediately. The show of patience surprised her.

Maybe ten seconds had passed, but Lindsey's perspective had changed. If she wasn't going insane—and she'd never really entertained that possibility—the voice was stronger here. She'd need to stay to find out why.

Lindsey could live with Dax. When compared to the other weird stuff happening, he was the least of her worries, assuming he could protect himself. Especially when he followed unspoken orders so nicely.

Sabine wasn't as easy-going. "Lindsey? You better not have hung up on me. I thought we were friends."

"I'm still here. I promised I'd stay, and I'll stay. Next time, give me a little heads-up, okay?"

Sabine cleared her throat. "Of course. Do you need anything else?"

"No, I'm good. If I have any other questions, I'll call."

"Great." Sabine hesitated, then spoke softly. "You can trust Dax, you know. Whatever you're dealing with, he might be able to help."

Lindsey scoffed. "I'll keep that in mind. Go back to whatever you were doing before I interrupted you. Crisis averted."

Sabine chuckled. "Gladly."

The call ended, but Lindsey took a moment to gather herself before she lowered the phone. Dealing with strange half-naked men was a skill she'd had to hone for her job, but she'd left the zip ties in the SUV with the rest of her gear, and she suspected that method would lead to a whole different place with this particular man.

The moment she lowered her arm, Dax's smile returned. "Am I cleared?"

"For now."

If she hadn't been well-trained, she might not have noticed the minute release of tension from his shoulders. Then again, it wasn't her training that had her staring at his chest. "Looks like we're roomies for the summer. Unless *you'd* rather go somewhere else…"

He laughed and crossed the patio toward her. "You're not getting off that easily."

Lindsey maintained her position, not sure what to make of him, but he stopped next to the hot tub stairs. "Want to join me?"

*Yes. Hard yes.* But giving in to temptation this early would be a mistake. "No, thank you."

"Such civility. I get it though. You don't know me. It's natural to be afraid."

Her brows rose. "I'm not afraid of you."

Dax hopped in and settled on the far side of the water. "Prove it. Stay and have a conversation with me. It might be nice to get to know the person you'll be spending the summer with."

Lindsey crossed her arms. "I think this manipulative little demonstration tells me everything I need to know."

His smile only widened. "How about if I ask nicely? Will you please do me the honor of keeping me company for a little bit?"

A twitch of her lips threatened to ruin her 'take me seriously' face. The man was charming; she'd give him that. The air outside wasn't cold—it was June in Texas, after all—but her muscles were stiffening up after the languid heat of the water. Maybe a few more minutes. Besides, gathering information about him might help her avoid him in the future.

Lindsey put her phone back on the chaise and climbed into the hot tub opposite him. He had the grace not to gloat, but triumph edged into his grin.

She sank down until the water lapped at her chin. "You can have five minutes of my time."

"I'll take what I can get. Why are you here, Lindsey no-last-name?"

Subtle, he wasn't, but Lindsey appreciated the straightforward approach, even if she didn't practice it. "Haven. My last name is Haven. Sabine asked me to house-sit. She wanted someone to take care of her cat and...other things."

He tilted his head. "Why did you accept?"

Lindsey shrugged. "Why not?" She deflected out of habit, then studied him. "What about you? Why are you here?"

Dax didn't sidestep the answer as she had. "Alex offered me my dream job on a silver platter, with one stipulation. I had to use my considerable skills on a different job, only for the summer, with his house as the home base."

He paused, searching for the right words. "I was already thinking of moving nearby. There's something about this place. Not the house necessarily, but the whole area. The first time I visited it just...clicked, you know? I'm supposed to be here."

Lindsey understood what he meant. Alex and Sabine had built the deck up next to the hot tub and put a couple of lounge chairs around the raised portion. Stairs led down to the stone patio and the path ended at the back door. On the surface, her view toward the house mimicked any other suburban backyard, but beyond the railing on every other side, the trees grew wild. A sense of purpose hung in the air.

He'd put into words the feeling she'd been trying to ignore since she'd driven up the gravel driveway. A click, as if she'd finally found where she belonged. She'd lived all over the country, but no place had felt like home in the way these woods did.

Except she didn't believe in fate or destiny or whatever he thought was happening. With her past, she preferred an untethered existence. Home only built disappointment.

Lindsey swiped at the bubbles floating near her face. "What's your dream job?"

The moment passed, and Dax focused on her again. "Cyber-security in the private sector. What do you do when you're not house-sitting?"

She pursed her lips. No harm in telling him what he could find out with a simple Google search. "Mostly I'm a retrieval specialist."

Dax grinned. "You're a bounty hunter?"

"It's not as thrilling as it sounds."

He studied the parts of her visible through the churning water. "I'll bet it's plenty thrilling. I can see you as a bounty hunter, actually. You're in great shape, and you're confident without being cocky. You should own the title though. For the coolness factor if nothing else."

"Yeah, well I'm not interested in the coolness factor, I guess. I also do odd jobs repairing things while I'm in town. People are more likely to cooperate if they think you're helpful."

"When I want people to cooperate, I tell them I'm a hacker for the government. The title impresses them."

She toyed with asking what Alex had him doing for the summer, but she wasn't ready to hear about Dax's 'considerable skills' just yet. "That's not what you told *me*."

He shifted, sending ripples of water toward her. "I'd rather impress you in more...meaningful ways."

His low voice scraped along her nerve endings and spread a flush across her face. Five minutes had come and gone, but despite her intentions, Lindsey wasn't in any hurry to leave. That realization alone blared a warning through her head. She was tired and unsettled, not the best mindset to deal with a seductive roommate. Especially when she kept involuntarily imagining what it would feel like to run her hands down the planes of his chest.

"I'd better go in. It's getting a little too warm for me."

Dax raised a brow and reached toward her. For a split second, Lindsey thought he'd read her mind, but his arm went past her to adjust the temperature. He smirked and took his time with the buttons.

The motion brought him closer than he'd been since they'd met, and Lindsey forced a slow, calming breath. She certainly wasn't immune, but she refused to give him the satisfaction of reacting. Dax was testing her, and she'd be damned if she'd give him a reason to think her weak.

As he returned to his seat, his leg grazed hers. A ghost of a touch, but reverberations shot through her. Heat pooled low in her belly, and Lindsey had to cover her gasp with a yawn. Sweet mother of dragons, she'd gone too long without sex if an innocent brush of skin had her ready to jump in his lap. Too bad for him she'd had a lot of practice taking care of that particular need herself.

He sat back with his arms spread along the lip of the hot tub and searched her face. "Better?"

At least she could blame the steaming water for her red cheeks. "Thanks, but I'm still heading inside."

He sighed, then levered himself out of the water and over the edge before she could act on her words. "I'm definitely getting a hot tub when I buy my own place."

Water streamed over lean muscle, and the late afternoon sun peeked through the canopy of trees to surround him in a golden glow. Even Mother Nature knew the man was beautiful, and the whole situation reeked of temptation. The fluid grace of his movements distracted her until she realized he was reaching for *her* towel.

"Hey! Hands off." Lindsey smoothly vaulted onto the deck using her good arm and made a grab for the material.

Dax was closer. He snatched the towel and held it behind him. "I was here first."

Lindsey's heart raced at the dare in his tone. "The hell you were, and what is this...elementary school?"

He shrugged—again with the maddening grin—and raised the towel out of her reach. "Finders keepers. You want it? Come get it."

The thrill of challenge set off her competitive streak. He wanted to play? That was fine with her. Lindsey didn't lose.

She faked a defeated slump, then lunged when he relaxed a smidge. Dax held his ground, not budging an inch, but she'd anticipated that. Surprise lit up his features when she edged past him and used the lounge chair to bound up at the towel.

Had he been any slower, the gambit would have worked, but the man had lightning-fast reflexes. He spun and caught her around the waist mid-air, keeping the towel out of her reach.

The maneuver pressed her flush against him as he absorbed most of her momentum. Dax's arm stayed around her even after her toes reached the wooden planks, and she could feel just how much he was enjoying this little exercise. He wasn't the only one. Her lips parted on a shallow breath, and his gaze dropped to her mouth.

Dax leaned in, and his arm lowered just enough. She braced one palm against his chest and leapt for the prize.

Her fingers brushed the towel, but a sharp pain shot through her shoulder and down her back, making her hiss. Dax's arm around her tensed, and Lindsey let him take her weight while the throbbing waves subsided.

She'd stupidly forgotten about her injury. Damn that asshole and his pipe.

Lindsey clenched her jaw against the spasm. In her current state, she was no match for Dax physically. Screw it, let him keep the towel. She could clean up any water she dripped on the floors later. Or *he* could.

Dax's eyes narrowed as she carefully straightened. "You're hurt."

"I'm fine." The ache had faded enough that she could move again, so it wasn't entirely a lie.

"You're not fine." He stepped back and draped the towel around her, breaking all contact. "What happened?"

"None of your business."

His stiff posture relaxed at her terse response. He tsked and shook out his wet hair with his hands. "Keeping it a secret only makes me want to find out more. One more question. For each of us. In the spirit of newfound friendship."

Lindsey took her time running the towel over her limbs. She still had several outstanding questions for him, but one would do. "Okay. In the spirit of friendship...but I get to go first. How do you know Alex and Sabine?"

"I met Alex in training. He was my only competition for top marks in class."

Sabine had mentioned something about Alex being in the Army, but honestly, Lindsey had only been half paying attention. She allowed herself a leisurely perusal of his body. Damn, the man had some fine assets. His shoulders were almost as big as his ego. Either way, she wasn't about to let the towel thief here think he'd finally impressed her.

Lindsey tossed the damp towel over one shoulder and sent him a knowing smile. "Clown school?"

To her surprise, he laughed. A rough sound that came from his belly and did funny things to her insides. Most guys with that much confidence didn't appreciate her delicate wit.

"You could call it that. U.S. Army. Cyber warfare division."

All joking aside, Lindsey had a solid respect for anyone willing to put their life on the line for the protection of everyone else. "Thank you for your service. Are you on leave?"

Dax leaned against the rail where he'd retreated and crossed his arms. "That's two questions, but I'll allow it. No, I served my term. And now for you."

She tensed, expecting him to repeat his earlier request. "Go ahead."

"Where are you injured?"

Lindsey pressed her lips together and mulled over his restraint before answering. She didn't talk about cases, but she could answer him without revealing any details. "Back of my left shoulder. Blunt force trauma put a kink in the muscles."

"Anywhere else?"

"Not today."

"Good to know. I've been told I have talented hands if you need someone to ease the ache."

His smile offered mischief, but Lindsey dismissed the promise there as careless arrogance.

"I think you've done enough with your hands." She hadn't meant it as a barb, but his slight flinch made it clear he'd taken it that way.

Dax inclined his head. "I'm sorry I hurt you."

The apology made her reassess her assumption. Careless arrogance would make him easier to disregard, but that didn't seem to be his style. He'd found a way to get the information he wanted without pushing her to give more than she was willing, and he'd taken responsibility when it wasn't necessary. The distinction made him all the more appealing, much to her frustration.

"Not your fault. You didn't know."

"You should have told me. I would've been gentler with you." The playfulness had left his tone, and even from across the deck, she could see he intended to hold on to the blame. Lindsey didn't want him assigning her the role of damsel in distress. She could take care of herself.

"I got the towel, didn't I?" With a parting smirk, she sauntered into the house.

She'd ice her shoulder later. For now, all she needed was a shower and a couple hours of uninterrupted sleep.

———

UNFORTUNATELY, sleep would have to wait. Lindsey gazed longingly at the neatly made bed in the guest room Sabine had assigned her. With the Dax drama, she'd forgotten that she'd left all her bags in her SUV. Her go-pack only held the bikini she currently wore and a change of undies. What were the chances her surprise roommate would be lingering near the front door?

As if on cue, the sound of water running in their shared bathroom answered her question. Like her, Dax had opted for a shower. Unlike her, he seemed to have unpacked already. Awesome.

Still in her bikini, Lindsey marched downstairs and outside to her pride and joy. She traveled all over the country, and she needed a vehicle that could keep up. One that had the latest GPS and front seats that reclined all the way back.

The dark grey SUV was the first thing she'd saved up for after finishing her criminal justice degree, and it had served her well until she'd traded it in for the newest model last year. Unlike the last one, this version didn't have the cage in the backseat for her quarry.

Dax had made an assumption that she retrieved people who skipped bail—and she had, for years—but that wasn't entirely accurate anymore. She'd started with people, but her real talent lay with finding missing objects. Honestly, she preferred it that way since priceless family heirlooms generally didn't try to kick out her back windows. Bonus:

she didn't have to stay in one state for years to make the licensing worth it.

Once she'd made the right contacts, there was no shortage of work. Hunting people paid well, but hunting trinkets paid better. Any time she got nostalgic, a metal pipe to the back was more than enough to remind her why she'd transitioned.

The nomadic lifestyle suited her. Since leaving home at eighteen, she'd had the itch to move. Before, even. Her mom had done more than enough to destroy any urge to put down roots. Nothing like constant belittlement to convince a young girl home was the last place she wanted to be.

Lindsey grabbed her two duffel bags from the back, then pivoted, wincing when the gravel dug into her bare feet. The hairs on her arms stood up as she stopped and surveyed the overgrown yard surrounded by forest. No one on the main road could see this far past the trees, but she became acutely aware of her lack of clothing anyway. Nothing stirred, but she still felt like she was being watched.

She turned and checked the front windows of the two-story farmhouse, but all were empty. Dax's bedroom over-looked the back of the property, just like hers. It was possible he could be spying on her from the living room or the master, despite Sabine's assurances. In Lindsey's experi-ence, people usually didn't know their friends nearly as well as they thought they did.

Lindsey dropped one of the bags and slammed the back hatch closed. Movement in the lower left window caught her eye, and she shook her head. She hadn't noticed the cat sitting in the shadows until it startled at the noise.

Suspicions assuaged, she hurried inside. The sound of the shower further confirmed that Dax probably hadn't snuck out naked to watch her retrieve her bags. Lindsey sighed at her quick jump to the worst possible conclusion. The constant skepticism was something she'd been working on, with little success.

The shower shut off with Lindsey halfway up the steps, and she treated herself to the memory of water sluicing down his abs to parts lower. Wrestling with Dax on the back deck had felt weirdly comfortable, as if she'd known him a lot longer than an hour. Lindsey liked him—what she knew of him—but she also knew people were made to disappoint.

How long before Dax disappointed her?

Lindsey hadn't told anyone about the voice or the light, and especially not about the fire she was pretty sure she'd accidentally caused with her mind. The fire department had blamed faulty wiring, but she'd been *right there* when it started. No wires had been involved.

Sabine encouraged her to trust Dax, but even Sabine didn't know the truth. And she was probably Lindsey's closest friend. Besides, how could he possibly help her when all the evidence pointed to either latent mutant powers or mental illness? Both of those she could handle on her own, thanks very much.

Lindsey dropped her bags next to her bed and turned to close the door, but a sleek little tortoiseshell cat sat in the threshold. She crouched down and held out a hand.

"Aren't you pretty? You must be Calliope. Sabine said you were a picky eater, but as long as you leave my stuff alone, I think we can come to an arrangement."

The cat sniffed her hand, then met her eyes. *I have no interest in your belongings, and we have bigger issues to discuss than my eating habits.*

Lindsey fell backward onto her ass with her mouth hanging open. The voice had been barely a whisper—one she couldn't understand—until that afternoon. Through her shock, she hoped this development pushed the answer closer to latent mutant powers.

"You can talk," Lindsey whispered. "Does Sabine know?"

*I can talk. Sabine knows, though I daresay she isn't aware you can hear me.*

She hadn't expected an answer, but a couple of other things made sense with this information. Sabine had been adamant that her cat needed special attention. She'd also insisted that Lindsey stay close to the house in case any wandering strangers randomly showed up.

Lindsey snapped her mouth closed as the cat continued to stare at her. The world shifted, and she realized Dax wasn't the one she should have been worried about.

Sabine had kept one hell of a secret.

## 2

*Dax*

DAMN ALEX AND HIS MEDDLING. Cold water pounded down on Dax's shoulders as he tried in vain to think of anything other than the satisfied smile Lindsey had tossed his way. His best friend and boss had failed to tell him that the nice cat-sitter would be living with him at the house.

He didn't fool himself into thinking that Alex had forgotten. Alex never forgot things. More likely, he and Lindsey had been set up.

The deal had sounded too good to be true from the beginning. Guard a relic and do some prelim work in exchange for lodging, and he didn't have to worry about actually taking care of the house? No hesitation in accepting. Then he'd arrived to discover Lindsey in all her glory.

If he hadn't found her all flushed and disheveled, he might have had a chance at resisting. Even then, if she'd been shy or nervous, he'd have done his best to put her at ease and kept his distance. Lindsey was *not* the shy type.

Prickly, confident, beautiful, sneaky...yeah. He'd never get that smile out of his head.

Dax shivered and twisted the knob to stop the flow of cold water. The effort would probably be in vain since Lindsey's answers hadn't exactly been forthcoming. He should probably accept her rebuff and leave her be, but she intrigued him. No harm in being curious about the lady bounty hunter.

Now that he thought about it, Lindsey was also uniquely qualified to guard a priceless artifact. How much had he been played?

Dax had already been prepping to move to the area after signing on with Alex's company, so the opportunity seemed perfect to scout around and decide if he wanted to stay. His family would be pissed that he wasn't returning to the fold, but he craved isolation and independence after all the years following orders.

Isolation that Alex had promised, but hadn't delivered. Dax couldn't bring himself to be upset. He stepped out of the shower and glanced at the closed door opposite his open one. Was Lindsey waiting on the other side?

He shook his head and took the towel into his own room before he did something stupid.

His phone belted out the chorus of Bohemian Rhapsody as he pulled on his jeans. The tune made him smile because his mom insisted that Queen was the only appropriate ring tone for her.

Dax stood for a moment letting the music play before sending the call to voicemail. She'd been reaching out more often in the last couple of months since his grandma had died—like she had after Beth's death. He sighed and sank onto the edge of the bed. She was used to him not answering because of his job, and he tried to make sure he called her back so she wouldn't worry. But recently, she'd been pushing hard for him to move home now that he'd been discharged.

He loved his family, but something held him back. The certainty that he needed to be somewhere else. Dax couldn't explain it, but his grandma had understood. She'd told him to listen to his heart. From anyone else it would sound corny, but Elle Kendrick *knew* things. She claimed she had the Sight, and Dax had never questioned her advice.

The last time his mom had called, he'd nearly caved. Then Alex had offered him the job here, and everything changed.

Dax eyed the now-closed bathroom door again. Grandma Elle would tell him not to waste time lollygagging. If the choice felt right, it felt right, no matter how many ways he examined it in his mind.

This job felt right. The place felt right. Even Lindsey felt right, especially when she'd been pressed against him. But he was no Grandma Elle with the infallible intuition. He'd followed his heart to serve his country, and he hadn't been there when his grandma had needed him.

Without her guidance, caution was the safer bet. He shoved his phone in his pocket and yanked a tee-shirt over his head.

A flash of light streaked across the ceiling, like the reflection off a moving car. Only his window faced the hot tub and an expanse of woods. Dax frowned as a frisson of unease rolled down his spine. The flimsy, see-through curtains didn't offer much protection, so he stood to the side of the window and peered out.

The sun had dropped behind the trees, casting the patio in shadow. Everything looked the same as it had when he'd come in. The hot tub cover appeared secure, the chairs remained scattered from his impromptu battle with Lindsey, and his towel still sat wadded up on the far side of the stone patio where he'd tossed it.

Dax controlled his breathing and kept absolutely still, watching for movement. Flowers swayed in the light breeze, moving with the tree branches higher up, but nothing that could have caused the flash of light. Deeper in the shadows of the forest, well past the cleared area, something flickered with a barely discernable glow. Not quite firelight, but close.

As he watched, the glow disappeared. Satisfied that nothing posed an immediate threat, Dax eased away from the window. He stared at the ceiling and figured the angles. Whatever it was had to have been in the backyard for the reflection to end up in his bedroom. Closer than the hot tub. He'd been at the window in seconds, so there was no way the light in the trees could have been the source.

When he'd offered the job, Alex had pushed the remoteness of the house and their need for someone to guard the things inside as grave concerns. Dax hadn't taken him seriously. East Texas wasn't exactly a hotbed for the tomb raider underground, and who else would be interested in old pottery?

That had been before he'd known Lindsey would be living there. If a threat existed, she was in danger too, and he needed all the information available. With the disquiet still flitting across the edges of his mind, Dax thought it might be time for a more explicit conversation with his best friend.

He dug the phone out of his pocket and took another look outside while he waited for Alex to pick up.

"What's wrong now?"

No change from before, but the shadows deepened as they headed toward twilight. "Why does something have to be wrong?"

"Because you hate talking on the phone."

Dax grimaced. "Everyone hates talking on the phone. I'm not special. Are you alone?"

A somber silence descended as footsteps echoed and a door shut. "I am now. What's going on?"

"I need you to tell me why you were so adamant that the house needs to be protected while you're gone."

"Did something happen?"

Dax hesitated. "I saw a weird glow in the woods behind the house, and another flash of light that I can't explain, unless someone was on the patio."

Alex groaned. "You're sure it wasn't Lindsey?"

The thought hadn't even occurred to him. Lindsey could have been messing around on the deck, but that wouldn't explain the light out in the trees. And it felt wrong. The heavy foreboding prefaced something else.

"Dax?"

"No. It wasn't Lindsey."

Alex's voice lowered to almost a whisper. "I know you thought I was embellishing the importance of the seal, but if you hadn't agreed to stay for the summer, I would have passed on this opportunity so I could stay near it."

"I need more information if you want me to do my job." Frustration made Dax's comment sharper than he intended, so he took a breath and tried again. "I can't work effectively if I don't know what I'm guarding against."

"That's the problem. I don't know where the threat is coming from, or if there even *is* a threat right now. Sabine and I had some issues a while back when we first found it, but it's been quiet since."

"What kind of issues?"

"Someone tried to take it. We convinced him that was a bad idea on his part."

Dax shook his head. "That's the poorest excuse for a report I've ever heard."

A knock sounded in the background, but Alex ignored it. "That's all you're going to get. You've worked with less."

"Not voluntarily." Dax ran a hand through his hair. Alex didn't mess around with assignments. If he couldn't provide more intel, there was a good reason. "This is more than broken pottery, isn't it?"

"Yes."

Dax blinked at the straightforward answer. "All right. I'll accept that, for now. But if anything—and I mean *anything* —happens that puts Lindsey in danger, you have to tell me every detail, or I'm out of here and I'm taking her with me."

Alex barked out a laugh. "You have a thing for her."

"I've only known her for a couple of hours. Even I don't work that fast." The instinctive denial slipped easily off his tongue, but it felt surprisingly close to a lie.

"Sure. And your sudden concern for my 'broken pottery' has no relation to a certain retrieval specialist with *do not touch* practically stamped across her ass?"

Anger churned in Dax's gut. "What would you know about her ass?"

"It was just an expression, man. The only ass I'm interested in is Sabine's. *You*, on the other hand..."

Dax relaxed his death grip on the phone at Alex's teasing tone. "I handled Lindsey's ass just fine."

"Handled, huh? And how does that not prove my point?"

"She started it. Mostly. She may have had some assistance in getting there."

"I don't want to know if you had sex on my bed. Actually, new rule: no sex on my bed."

"It's not like that. There might have been a small scuffle when I took her towel and she tried to take it back." Dax sank onto the bed, remembering the hot press of Lindsey's body against his.

"I hope you went easy on her."

Dax cleared his throat. "I did not."

Alex didn't even attempt to disguise the joy in his voice. "She got the towel, didn't she?"

"She did." Dax waited while Alex laughed. "Are you done?"

"Oh, I can't wait to see you mooning after her when she leaves at the end of the summer."

A pang of regret accompanied Alex's image, but Dax pushed it aside. They had three months to make those mistakes. "You're a sadistic man."

"I'm a realist. And you, my friend, are screwed."

"I do *not* have a thing for her," Dax muttered.

Alex gave an incredulous snort, then hung up.

Dax tossed his phone on the bed and considered taking another cold shower. The urge to search out Lindsey had grown so much that he didn't trust himself to leave the room. No way was he about to prove Alex right. The wariness had faded by the end of the call, so Dax spent some time unpacking and answering emails. Almost an hour passed before he realized Alex hadn't agreed to his terms.

He put his laptop aside and glanced at the door to their shared bathroom. It didn't matter what Alex agreed to. He'd been warned, and Dax had every intention of following through on his promise.

———

*Lindsey*

. . .

THE POSSIBILITY EXISTED that she'd made up the voice in her head and assigned it a convenient body. Lindsey stared at the splotchy feline, who blinked and stared back.

"If you're really talking to me, stand up and walk in a circle."

The cat gave her a disgusted look, trotted in a tight circle, and sat back down. Her tail twitched, but the voice in Lindsey's head remained smooth and emotionless.

*Was that sufficient?*

Lindsey nodded and did what any sane person would do when confronted with a talking cat. She scooted back on her butt until she'd cleared the door, then shoved it closed with her foot. And waited.

Did telepathy work through doors? Could the cat read her thoughts right now? The repercussions of this discovery spiraled into a stream of increasingly strange questions. Lindsey eventually wrangled her brain under control as she tried to work through the shock.

She spread her hands in the carpet and focused on the feel of the soft fibers against her fingers. Sabine's cat could talk. Lindsey accepted that she could be hallucinating from exhaustion after the long drive and the unexpectedly thrilling afternoon in the hot tub, but the floor felt real enough.

Despite the weird stuff over the last few months—one of them apparently being a cat that could talk in her head all the way across the country—Lindsey had never really harbored the fear that she was losing her mind. The air conditioner kicked on with a groan somewhere in the house, and for the first time in years, she considered yelling for help.

The water had turned off, which meant Dax had come

out of the shower. He'd hear her. But what could he possibly do for her that she couldn't do for herself?

She'd wanted answers, hadn't she? Sabine had even given her an off-hand promise that Lindsey would find what she needed. Of course, Lindsey had expected that to mean time and distance to do some digging, but a talking cat on the first day also applied. It certainly saved her some effort.

Lindsey rolled over and tried to peer under the crack in the door. A shadow darkened the middle of the space, so she assumed the cat hadn't moved. What now?

The cat—Calliope—didn't pose much of a threat. Granted, Lindsey didn't have a lot of experience dealing with telepathy, but her brain remained un-melted, which seemed like a good sign. A faint sigh drifted through her mind, answering her question of whether telepathy worked through doors. See, she'd learned something new already.

Feeling supremely silly, she stood and straightened her bikini before opening the door a crack. Calliope looked up at her and yawned. Her tail continued to twitch in an annoyed manner, but no more comments came through. If she was waiting for an apology, too bad.

"I need a couple of answers."

*I assumed as much.*

Lindsey glowered, but she chose not to address the sarcastic undertone. "Can you read my mind?"

*No. Unless you want me to. If you send a thought to me, I'll hear it. Otherwise, your mind is your own.*

The answer relieved her more than she expected. Especially considering her recent thoughts about Dax. "Are you an alien?"

*Do I look* like *an alien?*

"You *look* like a cat. If you're not actually a cat, what are you?"

*The short version is I used to be a Muse. For a while, I was a spirit. Currently, I'm trapped in a cat. Would you like the longer explanation now?*

Lindsey opened her mouth, then shut it again. She really didn't. Her eyes were dry and scratchy from being up for more than twenty-four hours, so what she wanted was a shower and a nap. Maybe after she'd slept, the world would make sense.

"Are you dangerous?"

Calliope cocked her head. *Not to you.*

While that answer disturbed her on several levels, Lindsey didn't have the energy to keep up the farce of normalcy. If she believed the cat—one of the weirdest things she'd ever thought—there was no hurry. Sabine's strange behavior suddenly fit into place, and offered another mark toward trusting Calliope.

Lindsey scrubbed a hand down her face. "Great. I need to sleep or I'm going to pass out right here. When I get up and my brain is in full working order, I'd like that longer explanation."

*I understand.*

"I'm locking the door."

She swore the cat smirked at her before sauntering away. Lindsey closed the door gently so as not to alert Dax. Calliope's gloating silence implied the lock wouldn't keep her out, but sharing the house with Alex's sexy Army buddy and the magical talking cat meant taking basic precautions.

Lindsey flipped the flimsy lock and dug in her bag for the baseball bat she always carried with her. Basic precautions. The bat went under the bed, within easy arm's reach, and her pepper spray went into the nightstand drawer. She'd unpack the rest when she got up.

AN ANNOYING BUZZ next to her face woke Lindsey out of a fabulous dream involving Dax and the shower they shared. She sighed and fumbled around until she hit the button to answer it.

"Too early," she mumbled.

"Then why did you answer the phone?" Sabine's cheerful question made Lindsey wince.

She cracked an eye open to confirm daylight, then rolled over and covered her head with her pillow. "I figured it was you. What do you want at this ungodly hour?"

"It's 10:00 a.m. there."

"I'm on vacation."

Sabine snorted. "Not for long. Calliope told me you can hear her."

That made Lindsey sit up in a hurry. "How?"

"Magic."

Lindsey rubbed her face and squinted at the window again. 10:00 a.m.? She'd slept until the next day. "Is that how she can talk?"

Sabine went quiet for a second. "What did she tell you?"

"Not a cat. Former Muse. Stuck as a cat. Not dangerous to me."

"That's all?" Sabine did not sound pleased, but Lindsey was too groggy to care.

"Yes. I was crashing, so I asked her to tell me the rest later. Which is pretty much now, I guess. Did you know I could hear her?"

A muffled sound of frustration came from the phone. "I suspected. The coincidence of the situation felt hinky, but I didn't want to get my hopes up that you'd be one of us."

"One of who?"

Another hesitation, longer this time. "I think I'll leave that explanation to Calliope. She knows a lot more about it than I do, but I should be around if you have questions."

Sabine's quick avoidance didn't inspire a lot of confidence that she'd answer the phone if Lindsey called. Then again, she'd reached out as soon as Calliope had blabbed. Either way, Sabine was here now, and Calliope was hopefully still locked in a different part of the house.

"Give me the quick version. I trust you more than a talking cat-Muse I just met."

"I'm not sure where to begin."

Lindsey rolled out of bed and tucked the phone against her ear to pull clean clothes and shower stuff from her duffel. "Stop stalling. Start with what you meant by 'one of us'."

Sabine groaned. "Fine. I'm a demigod, and if you can hear Calliope, most likely so are you. We're descendants of these powerful magical beings that lived as gods in ancient Greece."

"Are you saying they weren't gods?"

Clothing rustled as Sabine shrugged. "How do you define a god? All-powerful? All-knowing? Ancient humans needed an explanation for their magic, so they were described as gods. They weren't omnipotent though, or they wouldn't have gotten trapped in a seal for a thousand years."

Lindsey stopped with her shirt halfway over her head. Another piece of the puzzle fell into place at the mention of magic. The flashes of light, the fire. God magic, or demigod magic, technically. She filed the information about the seal away for later examination.

"I have magic powers."

"Yes." Sabine drew the word out, making it sound like there was a caveat she hadn't mentioned.

"But?"

"You won't be able to control them until you find your guardian."

Lindsey pulled off her shorts and switched the phone to the other ear. "You lost me again."

"See, this is why I wanted Calliope to explain it."

"Is this why you demanded I stay at your house while you went with Alex to Virginia? Was this a set-up to test me?"

"No. Calliope suggested I have you housesit, but she didn't give me an explanation beyond that she needed more care than a normal cat. I knew you were looking for some space, and even with Dax there, you'd have plenty of alone time."

Sabine sounded so forlorn that Lindsey took pity on her. "Don't worry about it. I'm sure the cat-Muse is still sitting right outside my door waiting to pounce."

"Thank you. In a desperate attempt to change the subject before I confuse you any more, how are you doing with Dax?"

A flash from the dream made Lindsey grin, but she wasn't going to share that tidbit with Sabine. "I haven't seen him since yesterday afternoon, so today will be the real test."

"He's a nice guy, Lindsey."

"So you keep telling me." Lindsey eyed the rumpled bed and decided to leave it. No one else would be seeing it. "Want to add any details to your assessment?"

"Just a sec." A muffled voice said something to Sabine, probably Alex, then she was back. "Sorry. I have to go."

"Another failed attempt at gathering information. I'm losing my touch."

Sabine laughed. "I'll be glad to gossip about Dax all you

want later, but I do have other things to deal with besides interfering in your life."

"Thank god," Lindsey muttered. The phrase felt weird on her tongue after what she'd just learned. "I'll talk to you later."

"Bye." Then Sabine was gone, and Lindsey stood naked, face to face with her locked door.

The cat-Muse could wait a little longer. She tossed her dirty clothes into a pile in the corner and headed for the shower with her bag of travel soaps. Lindsey hadn't had a lot of experience with Jack and Jill bathrooms, but she wasn't surprised to find the doors only locked from the inside.

Dax had access to her room through there, unless she locked him out completely. Lindsey bent to examine the lock. The same kind on her bedroom door that anyone could pop open with a butter knife. Anyone with opposable thumbs anyway.

A quick shower got rid of the chlorine from the hot tub and the lingering fuzziness in her brain. She dressed in her most comfortable clothes and set off in search of the cat or breakfast, whichever she found first.

# 3

*Lindsey*

THE HALLWAY WAS EMPTY. As were the stairs and the living room. Lindsey tried not to feel too relieved, but the lack of caffeine in her system made it significantly harder to lie to herself. She'd finally gotten some answers, but uncontrolled magic sounded insanely dangerous. Wasn't that why she'd come out here though?

To find answers, yes. But deep down, she'd worried she might be a danger to others. Lindsey stopped at the entrance to the kitchen and sighed at the full coffee pot. Dax was up. For some reason, she wasn't as concerned with his safety as she'd been about the generic people in the rest of the world. Or at least, the greater Detroit area. Did that make her a terrible human being? Could she even call herself a human being?

Her mom certainly hadn't.

She groaned and shook her head. What a useless line of thought. Why was she thinking about her mom so much lately? She'd put those memories behind her years ago when she'd left for college and hadn't come back.

Lindsey found the mugs on the first try and focused intently on the act of doctoring her coffee. She'd had enough of the panicky distractions, so until Calliope showed up, Lindsey would enjoy her drink in peace.

The kitchen included a small eat-in area surrounded on three sides by windows. They overlooked the back, so the view included the hot tub and the forest beyond. The trees calmed her jangled nerves, but the longer she stared, the more it felt like something stared back. So much for relaxing.

Lindsey sipped slowly and watched for movement. A couple of squirrels jumped from branch to branch, but they paid her no mind. She was on the verge of heading outside to check it out when Calliope trotted into the kitchen.

*Good morning, Lindsey.*

"Good morning. Is there something in particular you'd like for breakfast?"

Calliope hopped onto the table and sat with her tail curled daintily around her legs. *Sabine usually gives me some tuna and scrambled eggs. I am, of course, open to suggestions. Anything except that disgusting kibble.*

Lindsey got up and pulled out a pan for eggs. She wasn't much of a cook, but she could do the basics. "Scrambled eggs is fine. Sabine left instructions somewhere here, but since you can tell me directly, there's no need for me to try to find them."

With her back turned to the table, the polite conversation felt almost normal. She popped some bread in the toaster and tried to decide how to start a conversation about demigods. Calliope seemed to be waiting for Lindsey to bring up the subject, or she simply wasn't a morning person

—cat. Lindsey snuck a glance toward the table to find Calliope staring out the window.

The feeling of being watched had faded as soon as Calliope arrived, so maybe it had been her imagination after all. Sabine didn't have any window coverings in the kitchen, so despite the thick trees, Lindsey felt somewhat exposed. She'd lived in a lot of urban areas, but isolation and wilderness didn't usually give her the creeps.

"See anything out there?"

Calliope didn't answer until Lindsey had scooped eggs onto two plates and set them on the table.

*No. I don't see anything, but that doesn't mean much.*

Lindsey took a bite of her toast and chewed slowly before responding. "Are you going to eat?"

Calliope leaned down to sniff the plate next to her. *I have to wait a little longer than humans to eat. Apparently, a cat's mouth doesn't handle hot foods well.*

"It's weird that you don't seem to associate your body with yourself."

*It's not my body. Though the agility is nice.*

They ate in silence for a few minutes, and Lindsey's mind settled on a starting point. She waited until Calliope had finished her plate and begun to wash her face with a paw.

"Explain to me, in detail, what a guardian is."

Calliope paused. *Sabine answered your questions after all.*

Lindsey narrowed her eyes. "Did you tell her not to?"

*No. She was overwhelmed with what she's learned in the past few months and wasn't sure how to communicate it to you. I told her that I would take care of it.*

"Kind of you."

She resumed her bath. *Not particularly. I have much more*

*knowledge than she does, and I'd rather you learn the correct information from me.*

Lindsey's brows flew up. "You think she'll give me bad information?"

*I think she'll try to explain what she doesn't fully understand herself. Would you like to keep discussing Sabine, or should I answer your rude request?*

She almost replied with another rude remark, but Lindsey recognized that the response was rooted in trepidation as well as annoyance. The idea that she couldn't control her magic on her own raised all her hackles. As long as she kept up with the procrastination and distraction, she wouldn't hear confirmation of her worst fear. That she'd need to trust someone else to help her.

Fear would not control her.

"I want you to answer my request."

The cat studied her for a moment. *Good. Over a thousand years ago, the Fates tied the lives—and the magic—of the demigods to select humans they designated as guardians. Their lines, like yours, passed down through the centuries.*

"Meaning the status is hereditary?"

*Yes.*

"What are they supposed to be guarding against? And wouldn't it be more effective to have the ones with the magical powers guarding themselves?"

*They're meant to guard you from the gods. There's quite a bit of history here that would give you a better understanding. Would you like me to explain it?*

Lindsey sighed and pulled her hair away from her face. History had been her worst subject in school. "Can you give me the short version?"

*I can try. Magic, at its heart, is manipulating natural energy produced by humans. The humans are incapable of using the* energy, but gods can. *There is some speculation that they were once humans themselves, but no evidence other than genetic compatibility.*

Lindsey leaned back in her chair and crossed her arms. "Where do you even learn words like genetic compatibility?"

*I pay attention. There were many gods of various power levels at one time, but a quirk in our makeup made it impossible to reproduce effectively.*

"Are you saying the gods couldn't have kids? Because I feel like my existence contradicts that."

Calliope stopped cleaning herself to meet Lindsey's eyes. *The gods could have children with each other, but those children were barren, considered lesser gods. Many of the second generation couldn't collect and wield the kind of power necessary to maintain an essentially immortal lifespan, so they lived and died as humans would.*

Lindsey frowned, but Calliope kept going.

*In time, the gods turned to humans instead and found that those children were not only fertile, but produced more energy than a normal human. What better way to gather power than to tie it to them through blood? They chose their pairings carefully. The selective breeding led to twelve gods who amassed a majority of the power—the Pantheon.*

"Where do you fall in all of this?"

Calliope flicked her tail and turned to stare out the window again. *I, along with my sisters, were among the lesser gods who eventually died out.*

"I think your definition of 'dead' differs drastically from mine."

The cat's ear twitched. *We didn't all die. Some of us were able to collect enough power to endure.*

The explanation trailed off, and Lindsey squelched her impatience. Calliope's silence spoke of hard memories, and as much as Lindsey wanted to hurry things along, she gathered the best information when she let the informant set the pace.

Impatience made her restless, so she gathered the plates and brought them to the sink. There were a few more dishes, a coffee cup, bowl, and spoon, so she washed them all while Calliope brooded.

Lindsey shut off the water and made a note to discuss chores with Dax. She didn't want him to foist the dishes off on her for the entire summer. By the time she finished wiping down the counters, Calliope had turned her back on the woods.

*The gods couldn't create the energy used to make magic—that trait was unique to humans—but the Pantheon discovered that the offspring of a human-god pairing could do both. They ran the risk of their power sources suddenly choosing to use the magic for themselves, so they tried to keep the knowledge hidden.*

"Naturally, that plan didn't work," Lindsey muttered.

Calliope ignored the interruption. *The ensuing generations discovered magic on their own. They had all the benefits of the gods with only one drawback. They inherited a human lifespan.*

"Are you saying I don't just have magic powers, I have god-like magic powers?"

*For the most part, yes. You're also not limited by the humans around you. Different humans create different levels of energy based loosely on belief, so a god needs a steady supply of suppli-cants to maintain his or her power. Children inherently believe in their parents, but other humans required more convincing. You're constrained only by what you can produce within yourself.*

Calliope seemed to expect her explanation to make Lindsey feel powerful, but it had the opposite effect. The idea that she had access to potentially massive amounts of magic squeezed her chest and doused her in icy dread.

"Great, but I still don't understand how the guardians connect to this history lesson."

*Magic manifests differently for everyone. No one knows why, but the skills are shared among family lines. The Fates are blessed with the ability to see glimpses of the future. What they foresaw prompted them to act. They promised a war among the gods and their offspring. Their solution was to tie the fate of each demigod to a human. The connection would seal off the demigod's power until a bond formed with the human to restore access.*

Lindsey shot forward. "Wait, they only picked on the demigods? Why not do both groups? And why declare the humans to be guardians if their only purpose was to act as a restriction?"

A sigh passed through her mind. *The Fates weren't powerful enough to outright hinder the gods, but they could manipulate them. Without being able to access the power of the demigods, the Pantheon lost interest. By inhibiting their power, the guardian humans acted as protection to the demigods. Or so we were told.*

Helpless fury rose up in Lindsey, sticking in her throat as she tried to stop it from escaping in the form of an angry tirade. Or worse, god-like magic that seemed to really like the shape of fire. Her hands clenched into fists, and she wished she had something to take apart.

"That's the shittiest of shitty reasons."

Calliope walked over and nearly sat on Lindsey's hands. *I understand your anger, but this all happened centuries ago.*

"And yet, I have dangerous magic randomly leaking out of me with no way to control it unless I meet these arbitrary requirements decided by the Fates."

*To be fair, the leaking magic is my fault. A few months ago, I sent out a call to awaken the demigods and draw them here. I wasn't expecting it to activate your power, but in hindsight it makes sense.*

Lindsey took a deep, calming breath and spread out her fingers. She'd like to throttle the cat for messing around with magic without anticipating all the consequences, but she still had so many questions. To her surprise, Calliope leaned down and rubbed her face against Lindsey's wrist.

"Did you just mark me?"

*Ugh. I apologize. Cat instincts are strange and hard to ignore. It was an attempt at comfort.*

Weirdly enough, the attempt sort of worked. Lindsey's scrunched shoulders relaxed, and she sat back in the chair again. The frustration remained though. "Did you just do some kind of cat voodoo?"

*A tiny bit of magic, perhaps enhanced by the cat form.*

Lindsey blew out a breath. "Next time, let me handle it on my own."

The cat raised her chin and returned to her half of the table. *Of course.*

"Okay, so anger issues aside, I think I understand the history. As misguided as it is. Why aren't there more demigods descending on this place if you put out a magical want ad?"

*A thousand years ago, the demigods were plentiful, but I'm afraid the meddling of the Fates caused some lasting damage.*

Lasting damage sounded like something Sabine should have mentioned. "What does that mean?"

*Your magic is a natural part of you, and the Fates essentially took it away. I've heard that the demigods reacted poorly to feeling half-empty all the time. They spent their days sensitive to their magic—something inside that ached to be used—but unable to reach it.*

Lindsey sat stunned for a moment. She knew that sensation. Calliope had basically described Lindsey's life up until a few months ago. She'd always blamed the awareness on her mom. The woman had constantly talked about how she wasn't whole without Lindsey's dad, usually followed by a hefty dose of blame directed at Lindsey.

"What happened to them?"

*Most died alone, unhappy, and unfulfilled. A few forged connections and passed their power on, but I haven't felt any large bursts of magic that would denote a demigod regaining access.*

"None? In a thousand years, *none* of the demigods found their guardians? If it's fate, shouldn't they eventually meet up?"

*That's not how fate actually works. Free will plays a much greater role than humans realize.*

Lindsey scoffed. "I'd argue that most humans don't think fate is real, so they have a pretty good idea of the role free will plays."

She inclined her head. *That does appear to be true among modern humans. Your analysis is incorrect though. There was one demigod who regained her power. Sabine.*

Lindsey's spirits sank. If she had to guess, Alex was Sabine's guardian. Alex, who'd been Sabine's first love and happened to have elite training in protection courtesy of the U.S. Army. She glared at the cat, though she wasn't mad at Calliope specifically.

"To sum up: I have to find this bullshit guardian tied to me by the Fates and create a connection that will somehow allow me to control my magic."

*Yes. There's a high likelihood that the guardian is trained in combat. They tend to embrace warrior lifestyles, which is, I believe, why the Fates chose them. Your guardian will also be drawn to you. An allure that goes both ways.*

The memory of Dax easily countering her moves by the hot tub snuck into her mind and wouldn't leave. Trained in combat. Eerie fascination. Lindsey's gut clenched at the thought. On the one hand, if Dax was fated to be her guardian, the search would be over. On the other, she despised being manipulated.

"Is this connection a sexual thing?"

Calliope laughed. *Not necessarily. Bonds can be formed many ways, and I don't believe the guardian to demigod connection was always conducive to a sexual relationship. Trust is more important than physical pleasure. That said, Sabine believes sex should be the first thing you try to forge the bond.*

Lindsey groaned and pushed away from the table. She paced the length of the kitchen, circling the large island and trying to work past her reluctance. The wild magic posed a risk to everyone around her, and she didn't particularly want to end up unhappy and alone. But trusting someone she didn't know? Not to mention everything else Calliope had told her pushed the boundaries of insane.

Ancient gods and political maneuvering and magic. The whole story sounded so far-fetched, but she'd seen the magic firsthand. She'd nearly burned down an apartment complex.

At Lindsey's third turn around the island, Calliope hopped onto the counter next to her. *I understand this is hard to take in all at once, but there's more at stake than your comfort.*

The cat's words made her stop abruptly and backtrack. Her comfort? Clearly, the mind powers didn't include empathy. Lindsey leaned down close to Calliope's face and spoke slowly.

"My comfort is the least of my worries." Not entirely true, but finding a means to neuter any damage she could potentially cause came way, *way* ahead of trying to trust someone who'd only disappoint her in the end. "I could hurt people with this kind of power, so whatever it takes, I'll find my guardian and figure out how to make the damned connection."

Calliope didn't respond outwardly, but her tone turned icy. *People will be hurt either way. The gods are no longer contained, and unlike you, they're eager to use their power.*

A cold chill slid down Lindsey's spine. "Sabine said they were sealed away."

*They were. The seal was broken, and I need you to help me put them back.*

Dread churned in the pit of her stomach. She didn't know anything about the seal, but she'd bet powerful gods that had been trapped for a thousand years would want revenge on whoever trapped them. Lindsey had the feeling she'd been flung into the crossfire. "I think I need another history lesson."

*That will have to wait. Dax wants your attention.*

Lindsey spun around to find she wasn't alone with the cat anymore. Dax stood in the doorway, watching her with an amused smile.

---

*Dax*

Lindsey wore a ratty college tee-shirt and soft shorts that showed off long, toned legs. Her damp hair spilled past her shoulders in russet waves that he wanted to sink his fingers into, and Dax had to amend his statement to Alex from the night before. He *might* have a thing for her.

She glared at the black and orange speckled cat, who sat on the kitchen counter with her tail twitching back and forth, then turned her fury on him.

Dax had come downstairs with the intention of irking Lindsey, just to see how she'd react, but something had beaten him to it. Without knowing the cause of her anger, he'd be better off diffusing the situation.

Instead of entering the kitchen, he leaned against the doorframe and crossed his arms. "Good morning."

Lindsey straightened. "Morning. Thanks for the coffee."

Despite the gratitude, her stiff shoulders and tense jaw indicated wariness, but Dax could work with wary. "You're welcome, roomie. Sleep well?"

She huffed, backing away from the cat. "Can we skip the awkward morning after conversation?"

"Does it count as a morning after if there was never a night before?"

She skewered him with a withering look. "So that's a no then? We're just leaning heavily into the sexual innuendo?"

Dax shrugged. "Innuendo, invitation...take it as you like."

Her quiet indrawn breath gave away her surprise. So much for diffusing the situation. He'd spoken without thinking, but the comment stood.

Lindsey in a bikini was a goddess, and every moment after that first glimpse had made him like her more. As much as he'd denied his attraction, Dax had dreamed about her all night, then he'd come into the kitchen and felt that same gut punch from yesterday. If she took him up on the invitation, he'd enjoy the hell out of the next three months.

Her pause gave him hope, but he saw the moment she

decided not to engage. "To what do I owe the pleasure of your presence?"

"I heard your voice and figured you'd finally gotten up." He studied the cat—still standing on the counter—then the woman. "Who were you talking to?"

Lindsey scowled at the cat. "Calliope. Look, we need to agree on some house rules. Number one of which is that I won't be your personal maid service."

Dax made sure his amusement didn't show on his face. "I don't expect that. I clean up after myself."

She pointed to the sink. "I did your dishes this morning."

"I made you coffee."

"You made yourself coffee. I just got the extra."

He chuckled. "I made the extra coffee too."

Lindsey huffed again. "Fine. You get points for the extra coffee."

"Oh good, a points system. I do really well with those. Top of my class." A reluctant smile broke out across Lindsey's face, and he enjoyed the triumphant buzz from coaxing her out of her anger.

She cocked her head and raised a brow. "I thought Alex took top marks?"

Dax clutched his chest in a swoon, calling on every nonexistent ounce of drama he possessed. "You wound me. Second best was still roughly top of the class, and thanks for bringing up that painful memory."

Her smile went from reluctant to wide and welcoming. Dax's heart raced under his hand, and he regretted telling Alex he wasn't interested in Lindsey. The man would never stop gloating now.

She met his eyes, and the air around them charged with tension. Dax straightened from his slouch and finally entered the kitchen, but the step toward her wiped away the laughter. Lindsey cleared her throat and circled the island to lean against the stove, putting the full room between them.

Dax let her go and kept his distance. Lindsey didn't strike him as the kind of woman who wanted to be chased. "I promise to clean up after myself."

He walked to the island to stroke the cat, and Lindsey relaxed when he stopped moving. "Me too. Do we need to work out food?"

"How about we go to the store together when the time comes and work it out then?"

She hesitated as if she wanted to avoid even that much time spent with him, but in the end, she glanced at the cat and nodded. "Sure."

Calliope didn't tolerate his touch for long. Her ears flattened, and she jumped down out of his reach. Dax watched her make her way to the windowsill and curl up with her back to them. He was surrounded by prickly females.

Beyond the sunny window, shadows writhed as the trees twisted in the wind. He hadn't forgotten the flash yesterday, and the lack of blinds down here would make it easy for anyone to monitor them.

He stole a look at Lindsey, but she'd also trained her attention on the woods. What did she see out there? Alex had tasked him with protecting the house and the seal. Dax included Lindsey in that assignment, so the best course of action was to share his suspicions.

"I think someone's watching the house."

Lindsey started and shot a quick glance at the cat. "Yeah, about that. I thought someone was watching me earlier too, but it turned out to be Calliope. Her gaze is both weighty and judgmental."

"I don't doubt that, but I don't think it was the cat this

time. I saw a reflection of light in my bedroom come from somewhere in the backyard. Close to the house."

Her brow furrowed. "You saw a light—in your room—and you jumped to secret surveillance?"

Dax understood her doubt. He didn't normally assume the worst, but his instincts told him to pay attention. And after what happened with Beth, he always listened. "I know what it feels like to be watched."

"Me too, but that doesn't mean someone is staring at me every time I feel it."

"How do you know for sure? There are a lot of possibilities for someone to be monitoring you without directly using their eyeballs."

Lindsey pursed her lips as she considered his point, and Dax tried valiantly to keep his thoughts out of his pants. He mostly succeeded.

"Okay. I'll bite. That sounded like you have personal knowledge of non-eyeball monitoring."

He hadn't meant to take the conversation this direction. Some of his skills he wasn't at liberty to discuss. "I do. Someone was watching the house."

For a second, her mask of irreverence slipped and calculation crossed her face. "How sure are you?"

"Ninety-five percent. Be careful if you're out here alone." Dax didn't expect her to believe only his word, but at least the warning would stick in her mind if she saw anything unusual.

He *did* expect her to bristle at the order, and she didn't disappoint.

Her mask dropped back down, and she gave him a smug little grin. "And if I'm not alone? Am I supposed to come running to you for help?"

"If you could arrange it so you come running while

wearing something skimpy and transparent that would be great. I find that my heroics are better perceived while scantily clad."

"You're going to be sorely disappointed." She shook her head and reached back to brace herself on the counter, but her palm landed on the flat stovetop instead.

Lindsey hissed and yanked her hand back from the faintly glowing circle. Dax's heart jumped into his throat as he hustled around the island. She cradled the injured hand against her chest and didn't react when he reached for her. The second he touched her wrist, a bright light made him blink.

He scanned the room, but nothing obvious had caused the flash, so he focused on Lindsey's burn, gently flipping her wrist over. An angry red mark marred the fleshy part of her palm under her thumb. No blisters, she must have moved fast enough to avoid major damage.

Dax tugged her over to the sink and turned on the cold tap full blast. He thrust both their hands under the chilly water, and Lindsey clenched her jaw. His heart rate returned to normal as his fingers went numb.

"Why was the stove on?"

Lindsey spoke through gritted teeth. "Because I'm a dumbass and forgot to turn it off after I made eggs earlier. I got distracted."

Dax frowned. "Didn't you feel the heat?"

"Yeah, but not fast enough for my brain to process and stop me from touching it."

Lindsey tried to yank her hand away, but he held her steady. They stood shoulder to shoulder, but he could tell when the pain started to ease. Lindsey's tight muscles relaxed, and she exhaled softly.

"It feels better. You can let go now."

Dax examined her burn where only a fading pink spot remained. He released her and shut off both the water and the stove. "I guess it wasn't as bad as it looked."

Lindsey examined her hand, then closed her fingers over her palm. "Yeah. I must have only brushed it. Sorry for scaring you."

Dax waved the apology away. "It was only a couple of years of my life. No big deal. At least if you're accident prone I can ask Alex for hazard pay."

Lindsey scoffed. "He's paying you?"

"I mean, not yet, but when I agreed to be the guardian of the house, I wasn't expecting an alluring roommate to put me at risk."

Her smile dropped and a bit of color drained from her face.

"Lindsey? What's wrong?" She'd been warming up to him until his terrible joke.

*She just realized you're her guardian.*

Dax twisted and shoved Lindsey behind him at the unknown female voice. He expected to see a woman standing in the doorway, but the kitchen was empty.

## 4

*Dax*

WHERE HAD the voice come from? Dax double-checked, but the only ones in the room were him, Lindsey, and the cat, who'd developed a sudden interest in what they were doing. Lindsey yanked on his arm holding her back, and when he didn't release her, she pinched him in the side.

Dax flinched, but kept his arm right where it was. "Show yourself."

No sound from the mysterious woman, but Lindsey sighed behind him. "Calm down. We're not in danger. What did you do, Calliope?"

Lindsey's exasperated tone calmed him more than her words. She knew the voice. He had no reason not to trust her judgement, but her question forced a connection he never would have made on his own. Dax shot a quick glance at the cat. She watched them with luminous eyes, but other than sitting up and facing them, she hadn't moved.

*I helped. A little twist of magic to strengthen your bond and allow me to communicate with both of you.*

Lindsey groaned quietly, and Dax turned around to confront her. "Explain."

She raised her chin and slid away from him. "I guess you can hear her now."

"The cat?" Even with the influence of his grandma, he couldn't help his skepticism.

Lindsey nodded, then grimaced. "No wonder Sabine didn't want to explain this to me. There's not a good place to start." She studied Calliope. "Wouldn't it be better for you to do this part?"

The cat looked smug—most of them did as a default— and Calliope dismissed him to address Lindsey. *Your bond will help him overcome his natural distrust if you impart the information. Congratulations on finding your guardian. Share what you know, and when you're ready, I'll be here to finish explaining.*

She leapt down from the windowsill and trotted out of the kitchen while Dax wrestled with indecision. His previous brushes with the occult had all been subtle and at least partially feasible. Good instincts and keen observational skills could justify a lot of miraculous events, but a telepathic cat—she hadn't been physically talking—pushed well past the point of feasible. Then again, he had absolute faith in his grandma's Sight. If one aspect existed, why not others?

Lindsey sat heavily at the table and gestured at the chair next to her. "Might as well sit down. This is all going to sound insane, and I completely understand if you want to run away screaming."

Dax sat and leaned forward on his elbows. "Do I look like the screaming type? Tell me everything."

He listened intently while Lindsey talked, only stopping her a couple of times for clarification. She knew how to give a report, and Dax found himself thankful for the succinct style that made her easy to understand.

Lindsey shook her head when she'd finished. "Saying it all out loud, without Calliope speaking into my mind, makes me feel like I need a large alcoholic drink."

Dax laughed absently, but his mind whirled with implications. Alex and Sabine were a part of this world, and his best friend had pulled him into something dangerous without giving even an inkling of what he'd be up against. Gods? Actual gods with magic?

A large alcoholic drink wasn't too bad of an idea.

Lindsey met his eyes, and he saw the same overwhelmed apprehension he felt, though he expected hers stemmed from the forced connection part of the story. "So, you and me?"

She looked away quickly, confirming his guess. "That's what the Fates decided. I'm not fully convinced."

He had to choose his words with care here. "Lindsey, I don't expect you to enter into any kind of relationship with me. I have preferences, specific, mostly naked preferences, but Fates or not, it's your choice what you do with your life."

A smile flitted across her face. "Calliope and I were just discussing the role of free will among humans." She paused, then sat up straighter and seemed to shed all the doubt. "My magic is dangerous, and apparently, some kind of bond between us is the key to controlling it. Calliope assures me friendship is enough for the connection, and that's my choice. For now. Luckily for me, you don't seem like a total ass, so this relationship shouldn't be too painful."

"What a ringing endorsement. I might have shirts made." Dax hoped the sarcasm hid his disappointment. She wanted friendship, so he'd abide by her wishes. But nothing stopped him from letting her know he wanted more, and hoping she'd change her mind later.

Lindsey raised a brow. "I can see it now. 'Not a total ass' written in big letters across the front. Maybe 'guardian' and a picture of the seal on the back, just to drive the point home."

Dax tilted his head. "Have you seen the seal?"

"No, I didn't even know there was something to see until this morning."

He scooted his chair back and stood, suddenly pleased he had something to contribute besides status. "Alex keeps it in a safe in his office. He showed me before they took off."

Her nose scrunched. "That is the *worst* place to keep something valuable."

"That's what I told him." When she didn't immediately get up to join him, he reached over to pull her to her feet. "Come on. Might as well see what all the fuss is about."

Lindsey let him hoist her up with a reluctant sigh. "What does it matter? Calliope hasn't explained anything about trapping—or re-trapping—the gods, so I'm not even sure if the seal has any more use. Did Alex say why he wanted you to guard it?"

Dax drew her closer, tempted to stay put and see how far she'd come willingly. The scent of coconut wafted past him, and he recognized he was playing a dangerous game with himself. Just last night, he'd stressed to Alex that he wasn't interested in her, and now he'd gone so far the other direction that the smell of her shampoo was giving him a hard-on.

"No. He told me there were some potentially dangerous people looking for it, and not to mess with it. I assume the second part was his idea of a joke because he knew I would mess with it."

Lindsey quirked an eyebrow as she moved, her gaze locked on his, and Dax understood the challenge. She'd asked for friendship, but friendly wasn't the word he'd use to describe the heat building between them.

Dax stepped back, dropping her hand and conceding defeat. He turned and led her to Alex's first floor office. The safe was the approximate size of a microwave and hidden behind a non-descript painting of fruit. The frame had hidden hinges that allowed access.

Lindsey whistled when she got a good look. "Are you serious? An ugly, hinged painting? How is he rich when he makes terrible decisions like this?"

"He's brilliant with code. Right after he got out, he sold this program he'd been tinkering with to a private cyber security company. It's one-of-a-kind, so they wanted exclusive rights. He agreed as long as he got a percentage of the company's profits. Bam. Big money." He punched in the code and swung the door open.

Inside, a flat, round piece of bone-colored pottery sat on the top shelf. Dax reached in to pull it out, but stopped before he came in contact. Last time he'd done this, it had felt like holding a larger than average stoneware plate. Nothing mystical or weird.

This time, his fingers tingled when they got close, like pushing his hand through warm water. The faint pressure increased as he touched the gold rim.

He spoke over his shoulder. "Lindsey, do you feel that?"

"Impatience? Yes. Are you going to keep fondling it or do I get to see it sometime today?"

When nothing untoward happened, Dax carefully

extracted the seal and set it on the desk next to him. "Touch it and tell me what it feels like."

She stepped toward the desk and sent him a fake smile. "Not the first time I've heard that. Certainly the—"

Dax smiled when she stopped mid-sentence to stare at the seal. "So, you *do* feel it."

Lindsey moved her hand closer then farther from the stone. "What is that?"

"I don't know. It wasn't there before."

"I think it was, you just couldn't sense it." She ran a finger along the deep crack through the middle of the circle, then lifted her hand a couple of inches above it. "Whatever it is abruptly stops right about here. Like a bubble."

A pale orange glow appeared between Lindsey's hand and the seal. Before Dax could take more than a step, she'd gasped and skittered across the room.

"You need to put it away." She'd locked her hands behind her back, but she didn't look injured, like before.

"Are you all right?"

Lindsey didn't take her focus off the desk. "I'm fine. Put it away please."

Dax positioned himself between her and the seal, making sure not to crowd her, and trailed his fingers from her elbow to her wrist until he'd pulled her hand out where he could see it. She stared over his shoulder with her lips pressed together, but let him look.

No marks. Not even the one from the stove earlier. Nothing to explain why she'd panicked.

He gave her hand a squeeze then did as she asked. By the time he'd relocked the safe, Lindsey had drifted to the door on the opposite side of the room. She led him into the hall, where she stood cupping her elbows.

"We should find out everything Alex and Sabine know about that seal."

"Agreed, but wouldn't they simply be repeating whatever Calliope told you?"

"Calliope hasn't told me much about the seal itself, and they've been living with it for months. They may have noticed something Calliope didn't."

Dax wasn't so sure, but he wouldn't cut off any potential sources of information. "I'll call Alex tonight. He won't answer his phone if he's working."

Lindsey glanced at the closed office door then nodded. "I could call Sabine, but that seems redundant. We're probably fine waiting until tonight. In the meantime, I need to talk to Calliope again about some specific concerns."

He moved past her to return to the kitchen, and Lindsey followed. She visibly relaxed the farther they got from the office. Whatever had happened with the seal had shaken her.

Dax glanced at her unmarred hands again as he resumed his seat at the table. "That was magic back there."

She hovered in the doorway for a moment, then sighed and joined him. "Yes, and the seal made it worse. We need to keep it far away from me."

He warmed at her use of 'we', but he didn't understand how a bit of pressure and an orange glow cowed this fearless woman. "Why are you so sure magic is dangerous?"

"Personal experience." Her stiff shoulders said there was more to the story.

Dax covered her hand with his. "You can tell me."

She licked her lips and looked away. "I mostly destroyed my former apartment complex." The words were torn from her, but she clearly wasn't ready to share more just yet. Apparently, this fledgling friendship came with sharp limits.

He swallowed his disappointment and embraced the role of her guardian by changing the subject. She'd open up in time. "I'd like it noted that I find it completely unfair that you get magic and I don't. Why pair you up with a powerless human?"

Lindsey shrugged. "Political reasons? I don't know. It doesn't make much sense to me. I get the feeling the Fates didn't trouble themselves too much in explaining their reasoning to Calliope."

"And what reasoning they *did* share has been filtered through Calliope's distinct worldview. Too bad we can't talk to the Fates and get another perspective."

"Considering their complete disregard for the wishes of non-gods, I doubt they'd tell us everything. Or anything. As far as I can tell, they didn't leave any instruction manuals for the demigods and humans they tied together."

Dax studied the stubborn set of her jaw. She did *not* like the idea of fate. Noted. "Maybe they did and we didn't realize it."

Lindsey sent him an incredulous look. "And no one figured it out in a thousand years?"

"How would they? The only one left to share the story of what happened couldn't communicate with anyone until recently. Without the proper context, anything referencing the bond would be a mystery." Dax leaned forward. "The idea of magic has persisted despite all our technological advances. There are plenty of unexplained phenomena in the universe. This could be another example."

"Sure. Why not tie all the mythology together in one mess? Muses and Valkyries and Bigfoot all conspired together to entrap a bunch of gods, who have now been released. Only the Loch Ness Monster can tell us how to fix it. Makes complete sense."

"You forgot aliens."

"Don't be ridiculous. Everyone knows aliens advanced enough for space travel would fly right on past us."

Dax laughed, but his theory about fate unnerved him. How much of life *was* determined by a fate they couldn't fathom? His grandma's death? His sister's? He'd come to terms with his role in Beth's accident. Long periods of time went by when he didn't think of that day at all, but had his actions—and her loss—been pre-ordained?

Part of him wanted to share his thoughts with Lindsey, but she stood and stretched.

"I'm going to go find Calliope and hopefully get some more unhelpful answers." She studied him, then jerked her head toward the doorway. "You coming?"

Dax didn't hesitate to follow her. Alex had given him some projects to work on, but they could wait. Lindsey was endlessly more interesting. Not to mention, he had some questions of his own for the cat.

In the span of one morning, his life had changed drastically. As far as he was concerned, any situation that merited a guardian meant there was a need for protection. They might not know the details, but he wouldn't dismiss his role.

The mysterious watcher from the night before suddenly felt a lot more ominous. One thing was sure, sitting around in the kitchen wouldn't provide any answers.

———

TRUE TO LINDSEY'S GUESS, Calliope proved less than helpful. She couldn't provide any more details about the Fates or the binding, and Alex and Sabine only knew what Calliope did. Dax hated that they understood so little, but no amount of cajoling over the next week helped them discover anything new.

Calliope *did* explain a little more about the seal. The guardians offered the demigods a great deal of protection, but the gods still fought among themselves for power. The Fates had believed the only way to completely avoid the coming war was to remove the gods from the equation. The Fates had procured the seal—she didn't know from where—and given it to the Muses. With the help of her sisters and some expert-level manipulation, Calliope had gotten the gods inside, then locked it closed.

When Dax had asked what that meant exactly, all she'd said was it was bigger on the inside. They'd all had to give up their physical forms to lock the magic into place. She wouldn't talk about her sisters, and after hearing the pain in her voice, Dax didn't ask again.

She could manipulate the latent magic in the seal, which she used for the demigod assemble maneuver and to make two shields—a protective bubble around the seal itself and a larger circle around the house. Apparently, the magic couldn't get out, and the gods couldn't get in. She didn't explain it more than that. Calliope did *not* like sharing her knowledge.

After that first day, the three of them settled into a pattern of platonic hell. Calliope insisted that Lindsey needed to practice with what little magic she had, and if Lindsey's foul moods were any indication, it wasn't going well.

She often joined him for a workout or sparring outside after her sessions, and Dax recognized the need to sweat out frustration. It was the best part of his day, not only because he got to touch her, but because she taught him new moves every time they crossed.

They'd survived divvying up chores, cooking duties, and a trip to the local Walmart for supplies. Arguing with Lindsey over name-brand cheese versus generic felt surreal when he knew she'd spent the day trying to light fires with her mind. No, not her mind. Her magic. Calliope had corrected him on that point.

As agreed, Dax kept his hands to himself while they spent their evenings torturing each other with horrible choices on Netflix. When she stole his last piece of bacon in the morning, he resisted wrestling her to retrieve it. And every night, he went upstairs hoping she'd knock on his door, only to toss and turn alone as dreams of her taunted him.

Seven days of his best behavior, and Dax couldn't stop thinking about her.

Day eight looked to be the same as the others. After breakfast, he'd closed himself with the computers in Alex's office to try to get some work done, but his mind kept wandering to the seal locked in the safe. He leaned back in the leather chair and examined the fruit painting. It really was ugly.

Calliope had leaked that Lindsey couldn't conjure even a tiny glow, but she'd done it without trying when she was near the seal. He knew the idea scared her, but maybe all she needed was a little boost. It would be hard to learn control if she couldn't get the magic to work in the first place.

He glanced at his watch and decided to grab an early lunch. Really early. More of a brunch. Another couple of minutes got him to a good stopping point. The protocol for locking the computers only took a few seconds, then he was free to meander the long way to the kitchen. Maybe Lindsey would also be interested in an early brunch.

Dax shook his head at the mental gymnastics. He'd never resorted to borderline stalking before. How did other creepy, obsessed guys excuse their behavior?

Lindsey and Calliope had taken over the front room for their lessons, which as far as he could tell when he walked by, consisted of sitting on the couch and staring into space. Sabine had a desk in there for when she worked at home, but she rarely used it. Alex threatened at least once a week to knock down the walls to the "useless sitting room" and create a huge open space.

Dax didn't give a crap about floor plans, but the lack of a door made it convenient for him to catch glimpses of Lindsey throughout the day when he emerged from the nerd cave. Another point in the quasi-stalker column. The easy distraction made it hard to concentrate, but he suspected Alex hadn't expected him to get any actual work done this summer.

Lindsey sat on Alex's old couch with her eyes closed. Calliope curled up next to her in a bright sun spot. The scene made him hesitate. His idea had merit, but Lindsey looked like she was asleep.

He cleared his throat, but neither of them moved. Since he'd announced his presence and Lindsey couldn't see him, he let his gaze wander. She wore cargo pants with paint and oil stains all over them, unusual for her. The tight, blue tank top he'd seen before, but that didn't mean he appreciated it any less.

By the time he reached her face, Lindsey watched him with a raised brow, but Dax noticed her erratic breathing. She wasn't as unaffected as she wanted him to believe.

"What do you need, Dax?" Lindsey's voice caused Calliope to raised her head off her paws.

"I had an idea."

A smile flashed across her lips. "I'm still not interested in a rematch for the towel."

The memory of Lindsey pressed against him as she reached up for the fabric blazed through his mind. He'd suggested a rematch now that her shoulder had healed, but she wanted to go out on top. Hell, he'd let her win if it meant a repeat of that moment by the hot tub.

Dax grinned. "Because you know I'd take you."

She tilted her head and gave a little shrug. "We'll never find out."

Calliope yawned and jumped off the couch to stroll past Dax's legs. *I could use a break. Let me know when you're done flirting.*

"Don't hold your breath." Dax waited until she'd disappeared up the stairs to mention his suggestion. For some reason, he didn't think Calliope would like them messing with the magic around the seal. Especially now that they knew the "bubble" they'd felt was actually a protective measure created by Calliope to keep the seal's magic contained.

"Why didn't you want her to hear your idea?" Lindsey asked.

Dax came into the room and lowered his voice. "Because she doesn't like us touching the seal."

Lindsey shot up from the couch. "She's not the only one."

"Hear me out. You have to get your magic to turn on to figure out how to use it. The seal's magic helped you do that."

"That's precisely why I can't use it. If *I* can activate it, then I can deactivate it too. If the seal revs me up, we're gambling that I can stop it before something gets permanently destroyed."

The regret in her voice tore at him, but he wanted her to think it through instead of reacting out of fear. "Calliope would be right there to help you. Maybe you could finally get something out of all this training."

Lindsey shook her head. "Not worth it. It's too dangerous, Dax." She shoved at her hair then paced to the window and back.

Dax would have argued more—if for nothing else besides the joy of matching wits with her—but he noticed a dim glow emanating from her hand. Her brow furrowed and followed his line of sight, then flinched at the abnormal light.

Like he had the day with the stove, Dax strode forward and closed his fingers around her wrist. The orange glow coalesced into flames. Small licks of fire covered her palm, but Dax didn't let go.

Lindsey whimpered and fought to take shallow breaths, tugging half-heartedly as she gaped at her hand.

"Lindsey, look at me."

His words didn't penetrate, so he tried again, quieter. "Lindsey."

As if in a daze, she lifted wide eyes to his. "I don't know how to make it stop."

Dax didn't know either, so he went with his instincts. He slid an arm around her waist and pulled her into an embrace. "We'll control it together. Slow breaths. Like mine."

He inhaled for a four count then exhaled. Lindsey's free hand clenched a handful of his shirt over his stomach as she slowly matched his rhythm.

"Good. Close your eyes, keep focusing on your breathing."

She resisted for a beat, then her eyelids dropped down.

Dax made sure he maintained the four count and glanced at the hand he held. The flames had sputtered to tiny flickers of orange light, but they weren't completely gone.

"Don't think about the magic. Think about me. Focus on me."

"What if it gets worse?"

He brushed a kiss against her temple. "I'll tell you. You can trust me to do that, right?"

Lindsey didn't answer, but she lowered her head to rest against his shoulder and finally relaxed. Her tight fist let go of his shirt, winding around his back instead. A soft breath wafted across his neck, and Dax marveled at how well she fit against him.

She shifted closer, and her lips brushed his collarbone. Heat spread from the innocuous touch, and he had to adjust his stance to keep from pulling her all the way against his body. The move distracted him enough that when she rested her other hand over his heart, his lax grip didn't stop her.

Dax froze for a second when the little flames came in contact with his shirt, but instead of catching the cotton on fire, the warmth seeped into his chest and faded away. Lindsey curled into him, and he stroked her back with a light touch. She hadn't noticed her magic retreating.

The timing made Dax think the power related to her emotions. Her coconut scent surrounded him, and he wondered how long he'd get to hold her before she pushed him away. Not long enough.

She opened her eyes and sucked in a breath when she saw her formerly smoldering palm flattened against his chest. Dax knew the feeling.

Even though he knew it was coming, disappointment plagued him when she leaned back to gape. "My magic doesn't affect you."

"That appears to be true." His hand stilled, but she didn't untangle herself.

"How did you know what to do?"

"I didn't. You were on the verge of hyperventilating, so I helped you calm down. I had no idea that would calm your magic too." Except he wasn't sure he *had* helped her calm down. In the quiet moment, he could feel her heart racing against him.

"Thank you." She reached up to kiss his cheek, but Dax didn't want her gratitude.

He turned his head and captured her lips before she could move away.

# 5

*Lindsey*

THE WORLD STOPPED for a moment with Dax's lips pressed to hers. A tingly sense of anticipation rose inside her, flush with hunger, for the space of an indrawn breath. Then the wave crashed over and the world rushed back in.

Dax kissed as he did everything else, with complete confidence and utter skill. Lindsey groaned and gave into the ache that lit up every nerve ending in her body. After a week of unrelenting, highly sexual dreams, the reality of Dax put her imagination to shame.

Lindsey slid her hand behind his neck to pull him closer, savoring his spicy scent. She craved the taste and the heat of him. The kiss deepened, their mouths melding together over and over, in a desperate bid to satisfy the yearning.

His fingers pressed into her waist, holding her against him, but he eased back an inch, resting his forehead against hers. Like before with the magic, their chests rose and fell in sync. The hair at his nape brushed her fingers, and Lindsey savored the in-between moment. Amid breath and kisses and responsibility, Dax felt like home.

*Was this the fate she'd waited for?*

Her eyes popped open at the quiet, unwarranted thought—not from Calliope, but from deep inside herself. Of course, he felt like home. Dax had been chosen for her a thousand years ago by a meddling group of gods.

Reality intruded, and Lindsey back-pedaled out of his arms. His hands stayed on her until the last possible second, then fell to his sides, like he'd had to fight to let go.

Lindsey touched her lips. "That was a mistake." If she kept repeating it, maybe she'd be able to convince herself it was the truth.

Dax shoved his hands in his pockets, grim determination shadowing his face. "I disagree."

"I have to get out of here for a while." She reached for her purse before remembering she'd left it upstairs today. Her favorite cargo pants had big enough pockets to hold her wallet, phone, and keys.

"Running away won't help."

She sent him a tight smile. "I disagree. I want to think about what happened today. See if I can find a pattern for the magic."

He inclined his head. "Call me if you need anything."

His easy acceptance made Lindsey pause at the front door. He deserved at least a partial explanation before she bailed on him. "I don't like the idea of the Fates toying with us."

"The Fates have nothing to do with how much I want to kiss you again."

Warmth climbed her cheeks. "And I want to be able to use my magic without the assistance of your tongue."

He chuckled. "You pulled the magic back on your own. Well before any tongue action."

Was he right? Lindsey hadn't been thinking beyond Dax, which was one of the problems. She shook her head and opened the door. "I'll be back later."

"Take as much time as you need. I can wait."

---

THE TOWN AREA OF DECKARD, Texas wasn't exactly charming, but it was unique. Lindsey had visited many places with the picturesque square surrounded by quaint little shops, usually dominated by a park with a big white gazebo in the middle. There had to be a blueprint for "small town America" hidden away somewhere.

She never felt completely at ease in those places. The people there were quick to notice anything new, and often, they viewed change with suspicion. Whenever her job took her to a small town, she knew it would be twice the work for half the information.

Deckard didn't have a square, and the park took up a different part of town. The thick forest of pines closing in on all sides provided plenty of green if not space. Instead, they had two square blocks of one- and two-story buildings housing the necessities of modern life. A hardware store. A gas station. A chain restaurant. But they also had small businesses owned by the townsfolk, which she tried to frequent.

After parking at the local coffee shop, Lindsey surveyed the street. The fire station next to her had their bay doors open, and a discussion about the greatest superhero floated over on the breeze.

She smirked at the choices. Typical debate about who could kick who's ass. Personally, she preferred the ones who didn't have superpowers and fought for justice with their wits and their wads of money. Superpowers were overrated.

Lindsey flexed her fingers and blew out a breath. The sun warmed her shoulders, the air smelled like grilling meat, and the wind tossed her ponytail into her face. A normal summer day in a normal town. All she had to do was pretend to be normal.

Sabine had said to contact Moira if she ever needed anything, and at the moment, Lindsey needed something to think about other than magic, Dax, and the talking cat she'd left at home. Maybe Moira would have something for her to fix.

She set off walking the perimeter of the business district, searching for a sign of Moira's Yarn Shop. A glint of sunlight on metal in the corner window display caught her attention. An antique shop had prominently arranged a sword, slightly tarnished with age, on a wooden table stand amid a collection of orange Tupperware and creepy porcelain dolls.

While craning her head to stare at the sword, Lindsey plowed right into another person on the street. The small woman, with pixie-short honey-blonde hair and vivid green eyes, waved away her apology.

"It's as much my fault as yours. I should know better than to walk while digging in my bag."

The giant tote bag she had slung over one shoulder bulged with what looked like rocks. "I'm just glad I didn't knock you over. That bag might have done some damage."

The woman followed Lindsey's line of sight, then laughed. "Yeah, I'm pretty sure books will be my downfall one day. I'm Kora. I own the bookstore around the corner."

She held out her hand, and Lindsey shook it. "Lindsey. I just moved here. Sort of. I'm house-sitting for Sabine this summer."

Kora's eyes lit up. "Sabine told me you were coming. I'm new here too. Well, relatively. We've only been open for two years. Compared to the rest of the town, that's practically yesterday. Where are you headed?"

"Moira's Yarn Shop."

"Oh, she's on Azalea Street. Opposite side of town."

Lindsey pointed back the way she'd come. "So, a couple of blocks that way?"

Kora laughed again. "Yep. We like to say the close proximity keeps things interesting. But if you're looking for Moira, you're out of luck. Her shop's closed today. Could I interest you in a coffee instead? I was just heading to the café to drop these books off with Reggie."

Lindsey hadn't needed Moira specifically—only something to keep her busy—and Kora's infectious warmth meant she was probably a good source of information about the town. Calliope had been here the whole time, albeit in the woods, so Lindsey would love to know how the locals had explained away any oddities associated with her presence.

"Sure. I've got time." With a last glance at the sword, Lindsey followed Kora down the street.

Sweat dripped down Lindsey's back from the heat, but Kora didn't seem bothered. She bopped along in jeans and a black tee-shirt with nary a sweat stain to be seen.

Kora chattered about Reggie, the coffee shop owner, and his voracious appetite for murder mysteries. She seemed convinced that if the man weren't so nice, he'd be in the running for a serial killer.

"Isn't that what everyone says after they find out their neighbor murdered six nuns? 'You'd never know. He was so nice'." Lindsey wasn't sure why she'd said that out loud. She was usually better with first impressions.

Kora's face lit up with a sunny smile. "I know, but Reggie won't even kill a spider in his place. He makes his staff relocate them outside, and we get a *lot* of spiders here in the Piney Woods."

A blast of cold air dried Lindsey's sweat almost as soon as they walked in. Goosebumps raised on her arms, but after the ferocious heat outside, the relief felt fantastic. The scent of coffee and pastries filled the room, and she resolved to come into town more often.

Kora walked to the side of the counter to ask for Reggie. A skinny man with a shock of red hair and a surprisingly deep voice emerged from behind the espresso machine to lift Kora off the ground in a hug. She giggled and handed him the tote bag once her feet had reached solid ground again. He grinned like a maniac.

"You're the best, Kora. I'll get your usual. And for your friend?"

They both turned to stare at her. "Vanilla latte with an extra shot."

Reggie nodded and moved away, but Kora tapped her chin. "I didn't take you for the boring type."

Lindsey held out her arms. "What you see is what you get. I travel a lot and almost every coffee shop has a version of a vanilla latte. I try to save the extra shot for when I've had a particularly troubling day."

She hadn't meant to reveal the last part. Kora's gaze sharpened, but Reggie returned with their drinks before she could comment. Lindsey's brows shot up as Kora grabbed a pale concoction that looked more like a milkshake than a coffee drink.

"Thanks, Reggie. I should have new stock sometime next week."

"Just let me know when, sweetheart." He nodded at both of them then went back to pulling shots.

Kora took a long slurp from her straw then sighed with a dreamy smile. "Come on, let's grab a table."

They chose a high top with two stools, and Lindsey waited for the questions to begin. She didn't have to wait long.

"What happened today that necessitated an extra shot?" Kora sat cross-legged on the stool in an impressive show of flexibility.

Lindsey blew on her latte, then took a tentative sip before answering. "I kissed the guy I'm living with, and it's probably going to make the next few months weird."

"Did you enjoy it?"

Heat rushed up her face at the memory. "That's not the point. We're sort of working together in a possibly dangerous job, and there may have been a tiny bit of coercion involved."

"First, you definitely need to give me more details on the 'tiny bit of coercion'. Second, that's a lot of qualifiers for one sentence. It sounds like you're not one hundred percent on board with the kissing yourself."

Lindsey pointed at her. "*That* is not the problem. I wanted to kiss him."

"So, you *did* enjoy it."

"Yes, and I want to do it again, but I'm not sure it's a good idea given everything else that's going on." She frowned as she realized how much she'd just told a relative stranger. More than she'd have given anyone except Sabine, maybe not *even* Sabine. Then again, a relative stranger could give her a neutral opinion.

Kora didn't seem to notice Lindsey's indecision. "What does he think?"

"We haven't discussed it. I told him I needed some time and left." And he'd been clear that he wasn't going to give up, which she didn't mention.

Kora tapped her Converse against the seat, a bundle of energy that definitely didn't need the coffee and sugar she'd downed with alarming speed. "Is there anything stopping you from simply telling him what's on your mind?"

Lindsey laughed dryly. "Other than not knowing what's on my mind? The whole situation is confusing and scary and...complicated."

"And sexy?" Kora raised a brow.

Lindsey knew a dare when she heard one. She had a policy to not lie to herself, but it was harder to admit the truth to a relative stranger. "And sexy."

Kora tilted her head in a half-shrug. "You have to see the whole picture to get real understanding. Talk to him. Maybe you're a terrible kisser and he's no longer interested in a roommates-with-benefits situation." She got up to toss her cup in the trash and pushed in her stool. "Or maybe a connection between you two is exactly what he wants, coercion be damned."

The advice hewed uncomfortably close to what Calliope had told her. She'd insisted that Lindsey could try all she wanted to use her magic, but without the connection to Dax, it wouldn't work.

"Do you always give such impassioned advice to people you've known all of an hour?"

"It doesn't usually take me this long. It's been sort of an off day."

Lindsey laughed and raised her cup. "Thanks for the coffee."

Kora nodded. "Come by the shop sometime. You can tell me all about the coercion."

She waved on her way out the door, and Lindsey felt like she'd been released from a whirlwind. Not exactly the distraction she'd been looking for, but Kora had made the conversation enjoyable.

This town was full of surprises.

---

LINDSEY BOUGHT the sword before she came home. The owners of the antique shop were delighted to see it sold since they had a katana they thought would go better with the dolls. She shook her head as she turned off her car and stared up at the house.

Kora made it sound so easy. Just talk to him. Explain why they should keep their distance and leave it at that. Except she didn't really want to keep her distance. He made her smile. He made her *want*.

Something deep inside her lit up when he came into the room, and she'd started to look forward to the beginning and end of the day when they spent time together. He'd made no effort to hide his interest, but until this morning, he'd accepted the lines she'd drawn.

This morning. It seemed like so long ago. She'd tried all week to call her magic, with no results. What had changed? Calliope had left, and Dax had been there instead. Lindsey had assumed the seal had pulled out her magic last week, but what if it had been Dax?

Why today and not any of the other times they'd been together?

Kora was right about one thing. Lindsey needed to talk to him.

She'd wasted most of the day wandering downtown enjoying her free latte, so long shadows crossed the driveway as she grabbed the wrapped sword from the back and locked her SUV. The keys jangled in her hand as she jogged up the steps before she could lose her nerve.

After her abrupt departure earlier, she'd half-expected Dax to be stand-offish toward her on her return, but Lindsey could hear him singing when she walked in. Off tune and with mangled lyrics, but singing.

The savory smell of baking bread and sautéing chicken met her before she turned the corner into the kitchen. Dax stood at the stove with his back to her poking something on the stove with a spatula. Smears of flour on the navy hand towel thrown over his shoulder matched a set down the side of his dark jeans. The scene was entirely too domestic, and yet, she wanted her part in it.

He danced to his own terrible music, and Lindsey couldn't help but appreciate the shimmy he threw in for flair. Heat rushed through her at the memory of being pressed against him only a few hours ago. Before she'd let fear and uncertainty chase her away.

His silly antics released the remainder of the stress from that morning, and Lindsey wondered if he'd been right about running. "I don't think those are the right words. Shakira would be appalled."

Dax grinned at her over his shoulder. "*My* hips don't lie."

Lindsey sat at the island to get a better view of the show, massively relieved that things weren't awkward between them. "What are you making?"

"Chicken fettucine alfredo. I had a craving for pasta. There's wine in the fridge if you want some." He returned his attention to the stove, and Lindsey finally recognized the feeling she'd been denying. Happiness. Dax made her happy.

She considered the wine. Alcohol might make the next

part of the conversation easier, but after the apartment fire, she'd decided to hold off on drinking for a while. Now that she lived with Dax, lowered inhibitions were twice as dangerous.

"I'm fine." Lindsey set the sword on the counter while Dax switched off the burner. "I didn't know you could cook actual food."

"Only *some* actual food. All of it chicken based." He brought two plates to the island and set one in front of her with a flourish. "Remember this the next time you complain about my waffles."

Lindsey laughed. "I can't believe you burned frozen waffles. That smell lingered all day."

He took the seat next to her and scoffed. "Now you're exaggerating. It was gone by lunch."

"You didn't come out of the office for lunch until almost three."

"There, you see? Three barely counts as afternoon. Not all day." He took a bite, then pointed his fork at the package. "What's this?"

Lindsey stopped eating to unwrap the paper enough that Dax could see the sword inside. The tarnish didn't detract from its beauty. At only about a foot and a half long, she assumed it was a short sword. The hilt consisted of a simple T with a swirl design barely visible along the cross guard, and the double-edged blade curved in, then out, before coming to a tip. Symbols were etched down the length of it.

"I went through some of the shops in town today. This was in the window, and I couldn't stop thinking about it."

Dax chewed slowly as he examined her find. "What are you going to do with a sword?"

"I don't know. Something about it spoke to me." She

glanced his way quickly. "Not literally. And how weird is it that I have to make that clarification. I just feel drawn to it."

They finished eating before Dax ventured another question. "There's no sheath?"

Lindsey gathered both their plates and took them to the sink. "They didn't give me one, but since I'm not planning to defend myself with it, I didn't think it mattered. It's not even sharp."

"Do you know how to use one?"

She propped her hands on her hips. "Do *you*?"

"Actually..."

Lindsey had to laugh at his guilty expression. "You do, don't you? Are you good? What am I saying, of course, you are. I've never met a bigger over-achiever. Is there anything you're not good at?"

Dax got up and grabbed a clean hand towel to dry the dishes. "When I was a kid, I was obsessed with weapons, like most of my friends. We'd run around in packs using sticks to sword fight. They eventually grew out of it, I didn't. My parents put me in fencing to try to save the neighborhood trees, and from there I moved on to any kind of combat training I could find. The weirder the better."

She jerked her chin toward the island. "If you know so much, educate me."

"It looks like a xiphos. The hilt almost had me thinking a La Téne, but those markings are clearly Greek. It's a good reproduction."

Lindsey remembered the glint in the sunlight, and the slight pull that had been the reason she'd run headlong into Kora. "Are you sure it's a reproduction?"

Dax took another long look at the sword. "The tarnish makes it look old, but those swords were mostly ceremonial, and they were from the Iron Age if I remember correctly.

Any iron sword from that time would be nearly dust with oxidation."

The antique shop owners had said they didn't have a record of where it came from. The sword simply appeared in their stock one day. But when Lindsey had asked about it, they'd had to pull out a giant ledger to check—the kind made of paper and bound in leather—so she wasn't too confident in their assertion.

Dax made good points, assuming he was the expert he claimed to be, but something inside Lindsey responded to the sword—the same way she'd responded to the woods outside...and to Dax. As if she recognized it.

"Do you know what the markings say?"

He draped the damp towel over the faucet and leaned his hip against the counter. "Are you telling me you didn't Google it within ten seconds of picking up the sword?"

Lindsey mimicked his posture, facing him with the length of the sink between them. "Google wasn't as helpful as usual, and you seem to have the exact knowledge needed to tell me about an obscure ancient sword I found in a second-hand shop."

A slow grin broke across his face. "It's not ancient, and maybe you Googled the wrong thing."

She tried to frown, but a smile kept peeking through. "You take that back. My Google fu is strong. And I noticed you haven't answered my question."

"I don't read Greek, but it probably says something like 'dumb tourists will buy anything'. You could try searching for people who wanted random Greek symbols tattooed on their body somewhere." He tapped his chin. "Actually, that would probably just get you page after page of frat guys doing keg stands."

Lindsey furrowed her brow in mock consternation. "I'm not sure if you're insulting keg stands, frat guys, or tattoos."

He shifted closer, shaking his head sadly. "All of the above."

"You shouldn't knock them until you've tried them."

His lips twitched. "I'll keep that in mind if I ever decide to revisit my college days."

Lindsey found herself staring at his mouth and yanked her eyes up to clash with his amused ones. "You don't have any tattoos from your time in the Army?"

"No. I've never felt the need to get one."

"Isn't that essentially a prerequisite to being a badass?"

His gaze traveled over the length of her. "You tell me. Do you have any tattoos marking your status as a badass?"

Her skin tingled, and she struggled to keep her breathing even. Arousal hit her swift and merciless.

"You've seen me mostly naked. Don't you remember?"

"I was trying to show you respect by not checking you out in that tiny bikini—a decision that nearly killed me by the way—so no, I don't remember."

Lindsey grinned. "I have one tattoo."

Dax stepped closer, and his thumb swiped along her chin, grazing her lower lip. "Do I get to see it?"

His touch left a swirling, fluttering emptiness inside her, and he didn't move away. He traced her jawline, then tilted her chin up as if he could read the answer in her face. Lindsey's pulse quickened with the temptation to lean forward—just a little. To give in for one more kiss and test the electric response he created.

Dax leaned instead, bringing his mouth inches from hers as his fingers splayed to stroke her neck. But he didn't follow through. A deep breath shuddered out of him, warm against her lips, and Lindsey ached to reach out.

She clutched at the dregs of her willpower, and when she didn't move, he stepped back, breaking contact.

"Maybe next time. Good night, Lindsey." He lifted her hand to brush his lips over her knuckles, then turned and left the kitchen. For the life of her, she felt like she'd just been seduced without realizing it. Was that even possible?

Lindsey walked to her room and washed up as if in a trance. It was early for bed, but the day had exhausted her. As she crawled under the covers though, part of her hoped to hear a knock.

She punched her pillow into a more comfortable shape and told herself she wasn't disappointed. He'd obviously wanted to kiss her, and she'd frozen up. No, frozen was entirely the wrong word.

She'd burned.

From the inside out, one simple touch had burned away all her reasons for resisting. Made her forget about the Fates and bonds and magic. Like before, she'd only been thinking of him.

And that preoccupation could become dangerous. Not to him. They'd proven her magic wouldn't hurt him, but Lindsey knew alliances didn't last. In the end, people always put themselves first, and she had to be prepared for that eventuality.

As she closed her eyes, Lindsey realized she hadn't talked to Dax as she'd planned, but after that good night, she definitely needed to set some ground rules in the morning.

## 6

—————

*Lindsey*

DAX DIDN'T SHOW up for breakfast, and when she checked outside, his car was gone. So much for establishing ground rules. When Calliope showed up for her usual magic lessons, Lindsey explained about Dax's influence yesterday and his magic immunity.

The cat assumed her spot in the windowsill. *That makes sense. Your bond with him is what gives you access, which I've told you over and over again. The magic is as much a part of him as a part of you, so it shouldn't burn either of you. In addition, while I applaud your dedication to practicing, it's not going to merit any actual magic unless Dax is participating in some way.*

Lindsey scraped her hair back into a ponytail, wincing at the too-tight elastic band. "He wasn't around the first time."

Calliope sighed. *We've discussed this.*

"Yeah, and you still haven't given me a solid explanation"

The cat's tail flicked back and forth, betraying Calliope's annoyance. *If you dislike my guidance, why not look elsewhere?*

*Given your human job, I'm sure you could track down alternate sources.*

Kora's invitation to her bookstore popped up in Lindsey's mind. She doubted she'd find much help at a local bookstore run by someone who barely qualified as a local, but Calliope's attitude and Dax's absence had her feeling jumpy. She'd caught herself listening for the sound of Dax's car and wondering where he'd gone so early. At least the bookstore would give her an excuse to leave the house.

Lindsey grabbed her purse and headed toward the door. "I think I will check out some alternate sources today. You should take a day off and chase some mice or something."

*Your cruel sense of humor is wasted on me. Take your time. It's not like you need my shield to protect you. Besides, Dax was muttering about being gone all day with a lady friend when he left, so I'll enjoy my solitude.*

The sense of triumph from Calliope meant she knew she'd won that battle. Lindsey made sure she locked the door, and sent a heartfelt prayer to whoever was listening that Dax had left his extra key to the house on the kitchen counter as usual.

She managed to drive down the long driveway and turn onto the road to town without conjuring a mental image of Dax with another woman. A visceral jolt of possession tightened her hands on the wheel briefly, but Lindsey pushed it away by working on a plan to surprise Kora with a milkshake-thing from Reggie's.

Hopefully, the excellent coffee would wash away the bitter taste of jealousy.

FROM THE OUTSIDE, Kora's store, Soul Exchange, looked like all the other shops in the downtown area. Once inside, though, Lindsey swore she felt magic flowing through the place.

Light spilled in from the large front windows, highlighting the bright white columns in the middle of the space holding a rainbow of books. Rows of dark wood bookshelves stretched to either side, running the length of the room. Rich navy walls with swirls of black, white, and silver continued onto the ceiling, where a fabulous mural of the night sky twinkled.

Lindsey stood in the doorway gaping until Kora called out to her. Her plan half-worked. Kora squealed in delight at the sight of the Sugar Bomb, as Reggie had called it. But her own latte hadn't stopped her imagination from running wild. Kora's shop, though, worked like a charm.

A large, ornate clock with glossy silver panels dominated the space behind the counter, but Lindsey couldn't stop glancing up while Kora drained her drink as fast as the last time.

"Are those stars really twinkling?"

Kora nodded, then leaned back with a contented sigh. "We have LEDs strung through the ceiling. They're connected to a different switch from the main lights, so we can turn them on and off separately. You should see it at night."

Lindsey shook her head and looked around at the dark color scheme. "It's beautiful now in full daylight. I don't know how you did it, but this place is both cozy and bright at the same time. I need you to come decorate my apartment. As soon as I have one."

"Thank you." The woman glowed with pride, and for a

second, with actual light. Lindsey blinked, and the fuzzy halo disappeared.

She tilted her head back and forth to try to replicate the effect, but no luck. The bell over the door tinkled before Lindsey could bring it up. A young, lanky girl in an ill-fitting sundress and a backpack waved when Kora shouted hello, then continued past them into the darker portion of the store.

With one last slurp on her straw, Kora tossed the plastic cup in the trash behind the counter. She dragged a box closer to start neatly stacking books in front of her. Lindsey leaned against the high counter and used the reflection of the mirrored clock to watch the girl. Kora didn't even glance that direction.

"I'm glad you came by, and not just for the morning treat. Us new girls in town need to stick together."

"I appreciate the sentiment, but you've been here for years."

"Yes, well Moira has been here for centuries, so by comparison we've barely unpacked the moving boxes."

"I still haven't met Moira."

Kora rolled her eyes. "You will. Moira can't help inserting herself into everyone's business."

The girl stopped halfway down the first row and crouched to pull a book from the bottom shelf. She flipped it open, read a few lines, then surreptitiously stuck it in her bag. Lindsey glanced at Kora, but the woman had her head under the counter.

"Are you sure it's Moira who's nosy?"

Kora popped up with a big grin. "I never said she was the only one."

Lindsey checked on the girl again. She'd moved down to the end of the row with a book in her hand and a bulging bag. To tell or not to tell? The girl couldn't have been more than twelve, a little young to be embracing a life of crime. Then again, this area wasn't brimming with resources. Sabine's family was practically royalty in town, and Sabine had been living in a run-down apartment complex before hooking up with Alex.

The girl turned the corner into another row, and Lindsey leaned closer to Kora so her voice wouldn't carry.

"The girl that came in is pocketing your books."

Kora didn't even look up from pricing. "I know."

Lindsey pressed her lips together and straightened. There must be more to the story, but she wasn't sure how to respond to Kora's easy acceptance. "You know her?"

Kora sighed. "Her family situation is crappy. She's an avid reader, but the library is small and doesn't have the rotating stock that we do. I see her twice a week. Once to take what she likes, once to return the ones she's read."

Lindsey frowned. "Are you sure you should be encouraging theft as a solution to her problems?"

"I don't feel like I'm encouraging so much as looking the other way. The books are always in good condition, and I sell them at used prices. We can afford the difference, but she can't."

Kora finished the first stack and moved on to the next while Lindsey watched the girl with narrowed eyes. There were times theft was the only option, but this wasn't one of them. She barely knew Kora, but the forgiving attitude would only encourage more people to take advantage of her. The situation wasn't healthy for either party.

"You should talk to her. Come up with an answer that doesn't involve breaking the law. If you're okay with her taking the books then returning them, why not make it official? Offer her a deal that has repercussions if she continues to steal but gives her the chance to read the books with your permission."

She blinked, her leaf-green eyes appearing huge for a second. "I hadn't thought of that."

Lindsey smiled as the girl approached. "Here's your chance. I'll be looking through your occult section."

"It's along the back wall."

The murmur of voices softened as Lindsey put distance between them. She hoped the girl could move past her embarrassment and take the deal. So often, people learn at an early age to skirt the rules—or break them entirely—and the habit builds on itself until very little is off limits. She'd had to chase down the results of those stories.

Kora could make a difference today in her bookshop.

The occult section didn't take long to find. It stretched across the entire back wall as she'd said. Lindsey's brows rose as she surveyed the extensive selection. Kora hadn't been exaggerating. Was there really enough demand for this many books on—Lindsey grabbed the bright red hardback in front of her and checked the cover—tantric love practices?

Actually, she'd bet that one got a lot of sales. Curious, she flipped through the first couple of pages, then slammed the book shut when she got to a detailed diagram. A blush crept up her cheeks as she slid the book back into its spot. The illustrated people were very flexible.

"That one any good?"

Lindsey spun around at Dax's voice, cursing the timing and praying the pink had faded from her face. "I don't know. I haven't personally tested it."

Horror dawned along with his grin when she heard her words. What was wrong with her mouth?

To her surprise, Dax turned away to scan the shelves.

"This isn't a bad idea. According to the internet, or at least the ten seconds I spent on it, Kora has the best assortment of magic books in the state."

Her eyes narrowed. "You're not going to make a stupid sex joke?"

"One, my sex jokes are hilarious. Two, you made it too easy. I like more of a challenge."

Lindsey relaxed and shoved down the disappointment in his lack of interest. She couldn't keep up with his back-and-forth flirting. Besides, hadn't he left to see a lady friend? What was he doing in the back of Kora's store? The man frustrated her like no other.

"I thought you were some kind of computer wizard. Can't you just hit a couple of keys and find the information you want?"

"I'm acutely aware of the reliability of information people put on the internet. Some is legit, some is made up by a guy living in a bunker. Deciphering between the two takes time and effort, and I'm a firm believer in working smarter, not harder."

Lindsey cocked her head. "How is this working smarter?"

He lifted a shoulder. "Kora vets her books. She's done the work to make sure the information isn't from unreliable sources."

She thought again about the tantric sex book. "You sound pretty sure of that for someone who's only just moved here."

"I've been here before visiting Alex. Kora and I became friends. She doesn't really give people a choice once she decides, but it worked out since I enjoy her company."

Was Kora his lady friend? Jealousy roared to life, swift and fierce. Lindsey took a deep breath in an attempt to get a handle on her chaotic emotions. They'd shared one kiss, and *she'd* pushed him away. Not exactly a reason to think she had any claim on him.

Thankfully, Dax didn't seem to notice her clenched jaw. He chose a book from the top shelf and read the back. "Her husband, on the other hand, can be downright scary."

All at once, Lindsey felt better, followed immediately by feeling stupid for not realizing the plain silver band on Kora's hand was a wedding ring. In her defense, Kora wore a lot of rings, but Lindsey prided herself on her observation skills. She'd based her career on them.

A quick peek down the aisle revealed that Kora had disappeared from the front of the store. The open-backed shelves made it easy to see that she wasn't hiding in one of the rows, and no one had come near the 'employees only' door next to them. Did she leave with the book thief? The shopkeepers in Deckard didn't seem very concerned about their wares. Or their customers, for that matter.

If Kora and Dax were friends, maybe she trusted him to watch the shop while she stepped out for a bit. Lindsey cast a quick look at Dax, who'd chosen a different book to search through. He wore what she thought of as his uniform— jeans and a dark tee-shirt that pulled just right against his biceps when he moved.

Kora had never mentioned a husband. What kind of man would prompt Dax to describe him as 'downright scary'?

Lindsey had trouble imagining anyone like that married to the sassy, bubbly Kora. Dax looked up from the book and caught her staring, then glanced down at her empty hands.

"Nothing of interest?"

His question snapped her out of the useless musing. Wondering about Kora's husband wouldn't help her any more than Calliope's vague instructions on handling magic.

Lindsey waved at the books. "Kora may vet her books, but anything we find here will be pure speculation."

He chuckled. "Are you so certain you're the only one on the planet with magical powers? That none of these people know anything about what you're going through?"

"I know for certain I'm *not* the only one, but Sabine didn't give me any helpful information."

Dax shifted toward her. "That's an interesting distinction. So, she gave you information that wasn't helpful?"

That damn blush wouldn't leave her alone. There was no way Lindsey would repeat Sabine's suggestion that she use sex with Dax to jumpstart her magic. "I understand your point, but how could Kora possibly know if one source is more legitimate than another?"

"If you don't think the books are helpful, why are you here?"

Because she needed to get away from the house before she did something stupid, and Kora provided a good excuse. Something else she refused to tell him. "Kora invited me, and I thought it wouldn't hurt to take a look. I'm still going to keep Googling the shit out of demigods and magic powers when I get back."

Dax tapped the book in his hand. "Why not both?"

Lindsey's lips curved at his cheerful question. "Both it is."

They searched for several minutes in silence. She ran her hands over the smooth bindings, searching for any titles that would contain instructions on magic use, but a question nagged at her, getting louder until she couldn't ignore it any longer.

"How did you meet Kora?"

He smiled like he'd read through her forced nonchalance. "I always check out the local bookstores whenever I go somewhere new. I love computers and every advancement they offer, but for reading, I prefer paper and ink when I can get them."

Lindsey made a noncommittal noise, but her estimation of him kicked up a notch. She preferred books to screens too. There was something about turning the pages in her hands. The weight, the texture, the smell. Even before the fire, she'd basically lived out of her car. Not exactly conducive to lugging around boxes of books.

The way he'd flirted with her from the first moment had given Lindsey the idea that he hit on any reasonably attractive female in his proximity. His answer hadn't exactly dissuaded that idea, but it did allay the image she had of him following Kora down the street like a lovesick puppy.

Kora chimed in from behind them, and Lindsey cursed her inattention for the second time that day. "David, my husband, was working that day, but I'd come in to help with some extra stock we'd gotten."

Dax laughed. "Sure you did. It took a full five minutes before you two came out of the back room. He couldn't stop grinning, and your shirt was on inside out."

"My shop, my rules."

Lindsey took in Kora's unapologetic grin and faced Dax with her hands on her hips. "He doesn't sound all that scary to me."

Dax faked a shudder as Kora giggled. "Dax only thinks David's scary because he said Dax would find his fate here. You should have seen the color leech from his face."

Lindsey sobered and met Dax's eyes. Now that they knew the truth about magic, offhand comments like that took on a different subtext. He shook his head subtly.

Lindsey hesitated then summoned a bright smile for Kora. She could wait until they got home to grill him.

"Did you work things out with the girl?"

Kora didn't skip a beat at the change in topic. "Yeah, we worked out a system for her. Thanks again for the suggestion. I can't believe it never occurred to me."

"I'm glad I could help." Lindsey chose a book at random, well away from the one with the bright red cover—nearly in the farthest corner of the store—and turned her smile on Dax. "I'm ready to head home if you are."

Heat filled his gaze, and she had sudden second thoughts about getting him alone to pump him for information. They'd never established those ground rules, so maybe a public place would be safer. Kora muttered she'd meet them at the front and quickly walked away. Lindsey swallowed her protest, trying instead for option two.

"Maybe we could grab lunch at the diner." Her voice came out breathless, much to her chagrin.

"Afraid to be alone with me?" Dax spoke quietly, but she heard him loud and clear.

Her chin came up. "I already told you I'm not afraid of you."

Dax moved closer. "Are you sure? Because you ran off pretty quickly yesterday morning."

The same spicy scent from before surrounded her, making her breath catch at the memory. "In case you've forgotten, we have a lot going on right now. My uneasiness wasn't just from you kissing me."

He crowded her against the wall, but didn't touch her. "I seem to remember you kissing me back."

Lindsey clenched the shelf behind her in a death grip to keep from reaching for him. "I've since decided it was a bad idea."

He leaned down, close enough that she could see streaks of green through the dark gold of his irises. "Maybe we should try again. Just to be sure."

Her heart pounded in her ears, and she took a ragged breath. Like last night, Dax held his position, waiting for her to decide. Lindsey wasn't shy. She wasn't some blushing virgin, not that there was anything wrong with that, but it wasn't her style. Before the shock of Calliope and magic and demigods, she'd have probably jumped at the chance to spend the summer enjoying this man.

But knowing that fate tied them together—that her ability to use a skill depended on a connection to him—made simple enjoyment impossible. Not to mention, Calliope's arrogant declaration still circled her mind. She couldn't be one hundred percent sure she wasn't using him to gain access.

Still, Dax tempted her to throw all her good reasons out the window. Maybe she should take her own advice—and Kora's—and talk to him.

"I don't want to use you," Lindsey blurted. As explanations went, it could have been better.

His lips twitched as he tried to hold back a smile. "You have my complete permission to use me any time you need."

"I'm not talking about sex."

"Too bad," he murmured.

Lindsey felt her own lips twitch at his response. "According to Calliope, you're the key to my magic. I can't control it right now, which makes me dangerous in ways even Calliope can't explain. I need to be able to control it, but I'm not going to use you as a tool to get there."

"And you think denying both of us will help you access your magic? I heard what the cat said. Your magic is tied to a connection between us. If kissing or sex or anything else we do together has the side-effect of making that connection stronger and bringing you that much closer to control, then I'm completely on board. Also, for other reasons that have to do with my desperate need to find your mysterious tattoo."

"Desperate, huh?" Lindsey barely recognized the husky voice as hers.

He brushed his lips against hers, a touch so faint she could have imagined it, and left a scalding trail along her cheek. "Let me help you."

Her eyes fluttered closed. "I don't need help." The instinctive response sounded as if it came from far away.

"Then use me," Dax whispered into her ear, accompanied by the press of his tongue against the racing pulse point in her neck.

Her palms ached from the edge of the shelf as she let go.

Lindsey trailed her fingers down his chest then dipped under his shirt. Dax held himself still for a few seconds, letting her explore, then he growled low in his throat and captured her wandering hands. His mouth found hers, and Lindsey melted against him.

His weight pinned her against the shelves, and a book landed on the floor with a heavy thud. She giggled, but the laughter turned into a moan when his hands slid over her ass to lift her. Lindsey wrapped her legs around his hips and locked her ankles at the small of his back. He gripped her thighs, and for once, she wished she'd worn a skirt.

Dax's hair tickled her face as he nudged her head to the side for better access. The length of him pressed against her core, and Lindsey stopped trying to control the deluge of bottled-up longing. She dug in her heels and arched into him, making them both gasp.

The tinkle of the bell above the door broke through her cloud of need. Anyone could stumble across them with minimal effort. The back of the store was darker than the rest, but not dark enough that they were hidden from anyone with functioning eyes. A thread of panic started to creep in despite the truly fabulous things Dax was doing with his tongue.

Lindsey leaned away, unclasped her ankles, and dropped her legs to the floor. Dax maintained his grip on her until she'd steadied herself, then readjusted to her waist. He laid his forehead against hers and laughed quietly.

"I've developed a deep and abiding hatred for that bell."

His forlorn tone made her smile. "It's not like this was going to go any further in the back of Kora's store."

"Her shop, her rules." Dax dropped a kiss on her temple, then put a little space between them. "Just to be clear, I like and respect you as a friend, Lindsey, but that's not all I want. I don't give a shit what the Fates decreed. As much as I'd like to take you home before you come to your senses, I promised a friend I'd help her out today. She's supposed to meet me here."

Lindsey pushed loose strands of hair behind her ear and peeked around his broad shoulders. She couldn't see the front from where they stood—thank goodness—but she could hear Kora talking with another woman.

When her attention returned to Dax, a startling possessive streak made her reckless. If he was going to be spending the day with a lady friend, Lindsey wanted him to know exactly what he'd be missing. She grasped a handful of his shirt and pulled him down to her mouth. He responded immediately, threading his hand through her hair with a deep groan.

Lindsey wrapped her fingers around his wrist and poured herself into the kiss, which was proving to be addicting. He wanted more, and she wanted to take a risk. People never lived up to their promises, but maybe this time would be different. Before she could lose herself completely again, Lindsey broke away, moving well out of his reach.

"Enjoy your day."

Dax adjusted his pants with a resigned sigh. "I don't suppose I could convince you to come with us."

She smiled. "Maybe next time."

## 7

*Lindsey*

*MAYBE NEXT TIME*... The words repeated over and over in her mind as she strode to the front of the store. Lindsey waved at Kora, using the diversion to get a look at Dax's lady friend.

She stood at an angle next to the counter, so Lindsey couldn't see much of her face. She noted long blonde hair falling around a willowy figure in a flowy summer dress, small boned but with fantastic legs that seemed to take up most of her body.

Kora continued talking to the mystery lady, and Lindsey noticed a book clutched in the lady's arms. Maybe this wasn't the friend Dax was supposed to meet. Kora seemed happy enough to see her.

Curiosity got the best of Lindsey, and before she moved past the big front windows, she turned back for another glimpse. Dax had joined them by the counter, and the blonde woman faced him with her back to the window. Still not a great view. Lindsey's gaze shifted inadvertently to Dax, and she met his eyes as he watched her walk away.

She didn't react outwardly, but her heart pounded at the promise in that look. *Next time.*

———

LINDSEY DROVE HOME ON AUTOPILOT, but the dark house reminded her that she'd had words with Calliope before she'd left that morning. She scowled. The cat would be ecstatic that she'd given in to her feelings for Dax. Even if they were tentative and mostly sexual.

After dropping off her purse in the kitchen, Lindsey headed for the workshop in the garage. She didn't want to meditate or envision glowing lights or whatever Calliope would suggest she do. Sabine had mentioned they stored their broken appliances and things in the workshop and given her free rein to tinker.

Sabine's dad had built the room from part of the garage something like thirty years before, but the walls and tables seemed solid. Storage took up one whole wall with drawers and open shelves covered in dusty relics. It had one tiny window, and she suspected it had never been cleaned. No problem, since the switch turned on the bright overhead light and a couple of task lamps hung over the workbench.

Lindsey cracked her knuckles and breathed in the welcome scent of oil and sawdust. This room had history, what with the racks of odds and ends from multiple genera-tions. A twinge of longing wound its way through her at the obvious representation of Sabine's family, but she moved past it.

What was the point? Anyone could collect old junk, and eventually someone would come clean this place out.

Nothing lasted. Living in the moment would have to be enough. A radio old enough to have a tape deck sat in the corner, and she smiled as she cranked it up. Classic rock, perfect.

The room so exactly fit what she needed that Lindsey wondered if Sabine didn't have a little psychic premonition thing happening. She flipped the lock and gathered her tools to get to work.

Fifteen minutes into messing with a Bluetooth speaker, Lindsey knew she wasn't alone.

*Are you going to fix that?*

Lindsey glanced down at the cat who had somehow gotten through the locked door to join her in the workshop. "It's not a hard repair. And Sabine is letting me stay here for free, so I might as well help where I can."

*You're helping in other ways.*

"Sure." She'd finally gotten all the inside parts of the speaker cleaned, but the battery looked sketchy. As she suspected from the water damage on other parts, the connecting parts of the wires had corroded. They'd probably left it out in the rain.

*You're helping me.*

"I still don't understand what you really want from me."

*I want you to bond with your guardian, learn to use your magic, and assist me in restraining the gods as I did before.*

Lindsey snorted out a dry laugh. "You mean the magic that only shows up at the worst times? At least Dax can do his job without needing training wheels."

Calliope hopped onto the bench and pawed at a loose screw until it clattered to the floor. *The bond takes time to solidify.*

Lindsey put down her screwdriver to glare at the troublesome feline. "Are you naturally an asshole or have you been a cat so long you can't help yourself?"

She sniffed a canister of sealant then sneezed. *That's a pretty bold statement coming from someone who* does *need training wheels.*

Rewiring the speaker wouldn't help unless she got a new battery for it, so Lindsey set it aside while she reined in her temper. "I came out here to be alone for a while."

*Too bad. You've been gone all day. Did you learn anything helpful?*

She'd learned that given enough time, Dax could probably convince her to get naked in public. The possessive look in his eyes as he'd watched her leave sent a shiver over her skin. His lady friend had stood in front of him with her perfect posture and her mile-high legs, and he'd stared right past her.

The way she'd clutched that book though... She'd wrapped her arms around the words and herself in a white-knuckled grip. Pretty pink nails to match her dress, but her hands gave her away. For the first time, Lindsey wondered what she'd needed with Dax, and how Dax knew her. Kora too, for that matter.

Back when she'd been chasing people instead of objects, she'd seen a lot of women with hands like that. Perfectly manicured, but desperate when no one was looking. Lindsey spread her fingers and laid her palms flat on the workbench. Scars and injuries criss-crossed her hands. Short, unpainted nails didn't draw attention or get in the way of her work. Heavy calluses roughened her palms.

She hadn't been desperate in a lot of years.

Calliope nudged her arm, and Lindsey jumped. *You didn't answer my question.*

What had she learned? "I saw Dax's lady friend."

The cat watched her without reacting. *And Dax?*

"Yes. I talked to Dax. We looked at magic books together. He'll be home later tonight." At least, she assumed he'd be home.

How much had that kiss changed their situation? Would he call if he was going to be late? Were they supposed to check in with each other? Lindsey shook her head. Relationships were exhausting.

Why wasn't the one with Sabine this confusing? Lindsey grabbed the speaker again, then studied the creature who'd started this mess—the same one currently bathing while lying in thick grey dust.

"What are the chances that Sabine and I became friends because of this demigod thing?"

She paused in her licking to blink at Lindsey's question. *Highly likely. It's instinctual you would feel drawn to each other. Like you are with Dax. Think of it like vibrating on the same wavelength.*

There was a whole lot more than vibrating happening with Dax. Better to skip past that part of the explanation. "Will I feel the same way with other demigods?"

*Most likely.*

Lindsey fiddled with the screwdriver. Calliope had given her the answer she expected, but she'd shied away from the real question bothering her. Now that she'd made some kind of commitment to Dax—though they still hadn't set any ground rules—she should stop ignoring the concern. And stop hiding from the answers.

"What about other guardians? Would I feel drawn to them too? Or would they be drawn to *any* demigod?"

The cat sat up, apparently as clean as she'd get. *I'm not sure, but you might be able to answer that. Do you feel a pull to Alex?*

Lindsey thought back to the few times she'd met him in person. He was attractive, yes, but in a distant way. She could acknowledge his hotness without wanting his hands on her. That was *not* the situation with Dax.

"No."

*What about Sabine and Dax?*

Possessive jealousy tried to make her thoughts sharp, but Lindsey had seen Sabine and Alex together. They were...a unit. She couldn't think of a better way to describe their dedication to each other. Lindsey rubbed her chest to try to relieve the small ache there. What would it feel like to be that connected? To *know*—absolutely, without doubt— that her partner would put her first.

"I've never seen Sabine and Dax together, but she's only ever wanted Alex."

*Based on your data, it appears the guardian-demigod connection is specific.*

Lindsey snorted. "My data is severely limited. I wouldn't call that definitive."

Calliope jumped down from the workbench to explore the shelves. *Call it what you will. I've presented you with evidence, and if you choose to believe the opposite, then so be it. That said, I don't understand your aversion to logic. Humans are strange.*

"You're the one who stepped in to 'save' us."

*Not just you. A war between the gods would be disastrous for everyone.*

"But it wouldn't be between the gods, would it? It would be between the gods and their kids—or at least descendants." Lindsey gave up on the speaker. She screwed the lid closed and sat back, stretching her arms. "Petty jealousy seems like a terrible reason to start a war."

The cat tilted her head. *You have a better reason? Aren't*

*most human wars started for similar reasons. One faction wants
what another faction has.*

Lindsey understood that tenet better than most. People
whose things had been stolen by someone else supported
the majority of her successful retrieval business. "Still not a
good reason for a war. Here's a question for you. The gods
have been free for months now, and you've only had one
encounter. What makes you so sure they won't just blend in
to the modern world and live their lives?"

Calliope popped her head out from behind a tackle box.
*Besides Apollo telling us specifically that he wanted the seal and
threatening everyone?*

"I heard he only threatened *you*."

*That's because he was attempting to recruit Sabine to their
side. Do you think he'll simply give up and leave because he failed?*

"How would I know? The only magic I've had to deal
with is my own." And that had been enough to worry about.
As much as Calliope stressed the danger of the gods,
Lindsey hadn't seen any evidence that they posed a threat.
Much less that a war loomed on the horizon.

She leaned back and spun slowly in the office chair. "You
haven't told me much about the Pantheon specifically.
There're twelve of them, right?"

*Yes. Think of them as people, with diverse and complicated
personalities, histories, abilities. The myths passed down to today
capture aspects of the truth.*

Lindsey dragged a foot along the floor to stop her lazy
movement. As usual, Calliope didn't offer any specific information about the gods. She'd thought she'd gotten used to
that frustration, but fresh anger churned in her gut. "How
can I protect myself from them if I don't know what they're
capable of?"

*Your magic is equal to theirs even at their strongest. The current climate of disbelief only offers a fraction of the energy they previously had access to.*

"Except I don't have access to my magic either."

*You will. When you stop fighting the connection with Dax. He's the key to your lock.*

Before, she'd tried to ignore the familiar refrain, but recent events made her pay attention. "I'm detecting some serious phallic symbolism going on here."

*You're not wrong.*

Lindsey rolled her eyes at Calliope's arrogant tone. "Assuming it'll be a while before Dax sticks his key in my lock, what other options do we have apart from me? Is there another seal somewhere?"

*We don't need another seal. The one we have will work fine.*

"It's broken."

*Don't let the trick I used to hide the seal fool you. The power held inside it contained the gods for a thousand years, and it retains much of that magic.*

Lindsey jolted forward. "The seal is still juiced up? Why the hell would you leave something so powerful lying around with only two humans and a useless cat for protection?"

Calliope straightened and lifted her chin. *I don't like your tone. We have two demigods, two guardians, and a former Muse protecting it. Against the weakened gods, those defenses should suffice. As they strengthen, so will we. Also, it seemed like a good idea at the time.*

Lindsey's hands clenched into fists as she checked the urge to strangle the cat. No one would blame her. She hated that Calliope expected them to square up against as many as twelve gods without any kind of plan other than hoping their magic worked when it needed to. What were they even supposed to do with the magic?

She imagined an energy battle taking place where they threw colored lights at each other with the intention of inflicting damage, like something out of a sci-fi movie. Assuming they could even locate the gods. The world was a big place, probably moreso as a spirit.

"How do you plan to find the gods now that they're lost?"

*They're not lost so much as...well-hidden. I'm planning to use the seal and the presence of a group of demigods to lure them in, but not all of them scattered when the seal broke. I've felt the residual magic of one of them lingering in the woods. Before you ask. No, I don't know which one.*

Lindsey tilted her head. "What do you mean *felt*?"

Calliope crawled behind a box, but that didn't stop her voice. *Magic has a specific energy, like I've been explaining. It's unique, almost effervescent. Remember when you touched the seal?*

"I could feel the bubble."

*You should be able to feel magic anywhere you encounter it, but some are better at concealing the power than others. Teasing out the nuance of a magical trail takes a fine hand.*

A magical trail. Lindsey and Sabine had become friends on a forum for wilderness trackers. They both excelled at picking up the clues required for effective tracking, and though they used their skills in different ways, they'd found a lot in common. Something else she could thank the Fates for? How much of her identity had originated at the whim of others?

Lindsey put the speaker back where she'd found it, then realized she couldn't hear the cat pushing her way through the junk on the storage racks. "Calliope?"

The locked door hadn't stopped Calliope from entering,

but Lindsey didn't want to take the chance that she'd trap the cat out here. The amount of dust indicated that the room didn't get used often. She checked all the drawers, moved the broken appliances, even put away all the tools that had been left out.

Where was that damn cat?

"Calliope?" She crouched down to scan the bottom shelves, but the cat had disappeared again.

———

SEVERAL HOURS LATER, Lindsey panted through her last set of burpees and wished she'd stuck with her research in the air-conditioned house. Unfortunately, the computer couldn't keep her interest. Following a trail of information usually soothed her as much as taking things apart, but nothing worked the way it was supposed to today.

As time had ticked by, Lindsey hadn't been able to sit still. She'd paced from her laptop on the dining table to the front window to the kitchen door, not sure what she was looking for, but not finding it. Her preliminary attempts to suss out any information on the sword had mostly confirmed Dax's claim—a modern xiphos made to appear old for dumb tourists.

She'd decided to work out instead, in the middle of the afternoon, in Texas. In June.

Was it possible to die from being smothered by the air? Lindsey huffed out a breath that blew her hair away from her face. The oppressive heat was slowly wringing all the moisture from her body. She'd given up on her tank top, tossing it into a wet heap on the patio, while she struggled through the last few minutes of her regimen in shorts and a neon-blue sport bra.

As she'd transitioned away from finding people, Lindsey hadn't necessarily needed to keep up with her training, but the last job proved she never knew when she'd need to defend herself against an asshole with a pipe. A life lesson if she'd ever heard one.

The anemic breeze blew hot air against her skin but didn't seem to be drying any of the sweat. Lindsey stood on the patio, her hands on her hips, trying to suck in enough breath to merit one more set. As her heart beat slowed back to normal, she remembered Dax's concern about someone spying on them.

She walked to the edge of the yard, her sneakers silent on the sparse grass, and peered into the woods. There wasn't a line where the cleared space ended and the forest began, more of a gradual fade from purposeful to wild.

Lindsey pursed her lips and peered at the silent house. She knew the feeling of being watched, and she'd bet a month of cheeseburgers she was alone right now. A quick look around wouldn't hurt anything, and maybe it would give her top a chance to dry before she put it back on. She snorted. Unlikely, but a girl could hope.

The trees grew close together around the backyard, and the brush made it nearly impossible to forge a path without losing some skin. Lindsey hissed as a dead branch scratched her stomach, leaving a long red mark. Even a wet tank top would have been better than half-naked. Another life lesson she should probably remember.

After the initial fight with the bushes though, the forest spread out around her with a little more space. Lindsey turned and eyed the distance to the house. Not too far, and the wall of branches provided plenty of cover. A simple zoom lens would be enough to see into the house.

Pressing her lips together, Lindsey tried to recall the

texture of the magic around the seal. Effervescent, as Calliope described it, but with a zip—static electricity minus the shock. She rubbed her hands together, then feeling supremely silly, reached out to touch the closest trunks at chest level.

The bark felt rough under her hands, but it was just bark. No magic tingles.

Lindsey glanced over her shoulder at the house again and blew out a breath. She was working on a lot of assumptions here—Dax's phantom creeper, Calliope's magic trail, her own ability to *feel* magic she couldn't summon.

She hadn't had to do anything special with the seal. The magic had existed, and she'd stuck her hand in it. The brush behind her made a damn good vantage point, but there were any number of other spots that would do as well.

In the shade of the soaring pines, the wind seemed a tiny bit cooler, but the heat still roasted the vegetation. The smell of warm pine straw drifted up to her as she took a few steps farther into the woods.

If she'd come to spy on the house... Lindsey turned completely and had to lean far to the left to see the blue siding. First, she'd make sure she had a good view of the smoking hot new guy living there. She hopped over a tangle of honeysuckle and past two trees to another fairly open area. From there, she had a great view of the upstairs windows, but the hot tub and the first floor were blocked by a wall of blackberry vines growing over a boulder.

The canes drooped with ripe fruit, so Lindsey picked one and popped it in her mouth as she crouched to examine the dirt. Tart sweetness exploded across her tongue, and in front of her, smears of dark purple marked where fallen berries had been crushed. No footprints to speak of, and she'd bet animals loved to visit this area for a snack, so not exactly conclusive. But the area was well outside of Calliope's shield.

Her eyes narrowed as she stood and approached the closest tree. Calliope had said the gods were incorporeal, but what happened when they gained more power? Would they be heavy enough to leave evidence of their passing? Lindsey reached out for the trunk and jerked her hand back when her fingers prickled. Not the same sensation as being engulfed, but definitely magic tingles.

She smiled as she gingerly touched the bark until she found the spot smudged with magic. The next tree in a line away from the blackberries also caused tingles. A honeysuckle vine stretched across her path, and when she brushed it, she nearly jumped at the strength of the magic. After some trial and error, she discovered the best markers sat at around hip level to her.

If she walked slowly and ran her hand along whatever happened to be next to her, she could follow the trail. When the tingles stopped, she backtracked and searched around until she found the right direction again.

Dax and Calliope had been right. Someone was watching them, and whoever it was had magic that worked.

Lindsey became so focused on finding the trail that she wasn't paying much attention to where she walked. Her foot came down on a section of loose dirt that crumbled away below her. She shifted her weight back and fell on her ass, staring across what looked like a gentle slope. The overgrown brush hid a steep drop-off into a short ravine with the trickle of a creek at the bottom.

She grabbed a thick branch to stand and jerked her hand back at the strong magic under her palm. This was no trace, and it was higher than the others had been. Lindsey stepped to the edge of the ravine and looked down. If she were climbing up the wall here, she'd probably use this branch as leverage for the last pull.

In the mud at the bottom, the sun winked off a piece of metal, and Lindsey thought she could almost make out a footprint. A bare footprint. Would non-corporeal gods be hindered by all the spiky dead stuff littering the forest floor?

Who else would possibly be wandering around barefoot?

Lindsey sensed movement to her left, but when she pivoted, a sharp shove launched her forward. She released a panicked gasp before her shoes lost purchase on the loose rock and she tumbled over. In a slow-motion free fall, she instinctively reached for Dax, then darkness took over with a bone-jarring impact.

## 8

*Dax*

EVEN IN HIS WILDEST DREAMS, Dax had never imagined wanting a woman the way he did Lindsey. Kora slapped his arm, and he returned his attention to the two ladies in front of him.

"You weren't listening at all, were you?" Kora smirked at him. She knew full well that he'd been watching Lindsey; he hadn't been trying to hide his distraction.

"Something about heavy boxes." Dax made the assumption since Ana worked in the bookstore and had asked to meet him there. She and Dax had become friendly during his previous visits, but she'd never asked for help before.

"Ana finally decided to give up that guest room situation and come stay in the efficiency above the shop. She needs your muscles."

The woman in question flushed a pretty pink. Everything Ana did was pretty. When active, her movements flowed like a dance, and when she became still—like now—

her long lean lines arranged into an exquisitely balanced example of poise. Blonde hair, blue eyes, creamy skin, Dax considered it a miracle Kora's shop wasn't constantly swarmed with suitors.

And yet, her perfect features did nothing for him, even before he'd met Lindsey. Ana personified beauty and kindness, and he preferred a prickly retrieval specialist who had the ability to melt his brain with a single touch.

Ana looked at him now, making direct eye contact despite the blush. "I don't have much, and I could handle it on my own if there weren't so many stairs involved."

Kora snorted. "Your knee is only barely out of that brace. The place is furnished, but I think all the furniture is shoved together in the middle of the living room. Dax can do the heavy lifting of your measly possessions and arrange whatever you need while you lounge around giving orders."

Ana laughed. "You know I'm not great with orders."

"Strongly worded suggestions then. I'd offer up David, but he's working his way through the new sci-fi shipment."

Dax crossed his arms. "Why am I being conscripted if David is allowed to stay home and read?"

Kora patted his cheek. "Because I have other plans to make him tired and sweaty."

He didn't have a good response to that, so he turned to Ana. "I'm happy to help. Point me toward your place, and we'll have you moved in no time."

Ana thanked him while Kora returned to her position behind the counter and waved them on their way.

---

AFTER HOURS of carting boxes and shuffling couches, Dax wasn't in the mood to socialize, but Ana insisted on providing dinner. Since all of Ana's things were still in boxes, he suggested they order pizza at his place.

Dax hoped the pizza would be enough to lure Lindsey into joining them, but the house was empty when they arrived. He left Ana in the kitchen with the delivery number and did a quick search. Lindsey's SUV was parked in the driveway, but her bedroom—and every other room—was empty.

Ana thanked the person on the phone and hung up as he walked into the kitchen. She flashed him a smile. "Pizza will be here in fifteen minutes. I'm surprised it's so fast, but I guess this address is a regular customer."

Dax nodded absently. "Yeah, it's the only place we can get the weird vegetable pizza that Lindsey loves."

Her smiled dimmed. "Where is the infamous Lindsey?"

"I wish I knew." He wandered to the back window and checked the patio. No Lindsey, but a pile of wadded up white fabric caught his attention. Had the watcher returned or was Lindsey out there somewhere without some of her clothing? After their encounter that morning, he'd believe either.

"Excuse me, I have to go check something." If Lindsey had planned a surprise that involved naked time, he wanted to give her fair warning that Ana had come home with him.

He'd taken two steps onto the patio when a falling sensation tossed his heart into his throat. The strange awareness disoriented him, but the stillness that followed was much worse. Dax couldn't explain how, but he knew the feeling had come from Lindsey. Still came from Lindsey.

Bitter panic coated his mouth. Whatever magic switch she'd flipped had jolted him into a visceral connection with her, but after that initial vertigo, all he sensed was pain and darkness.

Lindsey needed help, and the pull in his chest told him where to go. Without thought, he took off into the woods.

"Dax, wait."

He hadn't heard Ana come out, but it didn't matter. He had to get to Lindsey. The crunch of running footsteps quickly catching up behind him made it clear she didn't actually need him to wait.

There weren't any trails in the forest, and Dax growled in frustration as the undergrowth blocked his path. The heat pressed down on him as he tried his best to hurry. In the back of his mind, he knew he should send Ana back— running over uneven ground in the woods was a good way to reinjure her knee—but he didn't spare the breath.

He almost missed the drop-off and had to throw out an arm to keep Ana from tumbling over. The ravine tore a swath through the forest, mostly hidden by the overabundance of plants. He could see the remains of a creek at the bottom, deeper than he'd expected, and another nearly vertical cliff face on the other side hidden by bushes and young trees.

The force inside him said Lindsey should be here somewhere. Dax edged closer and peered down. Frustration mounted as he scanned the shadows. Then he saw it. A strip of bright blue about twenty-five feet down, tucked into the side of the cliff.

"Lindsey!" She didn't move at his shout, and Dax pushed back his fear to summon the focus that had served him in the Army.

He started the climb down, concentrating on one handhold, then the next. When he reached the ledge, Ana was already crouched by Lindsey's prone form. How in the hell had she beaten him down?

She moved aside for Dax, and he winced when he got

his first good look at Lindsey. She lay crumpled on her side, her hair obscuring her face. Bruises and scrapes marred her torso, and for a split second, it was Beth all over again. But he could see her chest rising and falling.

Dax mercilessly shoved that memory deep down. Lindsey was *not* his sister.

He brushed the hair away from her face and checked her pulse just to be sure. Strong and steady. Lindsey groaned his name, and his eyes closed on a sigh of relief.

"Lindsey, can you hear me?" Dax repeated the question twice more, but all he got was a frown on the third one. Not awake, but responding. Ana shifted beside him, reminding Dax the three of them balanced on a dirt ledge that didn't inspire a lot of faith.

"How'd you get down here?" He didn't spare her another glance as he methodically checked Lindsey for broken bones.

"There's a ridiculous little trail up that way." She gestured to her right along the cliff, but Dax didn't see anything. "It's steep, but doable. And a heck of a lot easier than climbing down a cliff."

As far as he could tell, Lindsey had fallen from the cliff above and landed perfectly on the ledge to avoid any serious injuries. He glanced up and noted the abundance of bushes and branches that she'd have fallen through to get to this spot. That explained the abrasions.

"Do you see any injuries on her other than the cuts and bruises?"

"No, and I left my phone back at your place. I can run back and call for help—"

"I've got her." He knew from experience how slow rescue teams could be in the wilderness. Dax grunted as he lifted her, and once upright, Lindsey's lashes fluttered as she curled her body into his.

The trail was indeed ridiculous—probably a former deer path on its way back to obscurity. By the time they reached the top, Dax's thighs were on fire, but he'd endured worse. He found the landmarks he'd automatically memorized on the way there and started the trek back to the house.

"I'm not sure moving her after a fall is a good idea, Dax." Ana's tentative plea didn't slow him down, but he did put extra care into not jostling her as they hiked back.

The internal sense that had guided him to Lindsey ebbed and flowed as she fought toward consciousness. Dax assumed she'd reached out with her magic and strengthened part of the bond Calliope was always talking about, which let him know that she wasn't suffering from internal injuries.

As the backyard came into view, Lindsey surfaced enough to mumble into his shirt.

"Put me down."

Dax's arms tightened involuntarily as he headed for the cars parked in the front of the house. "I'm taking you to the hospital."

"No. Take me to bed."

With his hands splayed across her warm skin and her lips pressed against him, his body perked right up. "You fell off a cliff, Lindsey. I don't think you're up for a game of hide the salami."

She snorted then groaned. "Don't make me laugh. Hurts my head."

"Even more reason to take you to the hospital."

She hooked her hand loosely around the back of his

neck and levered herself up an inch. "I'm serious. I'll be fine once I get some rest. I can feel it."

His steps slowed. He could feel it too, but that awareness had faded from the absolute knowledge it had been before to a faint impression. Was he really going to trust Lindsey's well-being to a faint impression?

She sighed and whispered, "Trust me."

Dax readjusted her as she drifted off again. He *did* trust her, but it was his job to protect her. A role that had become vividly real in the last half hour. Then again, if she woke up in the hospital, it could destroy what little faith he'd managed to cultivate.

Ana had walked silently behind them to that point, but she stepped up next to him when Lindsey quieted. "I'm going to head home unless you need me for anything else. Thanks for your help today."

"Thank *you*. I'm not sure I would have found that trail without you there." They rounded the house, and Dax noticed a pizza box sitting on the front porch. He shook his head. "At least take the pizza. We'll have to try dinner again some other time."

Sadness tempered her smile. "Without any medical emergencies preferably." Her focus dropped to Lindsey for a moment. "She's lucky to have you, Dax. I hope she recovers quickly."

Ana limped heavily to the porch then back to her car, and Dax grimaced. He'd been right—she'd hurt herself trying to help Lindsey. He owed her a hell of a lot more than a pizza.

His arms screamed from the weight of carrying an adult woman that far, but he sighed and made his way back around the house. Lindsey wanted him to trust her, so he would. He'd take her to bed, as asked, but he'd do it his way.

She could sleep in her room, but he'd be right there with her—full observation. And if she showed any signs of getting worse, he'd break every traffic law in the state getting her to the hospital.

Dax managed to get the backdoor and her bedroom door open without dropping her, a feat considering he was losing feeling in his fingers. Lindsey didn't stir when he laid her on the bed or took off her shoes. Her bra and shorts were streaked with dirt and sweat, but he decided against removing any more clothes.

In their bathroom, he grabbed two washcloths and wet one with warm water. A quick wipe down of the areas he could reach would have to do until she could stand on her own and shower. Dax used the same technique on himself, but he had the benefit of sneaking into his room for a change of clothes. By the time he'd tossed everything into the laundry basket, the sun had begun to set. He sank down on the bed next to Lindsey to check her vitals again, preparing himself for a long night on the wooden chair in her room.

Her pulse beat against his fingers in a regular rhythm, and Dax reminded himself to set an alarm to wake her in an hour. Lindsey had other ideas. She grabbed his hand before he could move away and tugged.

Dax brushed her hair away from her face. "Get some sleep while you can. It's going to be a long night."

"Stay here."

"I am staying. I'll be right in that chair, annoying you every hour by waking you up."

Her brow furrowed, but she didn't open her eyes as she tugged on him again. "No, stay *here*."

In her bed. With her. Dax ran his free hand through his hair and thought for half a second about telling her no. She might not remember this in the morning, and he didn't relish being stabbed first thing. But Lindsey was worth the risk.

"Okay. I'll be right back."

She grumbled as he extracted his hand but didn't ask again. Dax had already changed into pajama pants and a basic tee-shirt, but he needed his phone for the alarm. He grabbed it off the bathroom counter, programmed the alarm to go off every hour, and rejoined her on the bed. She'd snuggled under the blankets, so he stretched out on top of them and set his phone on the nightstand.

Sabine and Alex had a pretty nice set-up for guests, but Dax wasn't a small guy. He took up more than his fair share of the mattress space. To his surprise, Lindsey didn't scoot closer to him. Instead, she stayed rolled in a ball on the far edge. He got the feeling she wasn't used to this much bed. His sore muscles started to relax as he tried to take his own advice and get some sleep. The adrenaline spike after Lindsey's mental body slam had faded, but the events of the day kept replaying over and over again in his head.

Laying on his back, Dax watched the deepening shadows on the ceiling. Speculating on what had happened to Lindsey wouldn't do much good until she could tell him the story.

The air conditioner kicked on, and Dax's stomach growled. They'd skipped dinner, but he didn't want to spend too long anywhere that he couldn't see Lindsey—as if having her within arm's reach would be enough to keep her safe.

She rolled over, reached out, and laid her hand on his chest. A fierce protectiveness surged to life inside him, more than he'd ever felt for anyone—including his sister. He swallowed the urge to gather her close, to be reassured by her heart beating against him.

Dax supposed he should blame the Fates for his fascination with her, but truthfully, he didn't give a damn. Lindsey was a gift. In their time together, she'd made his life better in a thousand little ways, and that wasn't counting the scorching attraction between them.

He'd ribbed Alex for not being able to go out of town without Sabine, but he got it now. Dax covered Lindsey's hand with his and closed his eyes. Guardian, protector, procurer of pizza—whatever Lindsey needed, he'd provide.

A tiny voice inside worried what would happen when the nomadic Lindsey needed space and freedom, but Dax silenced it. She'd be there until the end of the summer, at least. They'd deal with that eventuality when it happened.

---

IN THE NEAR DARKNESS, Dax awoke on his back to find his arm pinned between Lindsey and the mattress, numb from her weight laying on it. He flexed his fingers and welcomed the pins and needles that meant she'd turned to him in her sleep, kicking the blankets to the floor. The alarm blared for the fifth or sixth time—he'd lost count by that point.

She wasn't on top of him exactly, more like curled into a tight little ball against his side, but one hand had crept under his shirt to lay flat on his abdomen. As he considered the best way to shift her, she stroked his stomach and a bolt of lust shot straight through him.

"I'm not asleep," she whispered.

Dax abandoned his plan to restore blood flow to his arm. "How are you feeling?"

She sighed and goosebumps raised in waves along his

chest where her breath had touched him. "I'm tired and sore, like I didn't warm up properly before a workout, but that doesn't seem right."

"I think your magic and some epic first aid from a friend helped speed along the healing." He covered her hand with his, and to his relief, she didn't pull away.

"How badly was I hurt?"

Her raw voice tore at him, but Dax didn't want to pile his fears onto her. She wasn't Beth. She'd heal and be back to torturing him with separate rooms in no time.

"Hard to say. Ana got to you first—she's very limber. Once I found a way down, the bruises were already fading. Nothing broken, but you didn't wake up. Not at first. Not until we'd made it back to the house." Up until that last part, he'd nailed the neutral tone, but even he could hear the tension in his voice at the end.

She stroked him again, then twined their fingers together. "I'm sorry I scared you."

Apparently, he sucked at keeping his worries to himself. "There's nothing to apologize for. You fell off a cliff."

Her hair tickled him as she shook her head. "Something pushed me. You were right about someone watching us from the woods. I found a trail leading from the patio into the thick brush that someone had taken pains to hide."

Dax frowned. "I checked for footprints."

"There weren't any. Calliope said something that made me think about the texture of magic. The way it feels different against my skin than it does inside me. I could feel the magic used along that trail to hide it." Lindsey closed her eyes, and Dax wondered if she'd fallen back asleep. He stroked her hand, and she snuggled closer, tucking her face against his chest before she continued.

"I followed it to a ravine. Not too far down, but really

steep. The trail disappeared as if whatever left it floated out into space. I was debating climbing down a little to see if I could catch it again when I was shoved from behind."

She shuddered, and Dax fought to keep his touch light. He wanted to crush her against him as he remembered the mad rush into the woods with Ana. The breathless panic when he'd seen her halfway down that ravine in a heap.

"I felt you fall."

Lindsey levered herself up to stare at his face, though he doubted she could see much in the darkness. "You *felt* me fall?"

"I found your shirt in the backyard, then a whoosh like I'd stepped off a ledge...then nothing." Dax pulled her back down. "The nothing came across like white noise. Or like when a call is connected but no one speaks. You were there, but not."

Lindsey wiggled around until she'd twined one leg over his, then sighed. "That's new."

"And useful." Dax adjusted her knee down away from the danger zone, then caught himself before he stroked up her thigh. She'd asked him to stay, not fondle her, no matter how perfectly she fit against him.

"Do you feel it now?"

Dax's brows rose until he realized she was talking about the connection, not her thigh. He took a second to seriously consider her question. The underlying link hadn't disappeared completely, but the traces of *thereness* had abated.

"Not really. You think that was the bond Calliope keeps pushing?"

Lindsey lifted a shoulder. "Probably, but at this point I wouldn't rule anything out. I keep thinking it's a miracle I wasn't seriously injured in that fall. Then I remind myself it was most likely something to do with magic that protected me."

A visceral wave of possession urged him to stake a claim, but he clawed past it, fighting to keep his voice neutral. "Protecting you is supposed to be my job."

She stiffened, barely noticeable but there. "I can protect myself."

"That's debatable. You wandered off in the woods alone without telling anyone where you were going, then let someone sneak up on you. What if they'd had a weapon?"

He expected her to get defensive and try to kick him out of the room, but all she did was sit up again so she could poke him in the chest with a finger. "Seeing as how I'm not a child, I'm allowed to wander the woods on my own."

"I'm talking about basic precautions, not baby-sitting. I know you're not a child."

She poked him again, with more authority. "Prove it."

The possessive urge churned up again, stronger than before. Dax captured her finger, and in a flash, reversed their positions. He braced his upper body on one arm, but his leg pinned hers to the mattress. The sleep pants he wore didn't hide his reaction to having her underneath him. Her lips parted on a tiny gasp, and her hand twitched in his.

She could get him off of her if she wanted to—she'd done it before in practice, and all she had to do was ask. Dax didn't intend to take the move any farther, not when the reason for his presence in her bed directly correlated to finding her unconscious. Lindsey yawned, reinforcing his resolve to prove his point and nothing more.

This situation called for full honesty. "I want to finish what we started in the bookshop, but I also want you to be one hundred percent not concussed when we do."

Lindsey laughed. "That's fair. In my expert opinion, I'm

already one hundred percent not concussed. Before I get distracted again though, I should say thank you."

Dax cocked his head. "For what?"

"Finding me, bringing me back here instead of the hospital...staying."

Her breath shuddered out, and Dax recognized the need for reassurance. Lindsey had been vulnerable—still was to some extent—and she hadn't expected him to follow through. She had thought she'd wake up alone in a hospital bed.

Dax was determined to keep proving her wrong. "That part was easy. It's going to be hell getting me to leave."

"So don't." Her teasing smile nearly undid all his hard work.

He traced a raised scratch across her stomach, sliding both their hands along her skin. "You're much more lucid than earlier, but your body is still covered in marks from yesterday."

"I believe we've already established that I'm fine, and I can make my own decisions." She shifted her hips slightly, bringing him closer to her center.

Dax groaned, his body eagerly ready to take what she offered and his mind clutching at excuses. "Lindsey, we both need to rest."

"I don't want to rest. I want—"

He stopped her mid-sentence with a kiss. A slow exploration of her lips that he'd been dying to do since she'd whispered to him in the dark. Her fingers curled into his hair, but when she tried to pull him down, Dax held his weight off of her.

Lindsey dropped her head back onto the pillow. "This is some kind of torture, isn't it? I'm being punished for winning the towel."

He rolled to the side, pulling her back against his front with an arm around her waist and another under her head. "You won that towel fair and square, but the rematch will be a different story. Get some rest. You don't have a chance if you can't even stand on your own."

"You're not the boss of me."

Dax chuckled at her disgruntled tone. "I know."

A couple of seconds ticked by, then Lindsey laid her arm over his and linked their fingers together. "Are you going to keep waking me up every hour?"

Dax buried his nose in her hair, inhaling the coconut scent that seemed to persist despite all odds. "Affirmative, and I'll still be here in the morning."

And every morning after, if he had his way.

## 9

*Lindsey*

WAKING up to Dax curled around her in bed might be worth almost dying. Lindsey tended to sleep in a ball, a holdover from her youth, but this morning, she'd unclenched into a loose half-moon. Dax's arm banded along her ribcage to hold her against him, and his body curved to match hers, which meant her ass snuggled right up against his morning wood.

At some point in the many, many wake-ups during the night, he'd covered them both with the blanket. Lindsey tested her muscles, and though many of them were sore, none twinged in a way that indicated a problem. She was tired, but her head didn't ache and her vision seemed normal when she finally blinked the room into focus.

Ugh, mornings were bright in her room. She could leave the bed to close the curtains, but Dax didn't seem inclined to let her up. Instead, she rolled over and hid her face in his shirt. Lindsey inhaled and let out a contented hum. Dax smelled like warm, spicy cotton. Despite the attempted murder yesterday, she felt pretty good.

He sighed and wove his fingers through her hair, catching a tangle on his rough hands. Falling down a cliff wasn't exactly conducive to smooth, shiny locks, especially since she'd tied it back for her work out before the little detour. Lindsey leaned down to sniff near her armpit, then wrinkled her nose. Dax smelled great, but she needed a shower.

Totally unfair, since he'd carried her out of the woods. She wasn't small-boned, so he must have worked up a sweat. And yet...she breathed in deep. The bathroom offered a greater temptation than the curtains, but even the promise of clean pajamas wasn't enough to draw her away from the warm, comfortable bed.

She intended to go back to sleep, but the hand in her hair trailed down her neck, her shoulders, and her bare back to flatten just above her shorts.

"Good morning," he murmured in her ear. His rough voice sent shivers chasing across her body.

Lindsey tilted her head up and met his gaze, as sleepy and content as she felt, but with an edge of heat in the hazel depths. "Morning."

"How do you feel?"

"Not like I fell off a cliff. A little soreness, but like I repeatedly said last night, I'm fine." A lot of the wake-up time last night was a blur, but she remembered pushing him with those words. *I'm fine...I can make my own choices...Prove it.*

"Good to know." His thumb stroked a line of fire across her lower back, and Lindsey struggled to pay attention to what he was saying. "Please don't go off alone again. Especially now that we know the threat is real."

"I can take care of myself." Lindsey looked away. She remembered saying that the night before as well—something she'd always believed—but how true was it?

If Dax hadn't come for her, would she still be lying in that ravine? Her hazy memories and bone-deep exhaustion indicated that yes, she'd have spent the night alone, half-unconscious, in the woods where someone had just tried to kill her. Or at least tried to cause serious harm.

Her hands twisted in the cotton of his shirt, and her heart sped at the helpless feeling she abhorred. "I'm sorry. You're right. I need to take better precautions."

Dax lifted her chin and waited until she'd given him her full attention before speaking. "We should *all* take better precautions. I didn't fully believe Calliope when she talked about the gods. None of it sounded entirely real, and even touching the power in the seal didn't convince me of the danger. We can do better. It sounds like whoever shoved you took advantage of a convenient situation, which indicates they don't have a lot of magical power yet. They had the advantage of surprise, but now that we're aware, we can more effectively protect ourselves."

Lindsey nodded slightly, acutely aware of the tweaks in her muscles as she moved. "What did you have in mind?"

He traced her jaw with his knuckles, sending her heart racing for a different reason entirely. "I'm torn. On the one hand, I want to investigate and see if we can't learn anything about your attacker. On the other, it's hard to make another attempt if we never leave the bed."

Lindsey had made her decision yesterday in the bookshop. She hadn't wanted to use him, but willing, eager participation allayed that concern. As long as he didn't start trying to put stupid limits on her, staying in bed sounded amazing. They could investigate later.

She smoothed her hand down his chest to slip under his shirt, bunching the fabric as she traced the grooves in his abs. "If we're going to stay in bed, you're wearing too many clothes."

Heat flared golden in his eyes as he angled her onto her back. "That's easily remedied." He reached behind him to pull his shirt over his head, then tossed it across the room. "Better?"

Lindsey nodded as she spread her hands over all that glorious skin. Dax did some exploring of his own. His hand skimmed up the outside of her thigh, veering around to grip underneath when he reached the material of her shorts.

Need pooled low in her belly, and she maneuvered her ass closer in the hopes he'd keep moving upward, but Dax simply adjusted with her. When she trailed her lips across his collarbone, his fingers dug in, urging her legs farther apart.

She lifted a knee up next to his hip to settle him firmly between her thighs. His pajama pants did nothing to hide the firm length of him pressed against her core, exactly where she wanted him.

"So much better than the dream," he murmured.

Lindsey searched his face. "You had dreams too?"

Dax dropped a biting kiss on her lips, then bent to nuzzle her neck. "Yeah, but I much prefer the reality."

She snickered, embracing the moment and pushing aside the niggle of doubt. There'd be plenty of time later to examine the meddling of the Fates. "I'm sure the stench is a real turn on. I'm filthy. I should shower first."

Dax rocked his hips forward, making Lindsey hiss at the delicious pressure. "Do I look like I care?" He pulled back with both brows raised. "Unless you want me to join you in the shower. It looks like it's big enough for two."

Lindsey feigned deep thought. "Nah. I'm good. Besides..." She arched up to whisper in his ear. "Sometimes I prefer filthy."

She'd never bothered to tell that little tidbit to anyone before. Lindsey had always considered sex pleasurable, but not anything she couldn't handle on her own. Certainly not worth the drama that came from getting involved with sexy, confident men. Dax was quickly proving her theory wrong.

He smirked and backed away from her, only to haul her to the edge of the bed. Quivers of anticipation stole her breath as he slowly removed her shorts while kissing his way down her legs. She sat up to peel off the gross sports bra, then yelped as Dax nipped her inner thigh.

Kneeling between her legs, he looked up at her and grinned as he took in her naked figure tangled in the sheets. Lindsey had never spent much time thinking about her body other than keeping it healthy and fit, but the appreciation on Dax's face caused her stomach to clench.

He held her gaze and kissed the spot where he'd bitten her, then a bruise down a little farther, a scrape near her knee, a tiny scratch on her other leg. Soft and gentle, and not at all what she'd been expecting. Dax took his time and found every spot where she'd been hurt, ending at her mouth.

"I'm sorry I wasn't there to protect you." He whispered the words against her lips, and the sorrow in his voice pierced her heart.

For perhaps the first time in her life, Lindsey didn't immediately profess her utter capacity to take care of herself. He wasn't maligning her abilities—more than anyone, he knew her skills. For once, instead of feeling defensive, she felt cherished.

The air conditioning blew cool air across her heated

skin, and she shivered as she cupped Dax's jaw, his stubble rough against her palm. She kissed him, not with fire or lust, but with a different kind of need. Lindsey needed him to know she cherished him too.

They breathed together, lost in each other, as Dax lowered her back to the bed. Before she'd had a chance to recover from the emotional barrage, he'd returned to his position between her legs. The slow, wet glide of his tongue nearly shot Lindsey off the mattress.

She whimpered as he expertly played her, and called out his name when the sensation became too much to bear. His smirk returned when she recovered enough to relax the fists she'd clenched in the sheets.

"My god, how do you do this to me? You're still wearing pants, and this is already the best sex of my life."

Dax chuckled against her stomach. "I can't tell if that's high praise or a really low bar."

Lindsey buried her hands in his thick hair and tugged until he'd brought his talented mouth back up to her. "Both. It's both."

He shucked his pants and followed her as she scooted back on the bed. Lindsey pushed against his chest for a second, and he eased back with a frown until he realized she was reaching for her bedside drawer.

She rummaged around, thankful she'd planned for inevitably giving in, and sent him an eyebrow waggle when she emerged with a condom. Dax laughed and tried to snatch the packet from her, but Lindsey wanted the pleasure of sliding it on.

It was his turn to suck in a breath when she reached between them. His head dropped down next to hers as she teased him with leisurely touches. Dax growled into her ear, a rumble that sent lightning streaking straight to her core, and she rolled the condom on.

A quick flick of his fingers against her wetness, and he surged home. Lindsey groaned and locked her legs around him. Dax laced their fingers together and stretched her arms above her head as he moved, slowly at first.

Lindsey gripped his hands tight as the rhythm increased and she arched, straining up to meet him. He took her mouth in a deep, soul-delving kiss. Her eyes closed at some point, and Dax's touch became her anchor to the world.

For a brief moment in time, she let go of her need for control. Dax's hands released hers to lift her hips, and a riotous tension built inside her. Lindsey's nails dug into Dax's shoulder as her breath hitched. Waves of pleasure washed over her and starbursts exploded behind her closed lids.

Dax groaned against her mouth, then collapsed on her, gasping for air. Lindsey wound her fingers through his hair, struggling for breath herself. His arm tightened around her, and he kissed her neck under her ear. The sweet gesture caused another shudder. Apparently, she was sensitive there, and he'd figured it out before she had.

What else would she learn about herself from him?

He buried his nose in her hair and let out a satisfied hum. Lindsey didn't catch any words, but she understood the sentiment. She hadn't been this relaxed in...possibly ever.

Dax left a trail of kisses along her neck and jawline. "I'm not sure I can move my legs. How're you feeling?"

Lindsey surprised herself by giggling. She slapped a hand over her mouth but the giggle continued. "Fantastic, but now I'm sticky as well as filthy."

Dax rolled them over so she lay sprawled on top of him. "How about that shower?"

---

To Lindsey's great pleasure, the shower was indeed big enough for two. She'd have to thank Sabine later. Dax suggested they move to his room after they got clean, and he didn't have to do much convincing to get Lindsey to crawl into his bed while he raided the fridge for food.

After an impromptu picnic of grapes, orange juice, and peanut butter sandwiches, Dax had laid down, pulled her against him, and covered them both with the blanket. Lindsey couldn't imagine a better morning. She curled up with her head on Dax's shoulder and traced designs across the ridges of his abs.

He stroked her back, from her nape down to the curve of her ass and up again. She didn't think Dax intended the languid movement to tempt her, but that's how her body reacted to it. Everything the man did tempted her, but lying next to him naked added a pleasurable new layer.

Lindsey didn't usually spend time with her sexual partners after the fact, preferring a quick getaway. They'd served their purpose, and she had no more use for them. She'd been accused of being cold, but until Dax, she hadn't seen the benefit of cuddling. Honestly, she still didn't see the benefit, but she loved the freedom it offered her to explore his body on her terms.

Dax grunted and pushed the blankets to his waist. "This all feels so decadent, but also juvenile. Like, I *never* get to spend the day in bed with a sexy woman, but I'm also pretty sure I had that lunch as a kid."

She'd eaten more than her fair share of peanut butter

sandwiches because they were cheap and easy to make. If she'd been thinking, Lindsey would have suggested ordering pizza, but she'd switched off her brain some time ago.

"We still have the option of getting dressed and going god hunting."

Dax scoffed. "If I *ever* choose an activity that requires clothes over being naked with you, assume I've been replaced by a pod person."

The implication that there would be more instances of naked time together reminded Lindsey of her previous plans to keep things simple. "We should make some ground rules."

Dax's hand stilled for a moment. "If that's what you need."

Lindsey propped her chin on her stacked hands. "It's what we both need. Clear expectations make for healthy partnerships."

His brow furrowed, but he didn't correct her definition of their relationship, though she could see he wanted to. "Okay, first rule, no pajamas in bed."

She pursed her lips. "I'm not sure you get to decide what I wear at night in my own bed."

He nodded. "Right. I changed my mind. That's the second rule. The first rule is that we share a bed. Safety in numbers and all that."

Lindsey tried her best to keep the smile off her face because it would only encourage him. "We're not making that a rule, but I'll accept it as a strong suggestion. I was thinking more along the lines of no ties beyond what we have now. No drama if things don't work out."

"Oh, better idea for the first rule. We're going to need some silk ties—"

She put her fingers over his lips to quiet him, but the plan backfired when he met her eyes and kissed her palm instead. "Joking aside, I know you want clear boundaries between us. I'd prefer no boundaries, but I'll work with what makes you comfortable. I'm stating right here that I'm not looking for a fling. I want a real relationship with you. Until you're ready for that, I'll be whatever you need, but I won't share you. If we're doing this, it's only you and me."

His answer both elated and frustrated her. She'd been trying to make sure he knew they'd go their separate ways once the god mess was over, but his absolute surety that he wanted her sank deep into her heart. If only she could believe he wouldn't change his mind.

Nothing lasted forever.

Lindsey considered calling a halt to whatever was happening between them, but that seemed like too little, too late. He knew where she stood, and he'd been right before. There wasn't a good reason to deny them both when indulging would help her control her magic. Besides, she liked waking up next to him. Liked knowing he was hers, at least for now.

She nodded. "You and me."

Dax kissed her palm again then set her hand back on his stomach with a pat. "New topic. Did you see Calliope yesterday?"

Lindsey winced when she remembered the workshop. "Yeah, we had a somewhat heated discussion and she disappeared. Or I locked her in the storage space. One of the two."

"Don't you think it's weird that she wasn't here for all the excitement?"

"I think she wanders a lot farther than Sabine realizes. As for missing the excitement, I'm glad she's not here. She's been pushing me to forge a connection with you from the first day. It pains me that she'll get to be all righteous because we had sex."

"At least the sex didn't disappoint."

"It was..." She trailed off, unable to find the right description for what she'd experienced.

"Combustible?" He threw in an eyebrow waggle, and Lindsey laughed.

"Well, that's a word for it." She traced a crescent-shaped scar the size of her palm along his side. "What's this from?"

He glanced down, but Lindsey had the feeling he knew exactly what she was asking about.

"Shark bite."

She poked him in the ribs. "You know, I want to call your bluff, but with you, it could be true."

Dax's lips twitched, and he covered her hand with his, probably to prevent any more poking. "It's from my sister. We were fooling around, and I sort of got impaled."

"Please enlighten me. How does one get sort of impaled?"

"We were pretending to sword fight using these two swords I'd gotten for my birthday. The grass was wet, and my sister didn't have great balance to begin with. She lunged forward and slipped. I caught her, but the sword dug into my side and kept going. Turned out the swords were sharper than we'd thought. Luckily, she didn't hit anything important. The details are pretty gross. Just assume lots of blood and a skin flap that the doctors had to stitch back together."

Lindsey wasn't sure if she should laugh or be horrified. "How old were you?"

"I was thirteen. Beth was eleven, but she was taller than me so we sparred a lot."

"Who would buy a kid sharpened swords for his birthday?"

Dax clutched his chest in mock affront. "Hey. I was a newly minted teenager, and I made sure everyone knew it. The swords were from my grandma. Somehow she didn't expect Beth and me to immediately try to kill each other with them."

Being an only child, Lindsey didn't have any personal experience with siblings, but judging from Dax's wistful tone, being impaled by his sister was a fond memory. "Did she win the battle then?"

"Yeah, but we were both a lot more careful after that. For a while."

"It sounds like you were tight with her. Do you two still try to kill each other when you get together?"

Dax's smile faded to a faint curve of his lips. "Not for a long time. She died when she was fifteen. I was supposed to take her to some party, but I had a bad feeling about it so I backed out. Her friend picked her up, and they got sideswiped on the way there, only a few blocks from our place. I heard the sirens and rushed over, thinking I could help. There she was, covered in metal and blood, already gone."

Lindsey grimaced and cursed her stupid mouth. "I'm sorry." She wanted to say more—to offer comfort—but she didn't know how. Dax had clearly loved his sister, and he probably didn't want to be answering questions about her death.

She pressed a kiss to his chest, and he threaded his fingers through her hair. Dax eased her head back so he could lean down for a lazy kiss. The simple touch of his lips sparked the need inside her again, but he pulled back after a moment.

"I don't have anything to hide from you. Ask any questions you want, and I'll answer them freely."

Even with the encouragement, Lindsey didn't feel right probing for information. He could tell her about his feelings in his own time.

"It's okay. I already know the important part. She was loved deeply, and you miss her just as deeply."

Dax kissed her again, briefly, then laid his head back against the pillow with a sigh. "Since we're in a sharing mood, how long have you had the tattoo?"

Lindsey raised a brow, willing to play along if it lifted him out of his sadness. "I wasn't sure you'd noticed."

"I am a master of observation. Especially when it comes to your naked body. Tiny flame tattoo on your hip in the bikini zone. Spill it."

She smiled at the memory. "It was my present to myself on my eighteenth birthday. One of the few things I splurged on. I was finally on my own, and I wanted to prove it by paying someone to permanently mark my body."

"Why a flame?"

*Why not?* Lindsey wanted to throw that flippant answer at him and change the subject, but he'd told her about his sister. She'd endured years of emotional abuse from her mom, but in comparison, her past didn't seem quite as bad as the death of a loved one. She frowned. Now that she thought of it, she had no idea if her mom was even still alive.

Lindsey focused on the foot of the bed and took a deep breath. "I had to read the Divine Comedy in high school, and one of the lines stuck with me. 'From a small spark great flame hath risen'. I like the idea that beginnings aren't all that important. It's what comes after that makes a difference."

Dax wrapped both arms around her for a second and

squeezed her into a tight hug. "I had to read that too. Want to know the line I remember? 'Do not be afraid. Our fate cannot be taken from us; it is a gift'. My grandma had said something similar my whole life, and it made me wonder if that's where she got it."

The note of sadness in his voice helped her move past her discomfort. She tilted her head to look up at him. "Are you close to your grandma?"

His hand found its route again, soothing more than enticing now. "We were. She died not too long ago."

She thunked her head against his chest and groaned. "I'm sorry, Dax. Just to be clear before I put my foot in my mouth again, do you have any other dead relatives I should avoid mentioning?"

He laughed and lifted her chin to brush a kiss across her forehead. "No. Just those two."

"See, I'm really not good at the whole girl-friend/boyfriend thing."

"I disagree. Would it help if I called you my sugar mama?"

Lindsey's shoulders shook with laughter. "Please no."

"No, huh." Dax stroked his chin. "How about paramour? No? I've got it. Love bunny."

"You can call me what you want, but it's not my fault if I accidentally light your hair on fire."

He cocked his head and stared into the distance for a moment. "Do you think it's a coincidence that your magic manifests as fire?"

She rolled her eyes. "Do you think it's a coincidence that we both remember lines from the Divine Comedy? Or how about that we both ended up house-sitting the same house for the summer? Oh, here's a good one. You happened to know the exact kind of sword I had the random urge to buy a couple of days ago."

"I'm getting some very disbelieving vibes from you."

"You're right. You *are* a master of observation. I'm not a big proponent of coincidence. Even before I found out that the Fates were real and messing with people's lives. Now it seems like a front for meddling gods."

Dax's phone rang, and he leaned down for a lingering kiss before rolling out of bed. "Hold that thought."

Lindsey curled up in his empty spot and watched him search the floor for the jarring ring. He checked under the bed around the nightstand, growing increasingly frantic, until he pulled his phone out from the space between the headboard and the wall. Dax held his prize up in triumph, so she offered him a golf clap while he answered it.

All the playfulness drained out of her when she heard Ana's name. The lady friend from yesterday. The one who'd been with Dax when he'd found her.

Lindsey remembered the push and the bright rush of panic when she'd reached for Dax. Something else niggled at her mind. Something important that she needed to remember from right before that moment. Unfortunately, she couldn't tear her attention away from the naked man in front of her.

Dax sent her a quick glance, then assured Ana that everything was fine. He smiled softly, and Lindsey knew it wasn't for her. She kept her face carefully docile. This was another new sensation for her—raging jealousy. She hadn't cared enough about the other men that had drifted through her life to be jealous.

What a shitty time to break that habit. Dax laughed and demanded pizza in repayment for something as Lindsey fought to regain control of her irrational emotions. They were friends. Dax was allowed to have friends. Encouraged even. So what if Ana was beautiful and funny and limber?

Dax held the phone in place with his shoulder and walked into the bathroom. Running water obscured the rest of the conversation, but Lindsey didn't need to hear more. She pressed her lips together. Dax had insisted on the monogamy clause, and she trusted him to adhere to it. But that didn't mean she'd lay around warming his bed when there was work to be done.

She sat up and tossed the blankets off, then paused after two steps toward the door. If Calliope were in the hall and caught Lindsey doing the walk of shame back to her room, she'd never hear the end of it. Lindsey glanced at the open bathroom door and caught a snippet of Dax's teasing voice. Clenching her jaw against the inner bitch that wanted to break free, she took her chances with the hallway.

# 10

_Lindsey_

LINDSEY MANAGED to change into clean clothes and make it all the way into the kitchen without seeing Calliope. She paused in the doorway and glanced over her shoulder at the stairs. Dax hadn't come looking for her, so she assumed he was still in the bathroom chatting with his good friend Ana.

She grabbed a banana and ate it while she started the coffee-maker. If Calliope was right, Lindsey's morning with Dax should have cleared up any blocks to her magic. She lifted her hand and stared at her palm while the rich smell of brewed bean filled the kitchen.

After several seconds of intense concentration, Lindsey slapped the counter in defeat. She could feel the power, just out of her reach, but she couldn't get to it. All her worries about using Dax seemed to be for naught.

Could they all have been wrong? She glowered at her cup as she doctored her coffee, then transferred her annoyance to the damn cat. Calliope was supposed to be the expert, and she apparently had no fucking clue.

What if Dax wasn't who the Fates had chosen for her? Would that make things better or worse? Lindsey scalded her tongue on her first sip and cursed aloud. She'd wanted Dax from the first moment, and the feeling had only strengthened as she'd gotten to know him. Emotions aside, her magic didn't affect him. He had to be the one.

They needed a bond, but the one they had clearly wasn't good enough. Lindsey sighed into her coffee and took a large swig. She'd touched him from halfway across the forest during the fall. That proved they had some kind of connection. What more did the Fates want?

Lindsey emptied her cup and set it aside. Just to be sure, she'd try one more time. She took a deep breath and tried to will the fire into existence. All she created was the beginning of a headache from clenching her neck muscles so hard.

Failure pissed her off, so Lindsey chalked it up to not enough information and went in search of Calliope. For once, the cat was exactly where Lindsey thought she'd be—sleeping in the front room.

She crossed her arms and considered several rude wake-up calls, but Lindsey's frustration was only mildly caused by Calliope. She drew the line at spurious acts of petty retribution.

"Time to wake up, Calliope. Some things happened while you were missing yesterday. Your disappearing act isn't very helpful, by the way."

Calliope sat up from her sun spot in the windowsill and blinked sleepily. *I patrol the forest.* She yawned wide then jumped to the coffee table where she curled her tail around her legs. *You've made progress. Excellent. Shall we start magic practice in earnest?*

Lindsey's brow furrowed. "What?"

*You've finally consummated your relationship. I'll admit, you're more stubborn than I anticipated, but—*

"How do you know Dax and I had sex?"

*I can smell him on you.*

Lindsey pinched the bridge of her nose and took a couple of deep breaths. She hoped it was a cat nose thing and not a magic thing, but she wasn't going to ask. It didn't matter anyway. "I don't have access to my magic."

*I don't understand.*

"We spent the night together, but my magic is as trapped as it was before."

*That can't be right. I felt sure this would work.*

Lindsey straightened as a cold suspicion slid over her. "That *what* would work?"

The cat's ear twitched, a lone sign of her distress. *Don't give me that tone. I was honest with you from the beginning. I told you demigod magic was dependent on a bond between both parties. Since you were focused on your own issues, I attempted to speed along the relationship.*

"And how exactly did you do that?" Was this morning another example of magical manipulation?

*The usual human theatrics. Introducing the prospect of another woman. Highlighting the fruitless magic attempts without him. Giving the two of you plenty of space to—*

Lindsey held up a hand. "I get it. Please stop trying to manipulate me into a relationship."

*It seems you've overcome that particular hurdle. How do you know your magic is still caged?*

She ran a hand through her hair. "I tried to use it. Same results as all the other times."

*Not all.*

"Yes. Can't forget about those few unpredictable times the magic actually worked."

*All that means is your bond with Dax isn't complete.*

Lindsey shoved her hands in the pockets of her shorts as she tried to find the right words for her next question. "Are you sure—"

She snapped her mouth shut as Dax sauntered into the room. He'd found time to get dressed, and Lindsey's mind helpfully filled in the details of what exactly he looked like under the jeans and tee-shirt. At least his entrance had stopped her from asking the needy question circling her thoughts. Calliope couldn't know for sure if Dax was fated for her.

Either Lindsey believed, or she didn't—wanted him or didn't. She'd fought to make sure any mystical role assigned to him wouldn't cloud her decision to get involved. The lack of magic was a hit to her confidence, but it didn't change the way she felt about him. And his friendship with Ana shouldn't either.

Dax held up the phone he still carried. "Ana wants to bring over pizza tonight. What do you say? Up for meeting her while conscious?"

Before answering, she turned her back on the cat to slide her arms around his waist. Dax immediately pulled her against him, flattening the forgotten phone against her back. She claimed his mouth in a possessive, hungry kiss until they both struggled for breath.

He leaned back an inch and raised a brow. "Or we could tell her we're busy."

Lindsey swallowed the sarcastic response on the tip of her tongue and tried something new. Trust. "I like pizza, but

I want to go check out that ravine again first. How about we call her when we get back?"

———

THE RAVINE DIDN'T PROVIDE any new clues, except reinforcing the nagging sensation that Lindsey had forgotten something. Dax pointed out the ledge she'd landed on and the trail leading to it, but she didn't feel any telltale magic tingles to indicate her attacker had tried to venture down and finish the job.

Lindsey stood at the edge of the ravine for a long time, staring at the creek. The magic felt the same as before, but something about the visual was wrong. She tried to bring up the memory from just before the fall, but her mind was stubbornly hazy. Eventually, Dax pulled her away from the edge and teased away her frown with more suggestions for what he should call her instead of girlfriend.

Ana brought Lindsey's favorite pizza, courtesy of Dax's big mouth, and Lindsey's hackles slowly dropped over the course of the evening. She remembered Ana's desperate hands from the bookshop, and the quiet woman with the sly sense of humor managed to deflect any inquiries into her past.

She exhibited the kind of skilled maneuvering that usually made Lindsey suspicious, but since this wasn't a case, she let Ana keep her secrets. Besides, it was more interesting to hear tales of Dax's attempts to avoid Kora's husband. Since Ana worked at the bookshop, she had prime seats for the drama.

Calliope did her disappearing act after the obligatory hellos, and Ana stayed until Lindsey couldn't contain her yawns. Since Dax had woken her up every hour the night before, she hadn't gotten much sleep. As they said their goodbyes, it dawned on Lindsey that Ana didn't seem at all suspicious about her lack of injuries. She tucked the knowledge away to be examined at a later time. Maybe Dax would have an explanation.

Or maybe they missed something in the forest.

———

THE NEXT AFTERNOON, they didn't find anything in the woods, despite Lindsey insisting they spread out from the original trail. No more magic tingles, just an ordinary pine forest loaded with wildlife.

Calliope's protection only covered the house, but Lindsey didn't sense any threats. Her stomach tightened every time she stepped outside of the bubble, but as the weeks passed without incident, the reaction lessened until she stopped noticing it.

Life slowed to a crawl, but a pleasurable one that involved spending all her waking—and sleeping—time with a man she liked more and more.

Dax started splitting his day between the project for Alex, magic practice with Calliope, and physical training with Lindsey. He was always willing to finish up a training session with a walk in the woods, but none of the paths they tried to the ravine offered any new information. As the days passed, the two of them spent more time being physical and less time training.

His presence during Calliope's class meant that every once in a while, Lindsey could feel a prickling surge of magic—as if her hand had fallen asleep—which became flames along her fingertips. Each time, she failed to turn off the power. In the end, Dax would distract her with kisses until the flames vanished. Their mysterious watcher hadn't reappeared—not that any of them had noticed—and the lack of progress made Lindsey irritable. More than usual.

Kora insisted on making coffee dates with Lindsey, and after pizza night, Ana often joined her. Dax didn't like the idea of Lindsey going into town alone, but as she pointed out several times, he wasn't her keeper. For the first time in her life, Lindsey found herself on the receiving end of aggressive friendship, and she wanted to reciprocate.

Several weeks after the incident with the book thief—which Lindsey had mostly forgotten in the whirlwind of near-death and amazing sex that followed—Kora mentioned that the girl hadn't come to the shop that week.

They were sitting at their usual table in Reggie's as Kora tapped her foot against the table in a staccato rhythm that was slowly driving Lindsey insane. The last few nights she'd gotten shit sleep due to a recurring dream that involved a golden mirror caked in mud, but Kora didn't deserve her ire. Lindsey grabbed Kora's knee to stop the movement, and the other woman grinned.

"Does Dax know you're copping a feel?"

Lindsey immediately let go. "I know you're hyped up on sugar right now, but I need you to stop vibrating the table."

"Sorry." She moved her foot to the crossbar of her chair and picked up the wiggle again. "Like I was saying, I haven't seen Sophie in more than a week, which is weird because she's always so punctual."

"Maybe she developed an interest in something other than books."

Kora shrugged. "Maybe, but I kind of miss her. She always had something to say when I asked her which book was her favorite."

Lindsey smirked. "Have you considered that maybe *you* need to develop an interest other than books?"

"No, that's crazy talk. Books are mankind's greatest achievement. The guy who invented sliced bread can go suck an egg, and Mars is overrated." Kora's sweet smile didn't hide the fanatical devotion she had to her chosen hoard.

"If you're worried, I can go check on Sophie. It shouldn't be too hard to figure out where she lives."

Kora waved the suggestion away. "I know where she lives, but I don't want to intrude. She doesn't even have any books right now, so I don't have a good reason to go stalking her."

Lindsey nodded solemnly. "Yeah, stalking a minor is usually frowned upon." She dodged a wadded-up napkin that Kora tossed and shifted her cup out of the danger zone. "Where's Ana today?"

"David asked her to take the lunch shift since he had an emergency come up." Kora leaned closer and lowered her voice. "I wasn't involved, but I think he's planning something romantic. Ana said he smelled like roses."

Lindsey took a gulp of her latte to keep her pessimistic thoughts to herself. In her experience, secret emergencies involving roses generally didn't involve the wife. She stared out the front window, and an older woman walking by turned and met her eyes as if she'd simply been waiting for Lindsey to look that direction.

"Maybe during the Fourth Fest," Kora muttered.

Lindsey broke the strange eye contact and grasped at a chance to change the subject before she lost her ability to maintain a neutral face. "I can't believe the town actually calls it that."

"They're really fond of alliteration. From what I hear, it

used to be the Fourth of July Independence Extravaganza. Then like a decade ago, there was all this drama between the committee chair and the financial director about how the name was costing too much money to advertise. They ended up changing it to the Fourth Fest, written with the numeral, never spelled out. You're coming, right?"

This was the third time Kora had asked, but Lindsey had managed to deflect all the others. She wasn't necessarily anti-social—she'd just never enjoyed small town festivals. They mostly seemed like excuses to make poor fried-food decisions.

But unlike the casual invitations to small-town functions she'd received over the years, this time, she had Kora and Ana to contend with. Ana had gracefully accepted the refusal; Kora became more determined every time Lindsey made an excuse.

Of course, she couldn't very well tell Kora that she didn't want to spend an extended amount of time among people on the off chance her magic decided to show up in grand and inconvenient fashion. Spending an hour at the coffee shop here and there was a calculated risk, but a whole afternoon of dealing with the frustration of the human populace in general...yeah, pass.

"Kora—" Lindsey didn't get a chance to make a new excuse before Kora cut her off.

"Please come. I know it's not really your thing, but it would be fun to hang out somewhere other than Reggie's or my shop." She raised her hand to Reggie. "Fabulous, as usual."

He nodded at her, then went back to whatever he did behind the counter all day.

Lindsey sighed. "I'll talk to Dax and see what he wants to do."

In general, Dax's decision wouldn't weigh too heavily on what Lindsey did, but he'd proven himself skilled in calming her magic. If she intended to expose herself that way, she wanted him nearby in case of emergencies. He also provided a good cover if she needed another excuse for bailing.

Kora sat back with a satisfied grin. "David already roped Dax into helping set up a booth. You can keep me and Ana company while the menfolk put their muscles to good use."

"I have muscles."

"And you'll have Pie on a Stick to keep them busy."

Lindsey groaned. So much for using Dax as a handy excuse. "It sounded like there were capitals in there. Is that the official name? How do you even eat Pie on a Stick?"

"It's kind of a two-hand maneuver. Honestly, I usually dump it in a bowl and eat it with a spoon, but don't tell Maribeth at the bakery. She's very proud of developing the right consistency to get the pie to stay in one piece while speared."

Lindsey grimaced. "You're not selling me on the mastery of it. Why didn't she call them Pie Pops?"

Kora shrugged. "I've never asked, but if you're imagining cake pop-sized pie, you need to think bigger."

"Bigger?"

She held her hands in a circle the size of about half a regular pie pan. "Bigger. I'm not sure of the physics of it. There might be magic involved."

Lindsey jerked at Kora's word choice, but the other woman didn't seem to notice. She'd been focusing too much on magic and gods and Dax the last few weeks if normal conversation made her jumpy. Maybe Kora and Ana had the right idea. She could use a mundane distraction.

Despite the dubious charms of the Pie on a Stick,

Lindsey didn't want to commit without at least talking to Dax. Distraction or not, she'd need him there. What a difference a couple of weeks had made.

She shook her head. "I make no promises. Just because Dax is operating as slave labor doesn't mean I'll come."

Kora held up her hands in surrender, but her smile said she thought she'd won.

LINDSEY LEFT A SHORT TIME LATER, waving to Reggie on her way out even though she'd never said more than a few words to the man. He waved back without comment. She appreciated the strong, silent type, but apparently, she liked cocky and loud better.

Back at the house, she left her purse in the kitchen and went in search of her favorite embodiment of cocky and loud. He wasn't raiding the kitchen, so she assumed he'd decided to work while she was gone.

Dax sat at his computer in the office, headset firmly over his ears. Lindsey knocked, but he didn't respond. She crossed her arms and leaned against the doorframe to wait. His fingers flew over the keys as he offered a few noncommittal grunts to the person she heard on the other end. The tinny voice had to be Alex since Dax didn't deal with clients directly.

He huffed, then reached up to hit a button next to his mic and slid it up next to the earpiece. When he swiveled the chair toward her, she braced herself to deal with an annoyed tech genius, but his eyes warmed when they landed on her. And the smile he sent her was one hundred percent sex.

"You're back early."

Lindsey shrugged the shoulder not pinned to the wall. "Not really. Everything okay in here?"

"Alex is cranky because of a client miscommunication. They asked for a rush change that he can't handle without his set-up here. Ergo, I'm now the developer for this project." He studied her. "Everything okay at the coffee shop?"

"The coffee shop was fine. Kora asked me to come to the Fourth Fest with her and Ana. Again."

He tilted his head with a raised brow. "And you made excuses again?"

Lindsey grimaced. "I have valid reasons for not wanting to go."

"I'm not casting aspersions. You know I'd rather we didn't take chances. We haven't seen any indication that the person-slash-god who tried to kill you has left the area. I know Calliope said they probably used up most of their power becoming physical enough to push you, but it's been weeks since then. That said, you have to live your life."

Lindsey rested her temple against the cool wood and sighed. "I hate the uncertainty. All this waiting is tying me up in knots, and my magic is still dangerously unpredictable."

He patted his lap. "Why don't you come on over here and I'll see about making it all better?"

Lindsey couldn't help her smile. "I have no doubt you'd make it better, but you know I'm not setting foot in that room."

"The seal is safely locked away."

"I know, but I'm not taking any chances. Isn't that what you said you wanted?"

Dax swooned dramatically. "Hoisted by my own petard." His head popped back up. "Did you know that a petard is a bomb? I always thought it was a sail or something, then Alex corrected me a couple of years ago."

Lindsey squinted at him. "Why would Alex—" She shook her head and straightened off the wall. "Nice. I almost didn't catch that misdirection. You're getting better."

"So is that a no on lap time?"

She chuckled. "Go back to work. I'm doing dinner tonight."

Dax hopped out of the chair and rushed over to catch her before she moved out of the doorway. "Hold on. I'm missing something."

He cupped the nape of her neck and stroked her jaw with his thumb as his mouth came down on hers. Lindsey relaxed instantly. She savored the slow, sweet kiss until he pulled back.

"That's better." His rough voice reflected the shivery heaviness that always filled her with his touch.

Lindsey patted his chest, and he lifted her hand to drag his lips across her knuckles. "That did make it a little better. Go back to work. We can talk over dinner."

He held her hand until the last second as she walked away, and Lindsey felt his touch long after she turned the corner to the kitchen. Her mind drifted while she filled a pot with water for spaghetti.

Whatever god had stuck around posed a constant concern, so she'd tried to limit her time outside the house in an attempt to make a second ambush more difficult. If she had some kind of guarantee that she could access her magic, she'd be fine with waiting, but the timeline sucked. For all Lindsey knew, she'd still be playing house with Dax years from now and be no closer to control.

The water came to a boil, so she added a generous handful of noodles. Her problem was two-fold—the threat of Lindsey against the general populace and the threat of a god or gods unknown to Lindsey personally. Sabine's generous offer of her house had kept Lindsey's costs fairly low, but eventually, she'd have to go back to work. What would she do then, only take jobs in the middle of nowhere?

Added to that, Calliope needed her help. Judging from her own experience with the gods, even without much power they were dangerous. After the fall, she hadn't noticed any creepy watcher vibes, so maybe the god left after causing some havoc? Or maybe he didn't have the energy to make it back to the house for his Peeping Tom act.

Either way, the Fourth Fest could provide a chance to lure him out, as long as Dax stayed close. Which meant she needed to share her plan with him if she intended to use him as a magic extinguisher.

"I think you should go to the festival with the ladies."

Lindsey looked up from the colander. Dax stood in the doorway with a half-smile on his face. "Why?"

"Kora and Ana seem pretty taken with you, and it might be nice to make some friends besides me and Sabine."

She sent him a teasing grin as she dumped pasta on two plates. "Who said you're my friend?"

"Oh, I'm confident I'm more than a friend, but I don't think the others are interested in the same special relationship." He walked to the counter across from her and leaned on his elbows. "I think you lead a lonely existence."

His words touched on an open wound she put considerable effort into ignoring. Lindsey concentrated on the tasks in front of her. Cover the spaghetti in jarred pasta sauce, add meatballs, sprinkle on parmesan. She didn't meet his eyes until she was certain only amusement would show on her face.

"I'm not lonely. I've got you." Lindsey presented his plate with a flourish.

Dax shook his head. "You don't have to hide from me. I see what's beneath."

Her smile faded. "I don't like most people on a good day. If given the chance to cheat and lie, they will. There are a few exceptions, of course, but as a whole, humans are selfish and horrible. And that was my opinion when I still thought I *was* one. After a while, you get tired of digging through the disappointment to try to find the few who are worth it."

Dax studied her as if trying to solve a puzzle, then nodded. "I can see that."

She relaxed, unaware that she'd tensed up in the first place. Lindsey had explained her world views plenty of times before to people she'd been involved with, but they always backed away from the stark reality of it. They wanted her to be more positive or try harder, and it usually prefaced the end of the relationship.

Dax didn't push. "In that case, I'm happy to fulfill all your needs, but avoiding the ladies this time won't stop them from trying next time."

"I'm well aware of that, but there are only a limited number of next times. In less than six weeks, Sabine and Alex will be back and probably more than ready to reclaim their house. I'm capable of avoiding them for that long if I wanted to."

He raised a brow. "But you don't want to."

"But I don't want to. If I go to the festival, I'll need your help."

"Anything."

The quick, confident agreement struck a sensitive place inside her. Anything? What if she asked for him to shun his friends? What if she demanded he give up his dream job and move with her to Backwater, Montana? How could he *know* that her request for help would be something he could give?

"I want you to stay nearby and keep an eye on me. You can tell when my magic is manifesting, and you know how to stop it. I can't go out in public for that long if it's going to put people at risk."

Dax picked up her hand from the counter and held it between his. "No problem, though I admit I'm more concerned with a god showing up and trying to take you out as if it were a superhero movie. At least here we have Calliope's shield."

"Would that be so bad? It would give us some idea of what we're up against. We can handle ourselves if he does show up."

He sent her an incredulous look. "A demigod who can't control her magic and a guardian who doesn't have any?"

Lindsey scrunched her nose. "Do we have a B team?"

"I think we *are* the B team." Dax grabbed his plate and took it to the little table in the kitchen where they usually ate.

She sat across from him and sighed. "The world is screwed."

# 11

*Dax*

THE TOWN HAD outdone itself for the festival, and the crowd moved slowly along the tents set up around the edges of the city park. The official start time wasn't for another hour, but that hadn't stopped most of the town from showing up early.

Despite giving in to peer pressure, Lindsey almost didn't make it to the Fourth Fest. Dax had promised David weeks ago that he'd help cart boxes of books and set up a booth for the shop, but the morning of the festival he found himself distracted searching for Lindsey and her entourage.

His fated roommate-with-benefits considered herself dangerous to other people, but so far, every time Dax had seen her magic, she'd been emotional and alone. He suspected her feelings had a lot more to do with the process than she wanted to admit.

Lindsey hated discussing her feelings though. She worked hard to separate the softer parts of her personality from the determined problem-solver she presented to the world. Dax felt honored to get to see parts of her closely-guarded private persona. He hoped one day she'd let him in all the way.

Kids shrieked on the playground nearby. Rides and games had been set up on the softball fields, and the lines had already started stretching across the grass. Some bureaucratic genius had positioned the food vendors near the market area to entice customers, but he hadn't caught sight of Lindsey yet.

He'd skipped breakfast, so his stomach growled at the smells of gyros and funnel cake. Kora had convinced Lindsey to head out early with the promise of coffee and cinnamon rolls, but alas, he'd been left out of that deal. The sun beat down on him as he stopped to shade his eyes hoping for a quick glimpse of Lindsey's long legs.

A crumpled piece of paper hit him in the chest, and Dax raised a brow at David. "Yes? Can I help you?"

The other man grinned and gestured at the boxes surrounding him. "I was under the impression you'd come to help, but all you've done this morning is stare longingly into the distance. I've never seen actual pining before."

Dax picked up the paper and threw it back at him, missing completely. "It's not pining. Lindsey was nervous about coming. I wanted to make sure she had a good time."

David grunted as he lifted a box onto the folding table along the back of their tent. "Am I finally going to get to meet her? Kora talks about her non-stop, and even Ana has opinions. Ones she actually said out loud."

He hadn't spotted Lindsey among the crowd, so Dax grabbed the next box and started unloading the contents onto the tables. "Seems likely."

"She won't freak out and leave on her own?"

Dax finished his box and pulled over another. "No way.

She said she'd meet me here, and she will. The sooner we get this place set up, the sooner she'll show up."

They worked in companionable silence until they'd emptied all the boxes and David had started arranging displays. Dax wiped sweat off his face and the back of his neck, taking the chance to leave the stifling confines of the tent in search of a breeze. He hoped David remembered to bring a fan or the couple would be in for a long day.

After trying to make a breeze by flapping his shirt, Dax gave up and tried to judge how much trouble he'd be in if he took it off completely. David interrupted his bad decision-making by joining him outside.

"It's not worth it, and it would annoy Sheriff Garrett if he had to come disperse a crowd of gawkers."

Dax grunted. "Your ability to guess my thoughts is uncanny, and I'm not sure how I feel about that."

The other man shrugged. "You'll get used to it or you won't. Go on. I can handle the rest. Thanks for your help." David held out his hand, and Dax shook it.

"No problem, man. I'd have helped anyway, but Kora is extremely persuasive. I'm afraid to think of her being unleashed on your poor customers."

David laughed. "She knows to only use her powers for good. I'd check near the carnival games. Look for the giant duck."

Dax nodded and set off. He checked the food trucks as he passed, but all of them had long lines. His hunger would have to wait. The carnival games were on the far side of the park, situated among the trees. Where the market had the food vendors to pull people in, this area had shade. A highly valuable commodity when the day had only begun, and he'd already sweated through his shirt.

He found them right where David had suggested.

Another mark in the disturbingly accurate column for that guy. One of the booths had something to do with rubber duckies and had an enormous stuffed duck sitting on the counter.

A large inflatable kiddie pool had been set up on a series of waist-high tables, and filled with floating plastic cups of various colors. Lindsey stood at a taped-off area with Kora a few feet behind her, shouting nonsense instructions. Dax searched the area for Ana, but he didn't see any tall, uncomfortable blondes in the vicinity. He *did* see the teenage volunteer leaning on his podium and leering at the ladies.

Lindsey leaned forward to take aim with a miniature squeaky duck, and the worker tilted hard to the side trying to get a look up her skirt. Dax moved into the kid's line of sight and crossed his arms with a glower, which was enough to send the budding felon scampering for something else to do in the stack of supplies nearby.

His lovely roommate bit her lip in concentration, then let the ball fly. It landed perfectly in the center of the lone red cup. Lindsey whooped and threw her hands in the air, and Kora nearly tackled her. Both of them jumped up and down shrieking, until Lindsey noticed him watching.

She grinned at him over Kora. "I won the ridiculous duck."

Dax's brows shot up, and he glanced over at the table where the now-blushing kid held out the fuzzy monstrosity. "Isn't it my job to win you giant stuffed animals at the fair?"

Lindsey laughed. "I told you I didn't need help. But I'll let you carry him around for me."

Kora disentangled herself from Lindsey and propped her hands on her hips. "I thought you were assisting my husband?"

"I was released early for good behavior."

She snorted. "Sure you were." Since Lindsey hadn't moved, Kora walked over and snatched the duck from the teen. Then she pointed a finger in his face. "Don't think I didn't notice your inappropriate attention. You better watch yourself, Dillon. Your mom is *very* chatty at book club."

Color drained from the kid's face, and he nodded. "Yes, ma'am."

Dax shook his head. Small town justice at its finest. He left Kora to intimidate the local youth and pulled Lindsey close to brush a kiss across her lips. She slid her arms around his waist and smiled up at him.

"I've never won a carnival game before."

He pulled away and took her hand to lead her toward the food trucks. "In honor of your thrilling victory, I'd like to buy you a late lunch."

Lindsey pulled him to a stop. "Hold on." She ran back to the taped off area and grabbed a paper bag off the floor.

Dax's breath caught as she returned to him. This was the comfortable, happy Lindsey she deserved to be. Her legs stretched out before her, and her hair streamed out behind in a tangle of auburn waves. But even the short skirt flaring up couldn't tear his gaze away from her face and the heated look in her eyes only for him.

Her brow furrowed as she slowed to a stop. "What?"

"You look happy. I like it."

She shrugged and held out the paper bag. "You were right about Kora. I got this for you."

Dax unfolded the top to find a cinnamon roll nestled inside. She might as well have handed him the keys to a Porsche. She'd thought about him during her girls' brunch and gone out of her way to get the pastry he'd been pouting about.

He wrapped an arm around her waist and pulled her

close. Lindsey tilted her face up in an invitation that Dax had no trouble accepting.

"Thank you," he murmured against her lips.

Before he could deepen the kiss, Kora tapped him on the shoulder. "I have Lindsey's duck, and I would also like a late lunch."

Dax turned his head, but kept Lindsey tight against him. "Shouldn't you be getting back to your husband?"

She raised a brow. "Shouldn't you be more discreet at a kid-friendly event?"

Lindsey eased away. "She's right. We're drawing attention to ourselves."

Dax groaned. He didn't give a flying crap about the delicate sensibilities of the crowd. They'd shared a fairly chaste kiss. It's not like they were tossing off clothes in the middle of the park.

He twined his fingers with Lindsey's, then gestured for Kora to go ahead. "Fine. Let's all go get some lunch. I'm sure David could use some food by now too."

Kora scrutinized him, probably suspicious that he'd given in so easily, but then she turned around and flounced off in the right direction.

He kept Kora in his sights out of habit, but he didn't put much effort into keeping up with her. "Where's the third member of the group?"

"Ana only stayed a little while. She couldn't handle the crowds, and I can't blame her. It's hot and sticky and a lot to take in on a normal day." She paused then glanced over at his face. "Do you know her history?"

"No. She hasn't shared, and I've never asked. I've picked up from other people that she came to town about the same time that Alex moved home, but you probably already knew that. She obviously has the social anxiety deal, but when she's comfortable, she can be feisty and smart. Like another new-comer I'm quite fond of."

Lindsey squeezed his hand and ignored his last comment. "I get the feeling whatever happened is still happening."

"If she needs help, she'll ask."

"Are you sure?"

Dax led her around a mixed group of pre-teens sitting in the middle of the walkway. "Not everyone is as determined to be self-sufficient as you."

"I think you'd be surprised," she muttered.

They'd reached the food area, and Kora had already gotten in line for the Burrito Bros booth. Not the option he'd have chosen, but it was hard to screw up a burrito. Besides, he had his cinnamon roll.

Dax offered to pay for Kora and David's lunch, but she politely declined his offer by sticking out her tongue and proceeding to pay for everyone's food herself.

She handed him his burrito from the bag, but paused before letting go. "You worked for me this morning, so here's your pay. Don't spend it all in one place."

Kora handed over Lindsey's duck then took off toward her own booth. Dax met Lindsey's eyes, and they both burst out laughing.

Lindsey caught her breath first. "You're zero for two today, Dax."

"How so?"

"You couldn't win me a stuffed animal, and you couldn't buy me lunch. Was there anything else you wanted to suggest but not do?"

The sassy smile on her face robbed him of a snappy comeback, so he kissed her cheek, then jerked his chin toward the benches set up in the center of the grassy area. "Let's go find somewhere to eat."

The benches were all full, but the grass proved dry and soft. Lindsey sat cross-legged next to him, and Dax fought to keep his focus on his food instead of on her thighs where her skirt crept up. From their spot, they had a pretty good vantage point of the Soul Exchange booth. David had done a fantastic job making a couple of covered folding tables look inviting with stacks of books, candles, and twinkle lights. Dax tilted his head. How had David managed to make their booth seem both darker and more intimate than the other standard white tents?

Dax nudged Lindsey and pointed. "What do you think? All my hard work on display."

Her brows winged up as she examined the booth. "It looks like they transported their store to the park." She glanced at him, then back at the tent. "Amazing what hefting boxes can do for a space."

David stepped through the back flap of the tent, and Lindsey's eyes went wide. "*That's* David? No wonder Kora always has that little smile on her face."

Dax cocked his head at her. "Haven't you met before?"

She shook her head, leaning over his lap to check out Kora's husband. "No. I've only come to the shop a couple of times, and he's always off doing something else. Kora and Ana usually meet me at Reggie's. You described him as scary, not scary hot."

He scowled and studied David. Compared to the tiny Kora standing next to him, David looked huge. The guy took care of himself, but he knew dozens of guys with a similar build. Anyone with a gym membership and some free time could get there.

Floppy black hair, grey eyes, cheekbones. Dax shrugged.

"I don't get it."

Lindsey patted his thigh and straightened. "Don't worry about it. You're hot too."

She left her hand on his leg, and Dax fought off fantasies of hurrying her home or simply easing her to the ground right there. Kora, as obnoxious as she was, hadn't been messing with them about the abundance of families.

She'd also not-so-subtly pulled her husband behind their tent when she'd first arrived. Not a bad plan for privacy.

They finished eating with Lindsey teasing him about his design skills, and Dax affecting a foppish accent to explain the aesthetic to her in a tangle of made-up words. As much as her skirt and her touch affected him, her laugh warmed him from the inside out. He'd spend all day entertaining her if it meant she'd keep smiling at him like that.

Hell, he'd gladly spend the rest of his life making her smile. Dax blinked at the sudden realization. He wanted to spend the rest of his life with her. The knowledge felt so natural that he was surprised it had taken him this long to realize it.

He loved the way Lindsey's mind worked, her inability to share the covers, the way she tucked her face against his shoulder in the dark—her prickly sensitivity and her generous heart. He loved her.

The summer day moved on around him, but Dax's life shifted irrevocably as the reality settled in his mind. He loved her. Lindsey licked her thumb clean, smiling up at him, and he struggled to keep the words inside. If she suspected the sudden turn of his thoughts, she'd run.

Lindsey offered to clean up, but Dax followed her to the trash can nearly hidden in a copse of trees at the perimeter of the park. Once she'd emptied her hands, he snagged her around the waist and swung her behind the trees, fuzzy friend and all.

The giant duck hit the ground as Lindsey wound her arms around his neck. "Excuse me, sir, but there are children around."

Dax leaned into her, sliding his hand up her leg and under her skirt until he could palm her ass as he'd been wanting to do all damn day. "Not back here there aren't." He nudged her head to the side and kissed the spot under her ear that made her moan.

Her hands clenched in his hair as he teased her with his fingers, brushing the bottom hem of her panties until she spread her legs for him. Lindsey whimpered when he dipped inside and sank into her heat. Dax captured the noise with his mouth while she writhed against him.

She tasted like cinnamon from stolen bites of his roll, and he desperately wanted to lift her against the tree and slam home. Dax would have given several years off his life for the ability to instantly teleport them somewhere private.

Lindsey jumped as something crashed into the underbrush nearby. Dax shifted his body to shield her from whatever it was, then cursed when he saw a red playground ball nestled in a tangle of honeysuckle vines. Several high-pitched voices shouted to each other as they got closer, talking about where the ball had disappeared.

Dax dropped his head to her shoulder and removed his hand from under her skirt. "I swear I'm cursed," he mumbled.

Lindsey snickered, but she was as out of breath as he was. "If all you wanted to do was make out, we could have stayed at home."

"That's not *all* I wanted to do."

The kids dared each other to go into the shadowy woods

looking for their ball, effectively destroying any hope he had of picking up again right away. He lifted his head, and Lindsey patted his chest.

"Don't worry. We'll be alone all night."

"Oh, I haven't forgotten."

She pressed a lingering kiss to his mouth, and Dax breathed in her coconut scent. Before he was ready, she slipped away to retrieve the kids' ball. She had to high step through some weeds to reach it, but it wasn't too far away.

Dax leaned against the tree he'd just had her pinned against and acknowledged that everything she did made him want to know more about her, spend more time with her. Lindsey heaved the ball back toward the park, to the triumphant shouts of at least a dozen kids. She shook her head and started making her way back to him, and declarations of love flitted through Dax's mind.

Lindsey claimed to only want a summer fling, but Dax had no intention of letting her go at the end of the summer.

She'd almost made it back to their make-out spot when she stopped, frowned, and stared off in the direction of the park. Dax straightened from his slouch and scanned the area. Nothing triggered any alarms, but Lindsey's senses were tuned differently than his.

He grabbed the duck and approached her quietly, but even when he put his hand on her arm, she didn't lose the far-away look in her eyes.

"Lindsey?"

A few seconds went by—causing his anxiety to skyrocket—before she blinked and focused on his face. "I felt it. The same magic from in the woods behind the house. It brushed by me then disappeared. I was trying to figure out which direction it might have been moving."

Dax glanced around again. Her spot, only a few feet

away from where they'd been fooling around, offered a good vantage point of the entire park. A stunted pine tree grew to her right, within easy reach, and Dax wished he had the ability to feel magic as well. He hated being relegated to observer status.

"You did this by touch last time, right? What about that tree in front of you?"

Lindsey placed her hand on the bark and her lips curled in a half-smile. "You nailed it. The god was standing here, touching this tree, at some point."

"Is there any way to tell how much time has passed since then?"

She shook her head and crossed into the manicured grass of the park. "Not that I can tell. And before you ask, Calliope can't help with this. She experiences the magic differently."

Dax kept pace with her as she walked slowly toward the tents, zig-zagging to touch things and adjust her direction. "Can you feel Calliope's magic?"

"Yeah. I didn't know that's what I was experiencing until after the tracking incident. The house is more or less coated in her magic at all times. Sabine's too. It feels..." She trailed off then took a ninety-degree turn toward the walkway behind the booths. "It feels reassuring—safe and comfortable, like I've known it my whole life. Which is ridiculous because pretty much nothing I've known my whole life is safe or comfortable."

They'd talked before—briefly—about Lindsey's past, but she never wanted to go into detail. She claimed she moved beyond it, and she'd rather forget. Dax wasn't so sure, but he wouldn't push her to talk about something that upset her.

On the way past the back of the Soul Exchange booth,

Dax dropped the duck next to Kora's extra supplies. She'd know what to do with it until they could circle back. He wanted to have both hands free while they tracked a potentially invisible murderous god.

Lindsey meticulously followed the trail the four blocks into the downtown area. Lots of people milled around, enjoying the holiday in the relative coolness of the awnings, but none of them paid any extra attention to Lindsey.

He followed her into an alley between the buildings that he hadn't noticed before. The stench of open dumpsters roasting in the midday sun made his stomach turn, but Lindsey didn't seem to notice. Or she was so engrossed in her task that she'd blocked it out. Lucky her.

"Here." She stopped in front of the back entrance for a business. "The magic goes into this building."

Dax inspected the sign on the door for The Soul Exchange and forced himself to ask the next question. "Are you sure it went in?"

"Yes. The trace is on the handle but nowhere else on the door."

"Why would a non-corporeal god need to use the handle?"

She shot him an impatient look. "I don't know. Maybe he's corporeal now. Maybe it's habit. Maybe I suck at this particular skill and we're tracking a pigeon."

He grinned. "Honestly, I hope it's the pigeon. Could you imagine what that would mean for bird-life if it turned out pigeons were magical?"

Lindsey shook her head and tried the door. It swung silently open into a dark storage room. Dax grabbed her arm before she could move forward and sidled past her. She sighed behind him, but didn't object. It wouldn't have mattered if she had. He wasn't about to let her take point into unknown danger.

Neatly arranged stacks of boxes—most taller than him —created dead end lanes to either side of the main pathway. Lindsey eased the door closed behind them, trapping them in near-complete darkness. A sliver of light shone across the room where another door must lead into the employee area. Dax reached back to grip Lindsey's hand and waited until he'd adjusted to the shadows before moving.

Their feet shuffled quietly as they moved across the concrete floor, and the lack of other such sounds suggested either they were alone in the room or any other parties had chosen to stay hidden. But as they got closer to the door, Dax could make out voices. He glanced back at Lindsey, but he could only see a vague outline of her face in the shadows.

Dax reached the second door and pulled Lindsey right next to him to whisper in her ear. "That sounds like Kora and David."

She nodded and leaned over to whisper back. "There's magic on this door too. Should we come back later?"

"It's too much coincidence that your magic trail led here. I'm going to crack the door open. If they're discussing inventory or something, we close the door and sneak back out."

Lindsey's fingers tightened on his. "What if they're not discussing inventory?"

"Then we find out how much they've been lying to us. No matter what happens, we're in this together."

She hesitated, then nodded again. Dax kissed her hand then shifted them to the left so they wouldn't be visible from inside. He hoped Kora and David weren't paying much attention to the storage room door, but just in case, he prepped a story that didn't involve following a magical trail to their business.

The door pushed inward a few inches, and another swath of light illuminated the boxes next to where they'd been crouched.

"Kora, you can't keep doing this. We agreed not to interfere." The voice definitely belonged to David, and he didn't sound pleased.

"I'm not interfering. I'm helping."

"You're courting disaster."

Clothing rustled, probably Kora stubbornly crossing her arms. "And you're paranoid. A little nudge here and there won't harm anything."

"Are you sure? Calliope has been hanging around a lot lately."

Kora scoffed. "Calliope doesn't scare me."

"She doesn't, but the others should." David moved across the room, and his voice lowered. "I know your heart is in the right place, but it's not worth the risk. Let them sort it out themselves."

Kora sighed. "What's the point of magic if I can't use it to do good in the world?"

David chuckled. "I know. We should get back. You promised Ana we wouldn't be gone long."

Dax met Lindsey's surprised glance and shook his head. He hadn't known about Kora's connection to Calliope or her magic, but now wasn't the time to discuss it. The light disappeared as the door closed, and Dax hoped the couple went out through the bookstore instead of the back. He also hoped the magic Lindsey felt hadn't been Kora's.

## 12

*Lindsey*

A COLD ANGER FILLED HER, but Dax's hand warmed hers. She focused on that touch and pushed aside the betrayal to sort through the possibilities.

Kora had magic that she clearly knew how to use. Calliope had said Lindsey might feel a connection to other demigods, which would explain their instant friendship, but it seemed like Calliope didn't know about Kora and David.

Or Calliope had even more secrets than they'd realized.

Questions circled her mind and fought for dominance. What others? Who had Kora and David made an agreement with? How had Kora been interfering? And the worst of all, why was the same magic from the woods in their storeroom?

Lindsey flattened her hand against the wall next to her, and a slight buzz tickled her palm. Now that she knew to look, a subtle undertone of power flowed through the bookstore. Even knowing the magic was there, Lindsey couldn't quite get a lock on the signature. Kora didn't leave magic tingles behind like the ones in the woods.

Kora may not have tried to kill Lindsey, but they'd still followed the trail of dangerous magic to Kora's storeroom.

Dax rose from his crouch and tugged her back into the main walkway, but Lindsey wasn't ready to leave yet. That magic hadn't just stopped at the door. She pulled him to a halt.

"We have to go inside."

The shadow of his head swiveled toward her. "What? No. They're probably still in there. Possibly naked."

Her jaw firmed. "You're welcome to stay here, but I'm following that magic trail."

Dax sighed, and his clothes rustled. "Well, you're sure as hell not going without me."

Relief washed over her, and Lindsey tucked the warm, little feeling of partnership away to examine later. "Then use all that special training you keep talking about and get us in the bookstore undetected."

"Do I look like I have x-ray vision or the ability to see in the dark? You're the one with magic powers. Maybe if I had some duct tape and a paperclip..." Despite his grumbling, Dax moved at a steady pace back the direction they'd come. She imagined the sassy look on his face when challenged and doubled down.

"I'm happy to do the breaking and entering if you can't handle it. Do you want me to walk you through it step by step?"

"I want you to be still and quiet so I can listen." They'd reached the door again, so Dax released her hand to lay with his head tilted to the crack that provided the only real illumination in the room.

She didn't hear voices like the last time, and the light

seemed weaker than before. Dax rose and peeked inside before opening the door wide. Kora and David had turned off all the lights as they'd left. A skylight kept the office from being a repeat of the storeroom. At least Lindsey could see clearly in the dim interior.

Dax walked directly to the retail door and checked the store. When he closed it again and shook his head, Lindsey relaxed. She wasn't sure how long it would take to find the trail, but she knew it had to be there somewhere.

An open plastic tub of junk—books, author swag, loose papers—sat next to her feet, so Lindsey started there. She checked all the contents and moved on to the armoire taking up a good portion of the wall. After running her hands over everything top to bottom, she realized she hadn't heard any movement from the other part of the room.

Still bent over the bottom drawer, Lindsey glanced back, and Dax belatedly raised his eyes. She glared at him. "Would you stop staring at my ass and help?"

"I can do both."

"Why don't you search the room for anything suspicious while I look for magic fingerprints?"

He ran his hand through his hair. "What are we categorizing as suspicious?"

Lindsey shrugged and stood to check the mini-fridge. "Lists of other demigods. Ancient artifacts of great power. A journal detailing her magical journey with a convenient index in the back."

He sent her a bland look. "A journal. In the office of a bookstore, full of book-like products."

"I have faith in you."

"I don't," he muttered.

Not her problem. She had a different concern in mind.

Nothing close to the back door felt like magic, but

several handles on the desk and a gold-rimmed hand mirror she found in a drawer all tingled in that particular way when she touched them.

"Lindsey." Dax's voice lost its playfulness.

She carefully replaced the items she'd been rifling through, then turned toward him expecting another joke. He held up a metal helm that could have been stolen from a gladiator movie, and Lindsey swallowed the rebuke on her tongue.

"Do *not* tell me you actually found an ancient artifact of great power."

Dax jiggled the helm. "How am I supposed to know? But it doesn't look like it belongs in a bookstore. At least, not this one."

In the weak light, the brownish-silver helm didn't seem intimidating enough to be an ancient artifact like the seal. The design appeared fairly simple—two sideburn-like pieces came down from the top along with another piece over the nose—but she could barely make out faint engravings around the edges.

Something about it stopped her from reaching out to touch it though. A repulsion that felt like it came from the metal itself.

"I can't believe you forgot the cash box twice in one day."

Lindsey's head shot up at Kora's voice in the bookstore proper. She met Dax's eyes, and he nodded toward the storeroom door before replacing the helm where he'd found it.

David answered her. "If you'll remember correctly, I was decidedly distracted both times we were back here today."

Kora giggled, much closer. Keys jingled as Lindsey yanked open the back door and squeezed through. When she turned in the darkness, Dax had caught the edge of the door so it didn't slam. A faint light shone on his face, and he lifted his finger to his lips for silence.

Lindsey pursed her lips. She knew how to hide.

The light disappeared as he eased the door closed for a second time. His form approached her in the dark and pulled her close. Lindsey's pulse took off, but Dax wasn't trying to be handsy this time.

He leaned down to whisper in her ear. "Can we go now?"

Lindsey nodded. She'd gotten what she needed from the office space. More, even.

They'd walked halfway down the main aisle when a scraping sound from their left made her pause. She peered into the darkness, trying to spot movement. When she finally placed the noise, she gasped as the tall stack of boxes next to her swayed perilously in her direction.

"Lindsey!" Dax swung her out of the way, then pushed her toward the outer door. "Go. I'll meet you at Reggie's."

She flinched at the thunderous crash of boxes onto concrete. Books burst out of the broken cardboard and skidded across the floor. If Kora and David were still here, they'd be along any moment.

Lindsey had mixed feelings about the destruction, but she'd deal with them later. Dax had placed himself between her and the now-horizontal stack of boxes. The damn man was going to get himself killed. She picked her way to him and laid her hand on his back.

"Don't be stupid. I'm not leaving you here to fight a god by yourself."

He growled over his shoulder. "I'm not planning to fight him. I want to see if I can get more information. Can you listen for once and let me protect you?"

"No. I'm not leaving unless you are."

She couldn't see the details of his face, but the quiet

growl told her he wasn't happy about her ultimatum. Another stack toppled toward them from the other side, and Lindsey gasped. Dax spun at her indrawn breath, but for once, he wasn't fast enough.

Acting purely on instinct, she raised her hands to protect them, willing the boxes to fall elsewhere. A surge of power swelled inside her, painfully filling her chest, then broke through, appearing in the world as a spear of flame.

The room lit up orange for a brief moment, and the boxes changed trajectory to fall harmlessly closer to the office door. Lindsey slowly lowered her hands as she stared unblinking at the smoldering cardboard.

Dax grabbed her by the shoulders and shook her gently. "Lindsey, you need to put the rest of the flames out."

She blinked and nodded, suddenly terrified at the prospect of failure. Dax shifted behind her, keeping his hands on her shoulders, a warm, reassuring weight. "Just like you practiced. Call the magic back and let it settle inside you."

Dax repeated Calliope's words again, and Lindsey focused on the texture of her magic—like heated silk sliding between her fingers. She tugged on the nebulous tendrils that connected her to the fire, expecting resistance. To her shock, the magic returned to her, lining her hands with the little flames she recognized.

Intellectually, she knew she had to hurry because the god was still in the storeroom with them and the two in the office would surely have heard the commotion, but the sheer joy in her magic responding as asked nearly brought her to her knees. She closed her fists over the tiny blaze in her palm, and the magic retreated inside her, crackling and warm.

Dax kissed her temple and whispered, "Good girl." Then he picked her up and carried her out of the storeroom.

---

THEY MADE it home in record time, and Lindsey spent the entire drive staring at the blurred trees beside the road. Magic simmered inside her, moving and spreading as she breathed. After so much time spent working for this exact moment, the aftermath felt anti-climactic.

Guilt wormed in past the shock and the thrill. Controlling the flames had been laughably easy, and calling them? She'd done that without thinking. Was she done? Ready to face off against an angry, murderous god who liked hiding and pushing things over?

Lindsey didn't feel done. She felt...sad.

Dax parked next to her SUV in the driveway, then simply sat and waited. The charged silence stretched between them, and Lindsey was suddenly tired of everything. Magic powers and talking cats and attempted murder. Life was solitary before, but at least she knew what to expect.

"I can deal with brooding, but can we do it inside? I'd like to make use of Calliope's protections while we sort through what happened today."

Lindsey tilted her head to study him. "Do you feel different?"

He rolled one shoulder and met her questioning gaze with a blank face. "Yes, but probably not for the reasons you think. Let's get inside."

She nodded and walked straight through the house until she got to the kitchen. Once there, she filled a glass with water, chugged it, then refilled it. Apparently, magic use made her tired *and* thirsty.

Dax joined her, and the tension returned. Lindsey didn't have a good explanation for the weird distance between them, especially after her magic had broken free. According to Calliope, only a tight bond between her and Dax would release the seal, but she hadn't noticed anything change in the storeroom.

The car ride home, on the other hand...

She had the choice to ignore Dax's annoyed attitude— her usual go-to—or she could suck up her own discomfort and face the problem head-on. Lindsey chanced a glance at him to find him watching her with that same poker face.

Relationships sucked.

"Okay, what's wrong?"

He raised a brow. "You sound upset."

"Oh no. I know why I'm upset. What I don't know, is why *you* are."

"You used your magic to save us."

She crossed her arms. "You're upset because I can finally use my magic?"

Dax mimicked her stance. "I'm upset because we had to be saved in the first place. You didn't listen when I told you to leave."

Anger burned in her gut, stoking the sizzling magic inside her. "I'm sorry. I must have missed the point where I agreed to obey you."

"I don't need you to obey. You agreed to take basic precautions, but instead of doing that, you threw yourself back into danger."

She marched over to poke him in the chest. "To save *your* sorry ass. What were you going to do? Stand really still and hope the boxes missed you? I mean, yes, it was a shitty attempt at murder, but he could have caused real injuries."

He closed his hand around the one poking him, gentle but firm. "I would have done the same as you. I would have listened and paid attention, dodging as needed, until I recovered some information that would help us fight him. When you refused to leave, we didn't know you'd have magic fire at your disposal, and I couldn't hunt him while protecting you."

Lindsey's stiff shoulders relaxed as the angry whirlwind inside her calmed to a warmth that filled her chest. He'd had the chance to make progress, but she'd forced him to make a choice. And he'd chosen her.

"I wasn't going to leave you unprotected any more than you were going to leave me, and now I *do* have magic fire at my disposal. My full power is unlocked. Even better, I can control it."

"Was it worth it?" Dax crossed his arms and leaned against the counter like it was any other night.

"Hell, yes. That whole situation was like my worst nightmare come to life. Except the fire didn't spread. People didn't die."

His jaw ticked—not as unaffected as he'd like her to believe. "*You* could have died."

Lindsey surveyed the backyard. "We all take chances."

He moved silently, but she sensed him approach. Not like before. Now she could follow him with pinpoint accuracy. Another new skill courtesy of her magic finally surrendering. Lindsey wasn't confident it would prove useful, but she wasn't going to fight it.

Dax stepped in front of her, blocking the view she hadn't really noticed. He tilted her head until she saw his face instead, no longer blank, but blazing with emotion.

"I don't give a damn about your magic. I care about you. When I saw those boxes tumbling toward you..." He shook his head. "It terrifies me that you'll save everyone except yourself. The Fates chose me to save *you*. Let me."

Dax's plea struck at the heart of her. She could handle being injured—it had happened many times before—but she didn't want Dax acting as her shield. The idea that he might be hurt because of her, because of her choices, filled her with fear she hadn't felt in years. He'd become too important, and Lindsey would do anything to avoid that.

To her horror, her eyes filled with tears. She didn't cry. Crying never accomplished anything good. First, Dax had her breaking her own rules and getting emotionally involved, then he had her making stupid vows in her head while she *cried*.

She blinked, but the prickling only got worse. "I'll save everyone *including* myself, and I'm definitely not going to sacrifice you because some haughty goddesses thought they knew best when it came to human lives."

Dax wiped the tear that escaped off her cheek. "Well, that makes two of us. I won't let you carry the weight of stopping the gods by yourself because you have awesome magic powers. We're in this together."

She'd heard that before from others who'd bailed when things got hard, but Dax had never given her reason to doubt him. Even now, the distance between them came from her, from an attempt to protect herself if he decided this was more than he could handle. It was so easy to assume he'd fail her, but Dax deserved better. She moved closer and slid her hands around his waist.

Lindsey pressed her face against his chest, and when his arms came around her, the rest of the unnatural tension fell away. A tiny part of her had been afraid he'd push her away, but Dax held her, let her tears leak all over his shirt, and stroked her hair.

"You don't always have to be the strong one."

"Yes, I do."

His hand stilled. "We all need help sometimes. Even demigods."

Lindsey knew he was right, that she couldn't take on a pantheon by herself, but working with a team had never been her strong suit. He was asking her to put aside a lifetime of lessons, pounded into her over and over again. For him, she'd try.

"I hate crying."

He chuckled. "I know."

She reluctantly released him to grab a napkin from the table. Lindsey wiped her face and took a deep breath. "Now that we're done fighting, I have new information I didn't get the chance to tell you in all the excitement. There were traces of magic on a few things in the office, but not all of it. Particularly, an ornate golden hand mirror that really didn't seem like Kora's style."

"You mean like the gladiator helm I found?"

Lindsey frowned as she thought about it. "Yes, actually. The mirror had the same 'do not touch' feel to it. Also interesting to note, the magic was on *both* sides of the storage room door."

Dax rubbed his stubble and the bristly noise sent a shot of pure, visceral need through her. Thanks to Dax, her body associated that sound with some very sexy memories.

"Could you tell if the magic was specifically Kora's?"

Lindsey smoothed her hair from her face and cleared her throat. "No. Unfortunately, the sensation doesn't come with nametags."

"That would make things a lot easier," he mused.

She threw her wet napkin at him. "I've spent a lot of time with Kora. She's a touchy person, but I've never noticed any magic around her. If she's that good at hiding it—and at this point I'm going on that assumption since we heard her admit she could use magic—then why would she leave sloppy magic trails all over the woods where Calliope spends a lot of her time?"

Dax tossed her napkin into the sink. "You have a point, but I'm not in the mood to take any chances on people who've been lying to us."

He meant chances with Lindsey's safety. She'd seen how much he liked Kora, but Dax was ready and willing to immediately throw that friendship aside for Lindsey. The annoying threat of tears returned. Why was she only now noticing all this loyalty and devotion?

"How did they even get those boxes stacked that high?"

"Magic?"

"Is that going to be your automatic answer for every-thing from now on?"

"I feel like it's a valid excuse for anything at this point. Car won't start? Magic. Milk still good a week after the expiration date? Magic. Finding the exact thing we were looking for in the office? Magic." He grinned. "See? As long as we don't really understand how it works, we can credit it for everything."

Lindsey sat at the breakfast bar with a huff. "I wish we had more answers."

Dax joined her and nudged her shoulder. "For which questions. You're going to need to be more specific."

She peered at the sword they'd left sitting on the kitchen counter. "Start with the mirror and the helm. Magic finger-prints are useful for tracking, but they're not doing me a whole lot of good without a reference point. It would be great if Calliope knew about any connections between items and magic power because they definitely exuded magic." Lindsey's brow furrowed as she searched the kitchen. "Where *is* Calliope? She's usually around by now pestering me for dinner."

"Honestly, I'm a little surprised she didn't just appear in the storeroom when you used your magic." His attention shot back to her face. "Kora and David mentioned Calliope. Remember? They seemed to be hiding Kora's magic from her, but they also mentioned 'the others'."

Lindsey nodded slowly. "Why would they hide from Calliope? How would they even know who she is if she didn't tell them?"

When was the last time she'd seen Calliope for that matter? Yesterday, maybe? The cat had been disappearing more and more lately, but for once, Lindsey had good news for her. She'd be ecstatic that Lindsey's magic finally worked.

Too bad the new crop of questions made her suspicious of her self-appointed guide to all things magical. Sabine seemed to trust Calliope, but did she know about Kora? One way to find out.

Lindsey put her phone on speaker, set it on the counter, and called Sabine. Dax glanced down at the screen, but didn't say anything as Sabine picked up.

"Hey, Lindsey."

"How much do you trust Calliope?"

Dax raised his brows, and Lindsey shrugged at him.

Sabine sighed. "We've gone over this. She's secretive and sneaky, but she's on our side."

"Has she talked to you about Kora?"

"No." Sabine drew the word out. "What about Kora?"

Lindsey shared a concerned look with Dax. "I'm pretty

sure she's a demigod, and she's hiding from Calliope. At the very least, she has access to magic and knows how to use it."

"Well hell," Sabine muttered. "That would have made things a lot easier. Look, I know Kora, but I wouldn't call us close friends. Her and Moira have a competitive relationship, so I tend to keep things light. If Calliope knows about Kora's magic, she has a good reason for keeping it a secret. If she doesn't know—and despite what she thinks, there's a lot Calliope doesn't know—then I have no good advice for you."

"That's what I thought. Thanks."

"No problem. But I'm going to remind you that you didn't know *I* had magic, and in my experience, the person hiding isn't usually the bad guy."

Lindsey laughed. "I can assure you that's not always the case."

Sabine scoffed. "Oh yeah? You hunt a lot of magic-users in your bounty hunting life?"

"One encounter with a god does not make you an expert."

"Then why do you keep calling me for advice?"

Lindsey pressed her lips together as Dax tried to hold in a laugh. Sabine had a point. "I'll keep that in mind next time."

"You do that. And be nice to Calliope. She's had a hard life." Sabine ended the call before Lindsey could respond.

Dax snickered, and Lindsey shoved his shoulder. The call hadn't answered any questions, only left them with more. Exhaustion started to weigh her down even though the sun had barely set, and like always, Dax picked up on it before she did.

He pulled out his phone and started scrolling. "I'm

ordering pizza. No arguments. You're barely keeping your-self upright on that barstool."

Lindsey propped her cheek on her hand so she could watch him. Calliope swore the bond with Dax was the key to her magic, but what had changed that afternoon? She'd been in danger before, and her magic had barely responded.

She'd let herself get involved physically and emotionally —a decision she couldn't bring herself to regret—but that had been growing for weeks. What had triggered the change? He'd ordered her to go, and she'd refused because she wasn't about to lose someone else she lov—cared about.

The slip worried her. She could care about him, want him, enjoy spending time with him, but if she loved him, he'd inevitably break her heart when he left. Was it too late? Was that the change?

During that moment in the storeroom, Lindsey had come back to him, determined to keep him safe, and touched his back. He'd lost his focus, and when she'd seen the boxes falling, she'd found hers. *Nothing* would harm him.

Shit. She *did* love him.

Lindsey stood and tried to shake off the fluttery panic that accompanied her realization while Dax finished with his order. "I'll be right back."

She hurried to the main floor bathroom before Dax picked up on her agitation. He'd want to know the cause, and she was *not* ready to have that discussion. Lindsey closed the door and sank down onto the closed toilet. Oh, she was so screwed.

He'd snuck his way into her heart when she wasn't paying attention—more important to her than anything else. She hadn't wanted this, but that hadn't stopped much in her life. What did she do now?

First, she ran cold water and splashed her face. The chill woke her up and helped ground her spiraling emotions. Until she figured out how to deal, Dax couldn't know. He'd make assumptions she probably couldn't fulfill, and Lindsey wanted to spare him that hurt.

One day, he'd realize she wasn't worth the effort and leave. She remembered her mom, selfish and needy, wailing about being saddled with a daughter, without the love of her life. Time and time again she'd come home to her mom passed out in bed, reeking of alcohol, only to wake up despondent that Lindsey's dad hadn't miraculously been resurrected.

She couldn't be bothered to cook or clean or get a job. Too much work. Too much effort. Despite Lindsey keeping them sheltered and fed with her dad's social security checks, her mom had only seen her as a burden. *You remind me so much of your dad... it hurts to look at you...if only I didn't have you, I could try to find happiness again.*

The truth hurt, but Lindsey adapted. And she learned. She'd applied those lessons every day of her life since then, until she'd met Dax. The man who made her feel worthy and loved.

Lindsey met her own eyes in the plain oval mirror, calm and resolute. She was done letting the fear from her past dictate her future. Dax was possibly the best thing that had ever happened to her, and she'd try her best to be the person he could love.

She washed her hands and left the bathroom with her chin high. Voices at the door meant she'd spent longer in her head than she'd thought, but no matter. Dax met her in the kitchen, where the savory smell of dinner surrounded them. He grinned when he saw her and held up the pizza.

"I have provided sustenance."

Lindsey's heart skipped, and she told it to settle down. People ate together all the time without devolving into lovesick puppies. He slid the box onto the counter, and it knocked the sword sideways. She laughed to herself, grateful for the distraction.

"As much as I like this thing, I'm not sure the breakfast bar where we eat is the best place to keep it."

She grabbed the hilt and held it up at eye-level to get a closer look at the engraving again. A split-second after she'd lifted it, a tickle of magic fluttered against her palm where the leather rested. Without thinking, Lindsey gasped and let go.

**13**

---

*Lindsey*

LINDSEY DROPPED the sword as soon as she felt the magic, but Dax, with his super speed, caught the hilt before it could skewer any of her toes.

He raised his brows, then spun the sword up into a relaxed stance. "What happened?"

Dax performed that frustratingly sexy maneuver with such ease that Lindsey reconsidered her stance on reincarnation. He'd have made one hell of an ancient warrior.

The sword looked the same as it had in the weeks since she'd bought it. She'd touched the metal countless times—tracing the symbols, cleaning the counter underneath it, once, swinging it around like a kid because she'd had the inclination and some free time. None of those instances had included magic.

Lindsey raised her eyes from the sword to the man. "It has the magic tingle. Like the mirror and the helm...and all the trees around where the god tried to kill me."

In a flash, Dax went from ancient warrior to avenging guardian. His jaw tightened along with his grip. "The same magic?"

Belatedly, Lindsey realized the sensation had been different than any of the magic she'd felt before. It carried traces of the god they'd been dealing with, but the majority had struck her as oddly familiar.

She shook out her hands. "I need to touch it again to be sure, but I think it's a new player."

Dax flipped the sword, extending the hilt to her. Lindsey wrapped her fingers around the leather, anticipating the tickle this time. Unlike the other pieces, it didn't give off the warning vibe. The magic reached deep into the weapon rather than sitting on top like what she'd been calling the fingerprints.

In those cases, someone using magic had touched those surfaces. In *this* case, someone had infused magic into the sword during its creation. As far as Lindsey could tell, the power was benign, curled in on itself until she'd touched it.

She held the hilt in her right hand and smoothed her left along the flat of the blade. The swirls followed, moving along the metal under her hand.

"Huh." Lindsey let her arm drop to her side as she tilted her head at Dax. "It's definitely different magic, and it's responding to me."

The intensity faded from his face. "Why now?"

Lindsey shook her head and carefully put the sword back on the counter where it had been before. "Maybe because my power is unlocked? I don't know. It's been inside Calliope's protection this whole time, so unless she imbued the sword somehow, I think the difference is me not detecting the magic rather than it not being there before."

"What does your spidey sense tell you?"

"The magic is subdued. It feels old. The whole thing feels old. I'm just guessing, but I'd say that the traces are from whoever owned it originally."

He didn't ask her how she knew, simply believed what she said. Lindsey hadn't realized she'd tensed up preparing to defend herself, so Dax's faith in her abilities caught her off guard. She focused on the sword again, but no more convenient knowledge popped into her head.

"What did you say it was? A xiphos?"

He jerked his chin toward it. "That style dates back to the Iron Age, but if it's magically preserved, it could have been made any time in the last fifteen hundred years. It was a well-known sword shape."

"Okay, so that doesn't narrow it down."

"The markings should help with that, if we could identify them." Dax finally relaxed enough to open the pizza, and Lindsey nearly drooled on herself as the cloud of spicy scent wafted up to her.

He offered her a plate with three slices, and Lindsey grinned. "I could eat this every day."

"We pretty much do. I saw the delivery girl in town, and she recognized me as, and I quote, 'the guy who eats all the veggie pizzas'."

Lindsey snorted. "I'm one hundred percent okay with that." She finished two slices before bringing the subject back to the symbols. "I know Calliope said they weren't familiar, but I think she's lying."

"Everyone else is, why leave her out?"

She pointed her pizza at him. "Precisely."

He held up both hands. "Hey, I agree with you, but it doesn't help us unless you can convince her to tell us the truth."

"Lucky for you, I happen to find things for a living,

which requires me to decode all kinds of obscure information. I might know a guy."

Dax lowered the pizza from his mouth. "Why didn't we contact this guy weeks ago?"

Lindsey shrugged. "The sword wasn't high on my priority list. Now it is."

She stretched her legs out, attempting to ease the sore muscles there, and her skirt rode up her thighs. The skirt had been her attempt to wear something fun and sexy for once. She'd had the wild urge to show Dax she could do more than fail to make magical fire, and judging by his preoccupation, it had worked.

Dax followed the motion, and when his gaze rose to her face, a different kind of fire burned there. "Tomorrow."

Liquid heat pooled, and Lindsey's breath caught. She nodded. "Tomorrow."

---

THANKS TO DAX, Lindsey was beginning to like mornings. Even when he needed to do some work for Alex, he started his day focused entirely on her. After leaving her a satisfied mess in their bed, he'd reminded her to talk to Calliope and contact her source on his way out the door.

Lindsey blew her hair out of her face and pulled his pillow close so she could bury her face in it. *Their* bed. They'd taken to sleeping in Dax's room exclusively, and at some point, her stuff had moved in too. Her hoodie lay next to his discarded socks beside a stack of books from both their collections. His headphones had ended up next to her side of the bed, but she didn't remember how they'd gotten there.

Magic, probably. She smiled at the memory of Dax's explanation for everything. Their bed, their space. How odd that she'd fallen so easily into sharing her life with him. Her smiles came regularly now and most of them were even genuine. He helped her be happy in a way she hadn't been in a long time, maybe ever. What would it be like to have that feeling forever?

He'd said he wanted more from her than a summer hook-up, but what did that entail? The possibilities fought for space in her mind while she breathed in Dax's scent. He'd said he was in the process of moving his home base to Deckard, but that didn't mean he wanted her to be a part of it.

After the apartment fire, she didn't really have a home. To be honest, she hadn't had a home even before that. The idea of putting down roots had always made her itchy—her mom had certainly never made her feel wanted, and avoiding permanent ties made it harder for other people to treat her the same way. But this space they'd created, filled with parts of both of them, gave her a taste of what she'd been missing.

Had Dax been missing it too?

Speculating would get her nowhere. If she wanted to know, she needed to ask. Just as soon as she mustered up the courage to admit she might have been wrong about a relationship with him.

No big deal, but maybe she'd wait until they'd stopped the murderous god wandering town before adding more drama. Lindsey rolled over and faced the fact that she wouldn't be going back to sleep. Better get up and do stuff.

She took her time showering and dressing, in a strangely good mood. And no wonder. Her power was free. She'd used it on command. More importantly, she'd called it back on command too. Granted, the ability had manifested under heightened circumstances, so she'd definitely be testing it, but the magic felt different inside her. Unrestrained. Fluid.

Once downstairs, Lindsey grabbed a cup of coffee and took pictures of the sword to email to her contact. Andrew worked as an adjunct professor in the classics department at a major university. An insignificant cog in a broken wheel, as he liked to phrase it. Lindsey had taken to him immediately.

His disdain for humanity was legendary, but only in very small, intimate circles. To his students, he was sarcastic, irreverent, and fun, and she'd overheard some underclassmen talking about a challenge to earn a date with him the last time she'd visited. He loved a challenge—or anything to distract him from his current job—so Lindsey knew he'd get back to her promptly.

Email sent, she settled down in the front room to practice with her new magic. A gentle nudge and a half-formed thought caused her power to unfurl and rush to her limbs. She watched as fire engulfed her hand but went no farther. Lindsey's chest tightened with excitement as she slowly turned her arm to watch the flames dance.

As if she'd been called, Calliope strolled through the doorway minutes later. Her steps faltered when she saw the fire licking at Lindsey's wrists, but she recovered quickly.

*You completed the bond. Well done.*

Lindsey shook her hand free of the magic. "Where have you been?"

*I've told you. Patrolling.* Her voice sounded tired, but Lindsey squelched the twinge of pity.

"For days?"

*I've been nearby the whole time.*

Lindsey wanted to push, but the effort seemed pointless. Calliope had already given her explanation, and if she'd wanted to go into detail, she would have. The damn stubborn cat guarded her secrets closely. Better to come back to that line of inquiry.

"I have more questions about your fellow gods."

The cat hopped delicately onto the couch and curled up with her head on her paws. *You always have more questions, but I'll remind you again—they are of a different status than me. We're not fellows.*

"As you've told me several times now. What does it take, specifically, to become corporeal?"

Calliope lifted her head. *You encountered the god again.*

Lindsey sat next to her. "He tried to flatten Dax and me with some books. A lot of books. It triggered the release of my magic."

*I imagine it was more complicated than that, but that's not important at the moment. To answer your question, they absorb power from human energy and combine it with a physical anchor to create a form that can interact with the world.*

Calliope put her head back down, and Lindsey didn't dare move. She'd asked the question before, but the sneaky Muse had avoided answering. For whatever reason, Calliope seemed to be in a sharing mood. Though her story didn't fit with the one that Sabine had told Lindsey.

"Like you?"

*The gods don't know I'm corporeal. I shouldn't be. I gave up a physical body long ago to protect the seal, and I have no anchor. Nothing in our history warned me it was possible to reclaim this existence, and yet, here I am.*

"As a cat."

*As a cat. I'm not sure I would have chosen this form, but it is what it is.*

"Didn't you like to appear as a spectral panther before you encountered Sabine and her taser?"

*To scare away humans. It was a delicate balance between a creature that would frighten them enough to leave immediately and one they wouldn't attempt to hunt for sport. I didn't always achieve that balance.*

Lindsey wanted to get back to the part about the anchor, but she also wanted to distract Calliope enough that she'd keep talking beyond where she meant to stop. Absently, she held out her hand and practiced calling and releasing her magic in tiny spurts of fire.

"How does the anchor thing work? Can we reverse it— use it to trap them instead?"

Calliope sent her a knowing look without moving her head. *Clever. I'd considered this idea, but rejected it as being too dangerous. The best course of action is still to repair the seal and return the gods to stasis, but until we have enough power for that, finding a way to contain them would be helpful.*

"Yeah, it would be nice to not worry about being murdered. Tell me and let *me* decide if it's too dangerous." Lindsey attempted a form a ball with the fire, and surprised herself by making a lopsided oval.

The cat snorted. *It's a tricky bit of magic. You have to open the seal on the anchor to expose the well of power inside and manipulate it so that it forces the rest of the god's power to respond.*

"And how do I do that?"

*You infuse it with your magic. Too much and you go in yourself. Too little and it has no effect. The artifact is meant to ground the god's lifeforce here, if you push enough of yourself into it, they have to choose between releasing their hold or diving back into it to root you out.*

Lindsey frowned and let her magic fade, relaxing the prickling hold she had over the power. "What happens if they release it?"

Calliope's eyes drifted closed. *They'll cease to exist, but there's a good chance you will as well. Your lifeforce will be trapped inside the object, and demigods can't survive without their physical bodies.*

She groaned. "Of course. Why would the answer be easy?"

*Meddling with lifeforces should never be easy. Remember, and this is very important, you have to be close enough for both of you to touch the object. If the god can't reach it, they won't have a choice. And neither will you.*

In that scenario, she had to essentially force a god to call her bluff. Lindsey would be depending on the god to both believe her and want to live enough that they wouldn't risk dying just to take her out too.

Not the best odds, but ones she could work with.

"I assume there's one anchor per god? This isn't a Voldemort situation?"

Calliope cracked open one eye. *What does that mean?*

"Right. I forgot you literally lived under a rock for the last thousand years. How do I find the anchors?"

She paused so long Lindsey wondered if she'd fallen asleep. Then she sighed. *The magic. Each god will be intimately connected to their anchor with their magic. They would be objects from before the seal. Ancient in your terms, but well-preserved. The gods would probably keep the anchors nearby, though proximity isn't necessary to use them.*

An image of the sword popped into her mind. Could it be that simple? Granted, she'd found it in an antique shop, but maybe the Fates were working in her favor for once. The magic hadn't matched the one on the trees though.

What about the helm? She hadn't touched it, so she couldn't be sure, but it certainly seemed like the type of thing that would be an anchor. They really needed to go back and investigate Kora and David. Or at least have an honest conversation with them.

"How accurate is the magic texture thing you taught me?"

*That is entirely dependent on you. It's a sixth sense, and you're learning how to interpret it. In time and with enough practice among your kind, the skill will become second nature.*

Lindsey scoffed and spoke without thinking. "I'm not planning to practice among my kind."

Calliope sat up and turned to stare at her. *Excuse me?*

Silently cursing herself, Lindsey forged ahead. "I'm only staying until the end of the summer. Then Sabine will be back and she can be your personal weapon. I wanted to learn how to control my magic so I didn't put people in danger, and I feel like I've achieved that. I won't leave the seal undefended, but I have a life to return to."

The cat's brows furrowed. *You'd be so selfish to put yourself before the rest of the human world?*

Anger began to bubble up in Lindsey's gut. "It's not selfish to need to support myself. I can't live in Sabine's guest room forever, and my job requires me to travel. I said I'd help until the end of the summer, and I don't see why we can't take care of this god by then."

*This god is only the prologue to the troubles coming. They want the power of the seal, and Apollo, at least, knows where it is. He could have shared the knowledge with his brethren.*

"Then why aren't there more gods here trying to get past your protections?" She thought of the sword again and

Sabine's description of Apollo as a warrior. "Apollo is probably the one who's been causing problems."

*Potentially, but opportunistic murder attempts aren't his style. On the other hand, I wouldn't have expected him to share the location, as he tends to think he can do everything himself. Like you.*

"Would he be more likely to use a helm or a sword as an anchor?"

Calliope scoffed. *A sword. He'd never risk ruining his hair with a helm. Focus, Lindsey. We need you here to work with the others when they arrive.*

Lindsey chafed at the assumed responsibility. Who knew how long it would take the other demigods to react to Calliope's magic and travel here? She refused to be a burden on Sabine and Alex, but her savings would only last her so long. Unless she planned to sleep in her car, she needed to deal with the mundane aspects of her life as well as the magical ones. She couldn't afford to be picky about which jobs she took because they might drag her away from her happy little bubble.

A sharp stitch of sadness twisted through her as she imagined returning to her life before this summer. The prospect of leaving Dax behind left her questioning her future, but he had to make his own choices. In the end, would it be easier to make a clean cut instead of trying to navigate a long-distance mess?

Her chest ached at the thought of Dax one day deciding that a relationship with her was too much work.

She shook her head. "The others will be fine without me. I'll help with this god, then you can contact me when you need me for the seal."

Calliope sniffed then stood and stretched. *You should continue your practice then. It will take more than light balls to defeat a god.* With that, she jumped off the couch and hurried out of the room.

The frustration from Calliope shattered her concentration. Licks of flame crawled up her wrists, and Lindsey cursed. With her Dax radar, she felt him leave the office and head toward the front room. By the time he appeared in the doorway, she'd crossed her arms, fire and all, ready to send him back to work.

He didn't stop at the doorway though. Dax walked directly to her, slid his hands into her hair, and seduced her with a slow, deep kiss. At the first touch of his lips, Lindsey sighed, unclenched her tight muscles, and leaned into him. Distantly, she felt the flames retreat back into the seemingly endless magic well inside her.

Lindsey grasped desperately for the reason she'd planned to make him turn around. "You can't come in here and kiss away my magic every time I need help. I have to be able to do this myself."

His mouth trailed down her neck, only stopping when he reached the v-neck of her shirt. "I'm not in here to kiss your magic away. I'm just in here to kiss you. Please continue. Pretend like I'm not even here."

Lindsey's lips lifted into a half-smile, and she tugged on his hair until he looked up at her. "You. Are. Distracting."

He grinned and hooked his arm under her knees to lift her. "I'm not even trying yet."

Laughter banished the last of her anger as Dax carried her up the stairs to their bedroom. "Really? Is this your answer to everything?"

He kicked the door closed behind them and did a quick scan, she assumed to make sure Calliope wasn't lurking somewhere. "Of course not. Magic is the answer to everything, but getting you alone and naked is a close second. Everything else falls away."

Dax set her on her feet, and Lindsey had to admit she liked his order of priorities. Still, he needed to know what Calliope had told her. He ripped his shirt over his head and followed with hers. Lindsey covered his hands on her stomach as he reached for the snap on her shorts.

"Hold on, I have to tell you some stuff before we pass the point of no return."

He tugged his trapped hand. "Too late. I can listen and get you naked at the same time."

Lindsey tightened her grip and gave him the short version. "Calliope told me we can trap a god in an object that they use as an anchor in the physical world, something ancient but well-preserved."

Dax yanked his hands free and pulled her closer to nuzzle her neck. "And she told you how to do it?"

She let out a shaky breath. "Yes. It could be Apollo following us around, and I think we have his sword."

"Not that I want to add to your distraction, but doesn't that feel too easy? What about the helm we found?"

"It's not a perfect theory, but Calliope confirmed Apollo would be a sword guy over a helm guy."

"Okay, I have one more question." He kissed her throat and trailed his lips down to the tops of her breasts, stopping at the edge of her bra. "Is that skirt from yesterday still around?"

Lindsey giggled as he lifted her again, this time depositing her on the bed. He didn't wait for an answer, but made quick work of the rest of their clothes. Dax teased her with his hands and his mouth, driving her need ever higher. Through it all, his touch centered her.

They'd had weeks to learn each other, to find what

brought quiet pleasure and wild hunger. Last night, they'd come together in a frenzied rush, but today was slow and reverent. Today, he made her feel loved.

The words bubbled up from deep inside her until she caught them on her tongue. *I love you.* She thought it over and over again as they moved together, as she soared and sighed, as he went taut above her and dropped down to whisper her name against her ear. Lindsey pressed her lips together to keep the words inside, but her grip on his shoulder—the way she curled up against him—must have caught his notice.

Dax shifted his weight off of her, but didn't move away. He rubbed his thumb along her cheek and cupped her neck, holding her close.

"Forget the skirt. You're perfect just the way you are."

She cringed at his description. "I'm not perfect. Your mind is clouded by good sex and fate mojo."

He laughed dryly and leaned away for a moment. When he rolled back, Dax pulled her against him, wrapping his arms around her. Lindsey snuggled closer, tucking a leg between his and laying her head on his chest.

His voice rumbled under her cheek. "How do you know it's not always fate? When someone becomes interested, maybe it's because they were created for that purpose. To find each other. Complement each other. Be *more* together than they could be apart."

Lindsey didn't have an answer for him. She didn't care about other couples—she cared about him. If he thought of her as perfect, he'd be disillusioned that much faster.

LINDSEY DREAMED she stood barefoot at the bottom of the ravine. Daylight filtered through the trees high above, and the gap between growth on the two cliffs left a strip of bright light down the middle. The sky didn't give her any clues about the time of day, but when she tried to shade her eyes to look up, she realized she clutched the sword in one hand.

"You think much of yourself to stand against the gods. Tell me, do you have as high of an opinion of your lover?" The androgynous voice echoed at her from the trees, but she couldn't pinpoint a direction.

Sword in hand, she spun in a slow circle. No signs of another person, but the world moved wrong. A slight delay between the movement and the change in scenery. Lindsey glanced down and saw herself dressed in a simple shift. Nothing she'd worn before, or would ever wear voluntarily.

"Come. Do you have no answer for me?"

Lindsey scowled. The voice sounded deep and high at the same time, distorted enough that she couldn't detect any identifying information. The old-timey formal language gave her a pretty big clue though.

"To whom am I speaking?"

"She *does* have a tongue. You speak to a god."

Though she'd known, the answer still sent a shiver down her spine. Lindsey recognized the feel of foreign magic in her head from all her time with Calliope. She may be dreaming, but the voice was real.

"What do you want?"

The god tsked. "So insolent. I came to propose a simple exchange. The seal for your lover's life."

Lindsey's jaw clenched as anger and fear fought for dominance. She'd never given in to fear before, and she wouldn't start now. Anger won. "If you had the power to take his life, you would have already. I know your weakness, and I know I'm stronger than you."

The sky darkened, answering her silent question about who controlled the dream. "You *knew* my weakness. Your fledgling fire is no match for the blaze of my magic."

The trees crashed together in a sudden wind that didn't touch her. Branches tore from their trunks and flew across the ravine. Boulders heaved over the cliffs, shattering on the rocks below. Creatures born of mud and detritus rose from the creek to lumber toward her.

Then all of a sudden, everything stopped. A laugh, creepy with the two tones, drifted to her. Lindsey focused on a leaf suspended in the air. The world had paused mid-tantrum, an effective demonstration of power.

"You can't hide him away forever, but you don't have to. The seal is no use to you. Place it outside the circle, and our deal is complete. You have my word."

The world returned to normal. Mud people collapsed back into the ground, trees swayed gently in the breeze, and the sky became a slice of bright blue. The leaf floated down and landed on her foot. Lindsey used the tip of the sword to flip it onto the ground.

"I'm not making a deal with you. Dax can handle himself."

"Your faith in him is noble, and flawed. He's promised to protect you, yes? Is your love strong enough to do the same?"

Dax appeared on his knees in the mud, reaching for her. Lindsey took a step toward him before she could stop herself. At her movement, a vine wrapped around his throat from behind, and his face contorted in pain as his fingers scrabbled at the thin plant in vain.

The sword warmed in her hand as eddies of her magic

coalesced around the leather, but Lindsey refused to give in to the god's sadistic little display. She closed her eyes and told herself he wasn't real. None of this was real. Dax whispered her name in a strangled voice, and a sharp pain in her chest nearly doubled her over.

Lindsey reached in her mind for the foreign magic. She shoved against the jagged edges with all her might and felt a pop as she shoved the power of the god out of her head.

## 14

*Dax*

HE'D NEVER GET tired of waking up next to Lindsey, but her habit of stealing the covers probably wouldn't be as cute in the winter. And he planned to have her next to him through the winter and well beyond.

The sun had begun to peek through the window when Dax smiled ruefully and tugged on the blankets to cover both of them. Lindsey grumbled, but when he pulled her back against him, she sighed and relaxed. He wanted to enjoy the moment, but if the last few mornings since the storeroom were any indication, she'd be up and gone soon.

The coconut scent of her hair tickled his nose, and Dax drew it in. She spent her days researching the sword, practicing magic, and training on her own—a departure from the joint workouts they'd been doing before. But the nights were his.

In his arms, she shed her stiff, closed-off shell and

turned to him with a desperation he didn't entirely understand. Since she'd gained the ability to control her magic, she'd run hot and cold on him. At first, he attributed it to the frustration of not being immediately *good* at using her magic, but her behavior hadn't changed as she'd become more skilled.

If anything, she'd become more distant.

Lindsey yawned and turned her head into the pillow with a mumbled good morning. "What time is it?"

Dax chuckled. "I don't know. Daytime? Does it matter?"

She shrugged one shoulder. "No. It just feels really late. I'd better get up." Her body had already started to pull away, but Dax didn't want to start this morning like the others this week.

He caught her before she could slide out of his arms. "Stay. Talk to me. I know something's going on, and I want to help."

For a split second, she stiffened, and Dax prepared to let her go if that's what she wanted. To his relief, she rolled over instead. Her fingers danced over his cheek for a fleeting second, and his hopes soared that she'd finally tell him what the hell was bothering her.

She smiled, but Dax knew what her real smiles looked like, and that one only touched the surface. "I'm fine. Practicing with the magic is exhausting, and the sword is pissing me off. I'm sorry I've been cranky."

He nodded, disappointed that she'd deflected again. No doubt, the magic practice made her tired—she often took a nap in the afternoon if she spent the morning working with her fire—but she'd been tired before. Cranky didn't come close to explaining the walls she'd erected between them.

Dax wanted to push for a real answer, but he knew

Lindsey wouldn't respond well to that maneuver. She'd raise her prickly shields and do the exact opposite of his intended outcome. Maybe he needed to give a little first.

"My grandma Elle used to say magic wrung her out because she had to expend energy twice—once to See and once to believe."

Lindsey's gaze shot to his face. "How did I not know your grandma used magic?"

"Her magic wasn't like yours. She called it the Sight in front of the rest of my family, but they didn't really believe her. With me, she called it intuitive magic. Something she sensed and used every day even if it was subtle and small."

Dax rolled onto his back, and Lindsey followed, resting her cheek on his chest. The first time in days that he'd convinced her not to rush off in the morning.

"I wish I could have met her. She sounds like a fascinating lady."

He couldn't keep the smile off his face. First, because he had his Lindsey back, at least for now. Second, because grandma Elle would have loved her. Dax could imagine the trouble the two of them would have gotten into if they'd ever had the chance to meet.

"She was. She's the one who gave me my nickname."

Lindsey sat up. "Your nickname?"

Dax kissed her fingertips then eased her back down. "My dad is a cruel, cruel man. He had this idea in his head of what he'd name his first son, and nothing my mom could do would dissuade him. The story goes my grandma took one look at the name next to my crib and declared me Dax, after my late grandfather—the love of her life. My mom refused to call me anything else, so Dax stuck."

Grandma Elle had loved telling that story. Dax trailed

his hand down Lindsey's bare back and let the bittersweet memory of the last time he'd seen his grandma linger. She'd been fit and feisty up until the end, reigning over the kitchen in her little house. He'd shown up in the middle of the night, only able to get his leave request approved at the last minute, and there she'd been at the stove making gravy to go with the biscuits she'd put in the oven.

Grandma Elle always knew.

Lindsey shifted higher, and Dax realized his plan had sort of backfired. Yes, he'd convinced Lindsey to stay, but he'd gotten lost in his own thoughts instead of figuring out what was bothering her.

She tilted her head and studied him. "What's your real name?"

"I'll spill my secret if you spill yours. What's really bothering you?" As soon as the words left his mouth, Dax knew he'd made a mistake. Lindsey's eyes became wary, and her fake smile returned. He hated that fake smile.

"I told you, but feel free to keep your secrets. It would be weird calling you by another name. You'll always be Dax to me."

She shifted back, and in a desperate attempt to claw back from his latest snafu, Dax kissed her. He figured out right away the effort wouldn't work. She responded enthusiastically enough, but then she made an excuse and left the bed. He sighed and fell back onto his pillow.

Grandma Elle would be supremely disappointed in the way he was blowing this.

———

HE DIDN'T SEE her for the rest of the day, as expected. Twice Dax ventured to the front room, but both times, he only found Calliope sitting on the couch with her tail twitching. Lindsey had stepped out for a moment, according to the cat. He didn't bother a third time.

Around sunset, he started dinner prep, hoping she'd show up as usual. Burgers on the grill and the salad Lindsey would insist he eat. He cut vegetables and cleaned his mess, then went outside to grab the meat.

Her reticence worried him. Their conversation that morning had been heartfelt and real, but the moment he'd probed, she'd shut down. He didn't think her secret involved a problem with their relationship, but it could definitely be something she'd planned that would put her in danger.

Lindsey was hands down the most stubbornly independent person he'd ever met, and if she believed she could take out a god, she'd follow through. Dax had no doubt she'd try until she dropped, and he intended to be there if that happened. He'd lost Beth because he hadn't been there to protect her, and he wouldn't make that error again.

His heart skipped when he turned from the grill to see Lindsey. She leaned against the back door with her arms crossed and a half-smile on her face as she watched him.

"Did you remember to turn off the fire?"

Dax raised a brow as he walked toward her. "That was *one* time."

She stepped back into the house to let him pass with the plate of burgers. "It only takes one."

Boy, did he know that. Lindsey hovered by the back door and looked everywhere except his face. Something had happened, and she wasn't running off on her own this time. She'd come to him.

Dax set a burger on each prepared plate and carried them to the table. He wanted to be able to see Lindsey during this conversation. She took her seat, and he didn't have to wait long.

"Have you checked your messages lately?"

"Not in the last few hours. Why?"

She swallowed her bite then set her burger back on her plate. "Alex and Sabine are coming back early. They think in the next day or so."

Dax's brows shot up. That wasn't the type of news he was expecting. Why hadn't Alex called him? He pulled his phone out of his pocket and groaned. When he worked, he put it in airplane mode, and he must have forgotten to flip it back while chasing after Lindsey. Two calls, a voicemail, and a text from Alex. One text from Sabine.

He set the phone on the table and shrugged. "Okay. Did they kick us out?"

The question was a joke. Alex would never kick him out —especially when he'd agreed to let Dax stay for the rest of the summer—but Lindsey frowned.

"No. They insisted we stay, actually, but I got a lead on a job in Dallas."

"You managed that in four hours?"

Lindsey didn't answer him, and her uncharacteristic nervousness suddenly made sense. She'd been planning this for days. Alex and Sabine returning simply gave her an excuse.

"What about the seal? Calliope, the gods?" Dax held her gaze. If she lied to him, she'd have to do it to his face.

She didn't flinch away, but her tone hardened. "Turns out I'm not the heroic type. I came here to learn how to control my magic. I've done that. I agreed to help stop this god, but then it's time for me to go."

Dax pushed his plate away, no longer hungry when his

insides felt like they were twisted into knots. "What about me?"

Her rigid jaw softened. "You're the one thing I don't want to leave behind."

The table between them pissed him off. He needed to touch her. Dax circled to crouch next to her, taking her hands in his. "Then don't. Stay here and see it through. Stay with me." He heard the edge of pleading in his voice, but he didn't care.

A sheen of tears glistened in her eyes and tore through Dax. "I can't. I just...can't."

Lindsey's chair screeched across the floor as she got up, and her hands slid away from him. She paced to the doorway before speaking over her shoulder. "Be careful if you hang around here."

Dax stood—body taut with frustration and hurt but his hands relaxed at his sides. "Afraid something will happen to me?"

"Is that so far-fetched?"

"I thought you didn't let fear make you run."

She flinched, so his barb hit its mark, but then she turned and left the room with her chin high.

Dax imagined sweeping the remains of their half-eaten dinner onto the floor, could almost hear the crash of the plates and cups shattering on the hardwood. The thought of explaining himself to Alex kept his rage tempered, barely.

He finally knew part of what had been bothering Lindsey. Something had convinced her Dax was in danger because of her. Not the heroic type, his ass. She planned to throw away their relationship, the greatest thing that had ever happened to him, because she thought it would protect him.

Instead of destroying pieces of his best friend's home, he

gently collected the remains of the meal, threw away the food, and set the dishes in the sink. Washing plates was beyond him at the moment. A large part of him wanted to follow Lindsey and shake her until she admitted the whole truth.

Somehow in all this time, she still hadn't decided to trust him. That cut the deepest.

He'd heard her go up the stairs, but his parting shot had ensured she wouldn't go to their bedroom. She'd have gone back to her original room.

Lindsey wanted space right now, so he'd give her space. Even if it killed him.

Dax paced the kitchen until the movement upstairs quieted to give her a chance to retrieve what she needed for the night. The repetitive motion helped him focus his thoughts past his anger at Lindsey's fear.

His own fear tried to surface once the fury faded. Lindsey knew her own mind. He respected the hell out of her and everything she'd accomplished. If he ran roughshod over her plans, would he be making the situation worse? Maybe.

He rubbed the ache in his chest and thought about waking up every morning without her for the rest of his life. Watching a movie and not feeling her hair cling to his stubble when she laid her head on his shoulder. Using his towel after the hot tub without sparring with her for the privilege. Never feeling her breath catch in that quiet moment after the first rush of a kiss.

Dax shook his head and stopped to lean on the table with both hands. He loved her, and he'd fight for the life they could have together.

Tomorrow, the real battle began. He'd prove to her they belonged together. Starting with admitting his feelings for her. Dax ran a hand through his hair. If Lindsey needed to be in Dallas, he'd be right behind her. With that god still on the loose, he sure as hell wasn't about to leave her unprotected and alone.

Fuck the Fates. While he was at it, fuck the gods and the human race too. He'd call Alex and tell him to hurry his happy ass home if he didn't want his precious seal left protected only by a cat with possible loyalty issues.

---

*Lindsey*

LINDSEY HADN'T BEEN in the best mindset when she'd fallen asleep after the fight with Dax. Could it be called a fight? His parting words had certainly felt like a blow, but she hadn't intended to hurt him.

The wind blew her hair out of her face, and she realized she stood in the ravine, clad in her sleep shorts and a tank top. Lindsey sighed. The dream again. This would be the fourth time she'd gone to sleep and woken up here. Except she wasn't really awake.

The world around her felt real enough, but after multiple visits, she recognized the pattern. The god hadn't been able to get back into her head after she'd evicted him the first time, but that hadn't stopped him from trying. Each attempt—telepathic fingers clawing at her mind—became easier to rebuff with a simple push of power against that spot.

Her brow furrowed. This one differed from the last couple. For one, Lindsey didn't feel any pressure pushing her to surrender. For two, a malevolence she hadn't noticed from previous dreams was noticeably absent. Lindsey glanced up at the spot where she'd landed, then down at the mud near the creek, only a few steps from where she currently stood. The faint outline of a bare foot prodded her memory.

That was what she'd been trying to remember. A footprint and the shine of metal right before she'd fallen.

Leaves rasped together, creating a gentle shush, but another sound layered underneath it. A male voice, deeper than Dax's. She tilted her head to listen. The tone relayed urgency, but the message seemed to echo from far away preventing her from making out any words.

Lack of sleep combined with the persistent vision of Dax falling into the mud unconscious had her on edge, and even in the best of moods, Lindsey wasn't interested in playing games with the gods. She closed her eyes and focused on her breathing, like she'd done with Dax to settle her magic.

She imagined him lying next to her, his chest moving in sync with hers. Imagined the coolness of the room and the warmth of his skin. The sharp, sweet smell of pine began to fade, but while she hovered between sleeping and waking, one word came to her in a clear, deep timbre. *Sword.*

Lindsey sat up with a gasp in bed. Sunlight streamed through the window, and at first, she didn't recognize the room. Then the night and the dream and the fight with Dax came back to her. She'd grabbed her things from the other room and come to sleep in here. With a sigh, she flopped on the bed.

Dax wanted her to stay. Calliope wanted her to stay. Even Sabine and Alex wanted her to stay. Worse, Lindsey's heart urged her to stay. But what would she offer them? Untested magic and a weakness for the god to manipulate?

She'd been willing to bide her time until now, but giving

up the house meant she'd had to make a choice. Stay until Dax grew tired of her and broke her heart, or leave and try to salvage what pieces of her life remained.

Lindsey cringed and covered her face with her arm. *Was* she running because of fear? The question played on repeat in her mind, plaguing her with insecurity. Lindsey hadn't been afraid in a long time, but she recognized the feeling now.

She feared Dax being hurt, but she also feared Dax hurting her. Her chest ached from the disappointment in his tone last night. Lindsey had promised herself the summer would be temporary, but falling in love with Dax had screwed that all up. Even now, part of her wanted to cave— tell him she'd stay and play house and pretend they had a bright future.

But Lindsey knew her own faults. She wasn't good at families or relationships, and eventually, Dax would leave her for someone who was.

She'd promised to stay and deal with the god, but they didn't need her. Sabine knew how to defeat a god; she'd done it before. With Alex, she'd have full access to her magic, and without Lindsey, the god would have no reason to target Dax. Or...Lindsey could go after the god herself. She had an artifact and a trail.

Lindsey shook her head. If she went by herself, she'd be removing the threat to Dax but also eschewing backup if she needed it. Confidence in her abilities didn't translate to stupidity. She knew she was stronger with Dax than without, but would he go with her, even after yesterday?

In a fit of pique, Lindsey threw the blankets off and stomped through the bathroom. She flung open the door, then stopped short. Towels lay folded on the foot of the neatly made bed, and every surface looked like it had been wiped clean.

Dax was a borderline neat freak, but he normally had the usual junk that everyone collected on their side tables—coins, a flash drive, a sticker Kora had given him—and for some reason, he was incapable of putting his socks in the hamper. Today, nothing dirtied the floor and the nightstands were clear.

She checked the drawers, opened the closet, and looked under the bed. Nothing. All of Dax's belongings were gone.

He'd left.

After all the shit he'd given her last night, he'd left. Lindsey slumped to the carpet, her back against the bedframe. Her jaw clenched so tightly her teeth ground together, but she would *not* cry again.

The little part of her that had hoped he'd stand—the part that had begun to believe she could be more than a burden to other people—shriveled into a husk. She'd pushed him away, and he'd kept going.

Wasn't this what she'd wanted? To prove he was just like all the others?

Lindsey curled in on herself, drawing her knees up and resting her cheek on them. It was what she'd told herself would happen, but she hadn't wanted his desertion. She'd wanted his love.

What a stupid time to make that realization. Lindsey gasped for air, fighting the tightness in her chest, but moping and cursing the Fates for their blindness wouldn't help anything. She swallowed the hurt and anger to be dealt with later.

She'd promised to help with the god before she left, and that's exactly what she'd do—fulfill her last promise then get the hell out of town.

Lindsey climbed off the floor, careful to avoid noticing the bed they'd shared. After last night's dream, she didn't need Andrew's confirmation about the sword. The god had told her himself.

One good thing would come from Dax leaving, the god couldn't use him against her. Because she was fairly certain she'd sacrifice every human on Earth to save him.

After getting dressed, she headed for the kitchen and the sword she'd left there. Lindsey took the time to braid her hair and write a note for Sabine and Alex just in case. If her plan succeeded, she'd ditch the note before anyone ever saw it, but if she failed, at least the two of them—and Calliope—would know what happened.

Her stomach twisted in knots at the thought of food, so Lindsey took a deep breath, grabbed the sword, and hiked into the woods. When she got back, she'd pack her bags and load her SUV. No reason to hang around reliving painful memories. Or wishing for a future that had never been hers.

---

THEY'D WALKED to the ravine enough times by that point that a barely discernable trail had formed. Lindsey paid close attention to her surroundings, hoping she'd sense any magic before it reached her. The morning felt like any other, hotter than it had any right to be and stupidly humid.

Unlike the last few times, a breeze didn't help cool her off. The forest creaked and crunched around her, probably due to wildlife, but the trees remained still. Lindsey transferred the sword into her other hand to wipe her sweaty palm on her shorts and wished she'd found a sheath to wear. If she couldn't find the trail to the bottom of the ravine, climbing down was going to be a bitch with the sword in one hand.

To her great relief, she found the trail with a little effort. She'd trekked it before, but the steep, narrow path wasn't made for humans. Somehow, she didn't think fire magic would be much help against another fall. One day, she'd have to ask Calliope about other magic skills. Lindsey slowed. *If* she saw Calliope again.

The trail ended a ways from where she'd been before, but at least hiking along the bottom of the creek bed proved cooler than among the trees. Objectively, the place was pretty, but Lindsey hoped she never had to see this ravine again.

She stopped underneath the area where she'd fallen and touched anything she could reach. The traces of magic weren't as prevalent here, but the few she found led her farther along the creek. Luckily, the water had subsided into a trickle, leaving a crust of dried mud over a layer of slime underneath. The surface became slick if she wasn't careful, but it beat getting her sneakers soaked.

Lindsey almost walked right past the large boulder that looked like it had tumbled down a long time ago. From the front, it appeared to be imbedded in the cliff side, but when she placed her hand on the rough stone to steady herself, a strong pulse of magic made her jerk back. Her feet nearly slid out from under her, but she caught herself at the last moment, spinning in a half circle around the rock.

A shadow marked a break in the mossy stone, and as Lindsey crouched down, an opening revealed itself between the boulder and the rest of the wall. She activated the flashlight app on her phone, and her brows flew up at what it revealed.

A cave that looked like someone had been living there.

The mouth was about four feet across and sat several feet above the bottom of the ravine, probably protecting the inside from water when the creek rose. Lindsey didn't see anyone around or any other openings inside, but she didn't want to be caught in that tight space with only a sword and magic fire to defend herself.

The light showed a small fire ring near the entrance, cold now. Beyond it, a sleeping bag, blanket, and pillow sat next to a LED lantern. A ratty backpack rested against the wall, and weirdest of all, a stack of books leaned drunkenly to one side. Lindsey performed a quick check of the rest of the cave, then returned to the stack of books.

Who would go to the trouble of bringing books all the way down here? She'd barely made it with only a sword. Lindsey reached inside to touch the closest stone from the fire ring, and a familiar prickle of magic greeted her. Whoever stayed here was connected to the god somehow.

The hair on the back of her neck stood up a second before she heard a soft squelch behind her. Lindsey spun, her sword at the ready, but stopped short when she saw the thief from the bookstore holding a taser pointed directly at her.

She shook as she held the gun with both hands. Lindsey lifted her arms in a gesture of surrender and tried to look as unthreatening as she could while holding a sword. The girl's eyes darted to the sword in one hand and Lindsey's phone in the other, and Lindsey realized too late she'd missed her moment.

The girl—Sophie—apologized as she pulled the trigger. Lindsey felt the solid slap of the prongs hitting her stomach, pushing electricity right through the thin cotton of her tank top. She whimpered at the excruciating pain of her muscles trying to pull away from her body.

Lindsey crumpled to the ground, unable to catch herself. The back of her head struck stone, causing a secondary explosion of pain from the top down. Darkness closed over her, and she heard footsteps coming closer, slapping against the mud. From far away, Sophie said something, but Lindsey couldn't hold on to it. Dax would be so disappointed. She'd been taken out twice in this stupid ravine.

# 15

*Dax*

THE LINE at Reggie's moved at a snail's pace. Dax hadn't planned on the delay, and with every special order, he worried he'd get home to find Lindsey already gone. She'd be significantly harder to convince if he had to follow her to Dallas *without* talking to her first.

Last night, he'd thought loading up his truck with all his belongings would make things easier, but now he wasn't so sure. He'd never been to Reggie's in the early morning, though apparently the rest of the town were regulars.

Bribing Lindsey with a latte and a cinnamon roll had seemed like a fabulous idea when he'd been groggy from tossing and turning all night—without her next to him, he couldn't get comfortable. At this rate, she'd be long gone before he reached the counter.

The woman in front of him glanced back nervously, and Dax realized he'd been standing with his arms crossed, scowling. He sent her a smile and shifted to stare out the window, but she scooted forward a little more anyway.

Outside, he spotted Kora's blonde hair, newly colored with bright blue streaks. He almost didn't recognize her at first because of the surly look on her face. She stood close to Moira, gesturing animatedly with her whole body. A wink of sunlight reflected off of a golden mirror in her right hand.

Dax grimaced, abandoning his effort to appear non-threatening to the woman in front of him. Moira spoke calmly, and he wished he could hear what they were saying. Lindsey had lost interest in the other artifacts once she discovered the xiphos was an original, but he hadn't forgotten that the magic fingerprints, as she called them, had led to the helm *and* mirror in Kora's office.

Kora shook the mirror in Moira's face, but the older woman smiled and patted Kora's wrist. No one else seemed to notice them on the sidewalk. Under normal circumstances, he'd have probably ignored the scene too, but he wanted to leave Alex with as much data as possible since he and Lindsey wouldn't be there to help. Sabine seemed to think Kora was harmless, but they'd never gotten around to asking Calliope about Kora's potential as a demigod.

Dax considered leaving the line to ask some questions himself, but he didn't think making a scene in front of Moira would get him the information he wanted. Kora huffed, visibly huffed, and curled in on herself a bit. Her body language said she'd lost the argument, but her mouth hadn't given up yet.

Moira shook her head sadly and made a slashing motion with her hand, apparently ending the conversation. Kora glared and stomped into Reggie's, while Moira walked away in the direction of her shop.

The man behind him cleared his throat, and Dax moved forward with the line. Reggie called a welcome to Kora as she entered, but she ignored him and made a beeline for Dax. He forced a smile as she approached.

"Good morning, Kora."

She rolled her eyes and planted herself next to him, the mirror still clutched in her hand. "It's not good yet. Ana's going to kill me for being late. Buy me a coffee? I've earned it."

He tilted his head. "Have you *ever* paid for coffee here?"

Kora shrugged. "Probably, but I don't remember it. Look, it's good I saw you in here. I was just about to head over to your place."

Dax wondered how long she'd known he was here. He hadn't been subtle about watching them, and she hadn't looked his way until she'd come into the coffee shop. "Did you need something?"

She held up the mirror. "I need to return this to Lindsey. She left it in my shop the last time she was there."

Technically, Kora was right. They'd left the mirror there when they'd sort of broken in, but he knew for a fact it wasn't Lindsey's. What was she up to?

He raised a brow. "Funny, I don't remember seeing that with her things."

"And you've memorized all her things? Controlling much?" Her sarcasm felt forced, and she sent a quick angry glance out the front window.

Dax took another step forward, leaving only the nervous woman between him and Lindsey's bribe. "Sorry, it's not hers." He wasn't taking any chances, especially not after the lies she'd just told him.

She sighed. "It was a gift, and she needs to have it. Like *today*. Can you please just return it to her?"

He examined the mirror, making no effort to take it. If the artifact was booby-trapped, he'd have no way to tell, but if he refused, she'd simply go around him and deliver it to Lindsey anyway. After their last fight, Dax wasn't sure Lindsey would listen to him if he warned her. And why the insistence on today?

Before he could ask his questions, an intense, broad pain shot through his stomach and out to his extremities. Dax grunted and tried to stay upright. The clink of glassware and the quiet hum of voices disappeared as he nearly doubled over in pain.

Kora laid her hand on his back, and the pain diminished enough that he could breathe again. She'd almost certainly used magic, but he couldn't fault her in this instance. The pain hadn't come from him. Lindsey was in trouble. Again.

He straightened and met Kora's eyes. She raised a knowing brow and held out the mirror again. "She needs it today."

"Promise me this won't hurt her."

Kora rolled her eyes. "You're so dramatic. I'm not the enemy here. Take the mirror and run to her rescue."

Dax searched her face, but he didn't see any malicious intent. "You and I are going to have a long conversation later."

She nodded. "That seems fair."

He snatched the artifact from her, half expecting to be zapped or turned into a toad, but nothing happened. It was simply a fairly heavy golden hand mirror with magic fingerprints and the ability to save the woman he loved.

She'd already turned her back on him to say hi to Reggie, stealing his place in line, but Dax didn't care. He hustled out of the coffee shop and into his truck, tossing the mirror onto the seat next to him. His instincts said she was in the woods behind the house, probably the ravine again, and he didn't want to waste any more time.

The anxiety and fear churning in his stomach urged him to speed through town, but he stayed under the limit and came to a full stop at the stop sign. A good thing too since the sheriff was parked not a block down the street. The man raised a hand in greeting when Dax made eye contact, and for a split second, he considered asking the authorities for help.

Dax had weapons, but what did one use against a god. This could be a case of quantity over quality. Besides, if Lindsey was hurt—as the gripping pain had indicated—he could use another strong back with first aid skills. Then the moment passed, and he gunned it through the intersection. Sheriff Shane Garrett seemed like a decent guy the few times they'd met, but he'd be unprepared for magical warfare.

Hell, Dax was unprepared for magical warfare, and he'd spent months training for it. But he'd dive into hell itself for Lindsey. If she needed him, nothing would keep him away. Once outside town, he picked up speed on the road to the house and prayed he wouldn't be too late.

---

*Lindsey*

A SMALL CREATURE with a hammer had taken up residence next to her brain. Lindsey moaned and tried to rub the aching spot at the back of her head, but both arms lifted together. She squinted and examined the tape wrapped around both wrists. Shiny, but not duct tape. Washi tape?

She cautiously pulled her wrists apart, and the tape stretched. Worst. Kidnapping. Ever.

Lindsey tried to sit up, but the world spun and her stomach roiled. She squeezed her eyes closed until her head caught up to her body, then tentatively tried again. Her hand scraped against rough stone below her, and her gaze landed on the stack of books she'd seen earlier.

Someone had put her in the cave. She blinked, trying to bring the rest of the room into focus. The lantern cast light across most of the cave, and nothing else seemed any different than when she'd been peering in the opening. Only her hands had been bound, but the pounding in her head slowed her down pretty effectively.

She reached back again, then grunted and popped free of the tape when the angle tweaked her sore shoulder. A squeak came from the darkest corner of the cave by the entrance, and Lindsey hissed when she jerked her head sideways without thinking to peer into the shadows.

"I'm sorry. You weren't supposed to hit your head." The soft voice belonged to Sophie, sitting with her back against the wall and her arms wrapped around her knees. She wiggled bare toes, and Lindsey finally had an inkling of where the footprint had come from.

"What *was* I supposed to do?"

Sophie sighed. "Drop the sword and maybe fall down. I guess you did that part."

"How did you get me in here?"

"Aph moved you."

Lindsey stopped rubbing the knot under her hair and focused on Sophie. "Aph?"

The girl nodded. "Aphrodite. My patron goddess. She wanted me to save my energy for later."

"I'll bet she did," Lindsey muttered. Not a god, after all. A goddess.

"Where is she now?"

Sophie jerked her chin at the entrance. "Outside, checking for others. She's very protective of me, being the chosen one and all."

Lindsey tilted her head. The girl's tone continued to sound like a drawn-out apology. She'd thought she was caught up on the lore involved here, but 'chosen one' was new.

"What did Aph tell you?"

At Lindsey's friendly tone, Sophie uncurled from her tight ball, but bit her lip. "That a war was coming, and I was chosen among all the humans to help the gods right a thousand-year wrong."

She sounded like she was quoting verbatim, and Lindsey assumed Aphrodite had repeated the information as many times as needed to convince Sophie. The poor girl would make a terrible chosen one if she willingly shared information with the enemy and apologized when she tased someone.

Lindsey nodded and edged toward the bright light at the entrance. "Is that why you're living in a cave?"

Her face shut down again. "I like it here. Aph understands that and supports me."

"Like Kora?" The question had been a risk, but Sophie winced and looked away.

"Kora sort of gets it, but she can't really help. At least Aph doesn't pretend." She sighed. "It's fine. I can take care of myself."

The refrain hit Lindsey hard. She could have been listening to herself as a teenager. Then again, she'd never tased anyone without good cause. Kids these days.

Lindsey reached the hole and stretched one leg through it, then paused. Sophie paid her no mind, and the washi tape had been pathetic. Why would they want to keep her here anyway? Aphrodite wanted the seal, and Lindsey couldn't get it if she was tied up in a cave. Was Aphrodite *really* out scouting the area?

Their motivation didn't matter. Lindsey needed the sword, which she could see only a few feet away, and the goddess to force into it. She could also use exact instructions on *how* to trap a goddess in a sacred object, but she'd have to rely on the meager directions Calliope had given her. Whatever Aph had planned with the 'chosen one' business would become moot once the goddess in question no longer had the power to shove people off cliffs.

With a grunt, Lindsey emerged into the ravine and scooped up the sword. Mud slid right off the blade, and she shook her head. Of course, it had a magical cleaning spell.

From the entrance, Sophie peered out past Lindsey. "Was that what you needed?"

A translucent woman in a short, flowy dress walked around the boulder into view. "Good girl. You did just as I asked."

Lindsey took a few steps away from the cave to give herself room to maneuver. The goddess' amused eyes never left her. "Aphrodite, I presume. You wanted her to knock me out, stall me, then let me go?"

She shrugged elegant, bare shoulders. "I didn't intend for you to be rendered unconscious. The rock was fortuitous. Did you bring the seal?"

Lindsey raised the sword like a baseball bat in a tight two-handed grip. "I brought this."

Aphrodite's gaze lingered on the inscription, but she didn't recoil as Lindsey had hoped. A remnant of

Aphrodite's power definitely lingered on the metal, so why wasn't the goddess more concerned that Lindsey had a sacred object connected to her magic?

Was this another example of Calliope making a guess and passing it off as truth? She sincerely hoped not, since her entire plan hinged on Calliope's information and Lindsey's ability to improvise.

Aphrodite sighed. "Give me the seal or I'll kill your guardian. It's not an option I'll enjoy, but don't mistake my distaste for weakness."

Lindsey moved closer, brandishing the sword. "You should be more worried about me than the seal."

The goddess waved her hand, and the weapon jerked forward out of Lindsey's grip. It flew to Aphrodite who caught it smoothly and held it up to the filtered morning light. "I haven't seen this in a long time, but if you hoped to use it against me, you've made a poor choice."

She flung the sword behind her into the underbrush without a backward glance. Despite her filmy form, Aphrodite didn't waver when she used her magic. Calliope had been quite clear that the energy the gods used for magic came from the belief of humans, and that it was finite.

A human like Sophie, who'd tased Lindsey at Aphrodite's bidding, could potentially provide a lot of energy. Especially since the girl had bought into the story of a patron goddess. Aphrodite had found a devout worshipper, and she was using Sophie's faith to power up. More troubling, the sword didn't appear to be her sacred object after all.

Aphrodite smiled, but her eyes remained cold. "Last chance to prove where your loyalties lie. The seal or your guardian."

Lindsey scoffed, snarling on the outside while she ached in private. "I don't like ultimatums. I'm not bringing you the seal, and Dax is long gone by now."

The goddess raised a perfectly arched brow in challenge. "I'd almost forgotten how obtuse humans could be. Your Dax will be here shortly to protect you like a good little guardian. Tell me, do you think streaks of fire and a broken bond will be enough to protect *him*?"

Broken bond? Lindsey couldn't help it, she reached for the connection between them. Her sense of Dax came through bright and warm, and much, much closer than she'd expected. What the hell? He'd left. How would he even know she was in trouble? She shot a quick glance at the cave entrance, but Sophie had abandoned her post.

Aphrodite's sly smile widened. "I see you've accepted the truth I told you in your dream."

Most of the truth. Her bond with Dax hadn't felt broken, only her heart. Aphrodite had clearly been watching them, but she didn't know everything. For instance, she probably didn't know that even with a broken heart, Lindsey absolutely trusted Dax to arrive with a contingency plan. There was no one else she'd want at her back.

Without Aphrodite's artifact, Lindsey had to depend entirely on magic she'd never used offensively. Fire magic. In a forest. Against a juiced-up goddess with her own private power source.

The odds weren't in her favor, but she'd sure as hell try to make Aphrodite's attempt to lure Dax here backfire. Now the goddess had to face off against two instead of one. Even if neither of them knew how to get rid of a god.

Lindsey prodded her magic, and the flames sprang to life along her hands and arms, quicker and stronger than she'd been able to achieve before. Her Dax radar pinpointed him working his way down the wall of the ravine behind her current location. She hoped he had a better plan than she did.

The goddess sighed. "Very well. Let's get this out of the way." With a flick of Aphrodite's fingers, the sword lifted from the sparse grass where it had landed and spun to point at Lindsey. "I have no qualms injuring you again to prove my capabilities."

The weapon shot toward her, faster than she'd anticipated. Lindsey twisted and knocked the sword to the side with a blast of fire. It flew a few more feet past her, then suddenly dropped to the ground. Realization dawned and her eyes shot back to Aphrodite, who had a tiny line marring her forehead for the first time. The goddess could only use her power for short distances.

She wanted to shout *ha!* Or at least back up a few feet and do a snappy little dance, but the furrow cleared, and she had to dodge another sharp burst of telekinetic magic. Arrogance could be dangerous if she let it creep in.

Lindsey tossed a fireball at Aphrodite, but another flick of the goddess' fingers sent the fire to its death in a shallow puddle. If she survived this, she'd have to beg Calliope for lessons on magical combat. Thus far, her attempts had been nothing more than embarrassing. Thank goodness her mouth never failed her.

"It's going to be hard to take me out when there isn't a handy cliff or stack of heavy boxes nearby. I can dodge your pointy projectiles all day, and you'll never get close enough to Dax with your short-range magic." Okay, maybe she'd let arrogance creep in a little bit.

Aphrodite tilted her head and silky blonde hair slid over her shoulder. "I don't need to. How would he react to a young girl in need of help? Surely you noticed my young protégé has slipped away. Sophie will be sure to incapacitate your guardian, providing me with more than enough time to stop his heart."

Helpless anger burned through Lindsey, stoking the flames on her skin. Dax would definitely fall for the ruse, and Sophie didn't deserve the future Aphrodite had planned for her. "Why do you even need the seal when you have an acolyte?"

She spread her hands. "Sophie isn't enough power, and finding others of her ilk has proven challenging. Modern humans see love differently. They've forsaken me in favor of independence and swiping." Aphrodite shuddered. "In the aftermath, I've chosen to use love as a weapon. Your love for your guardian will net me the seal, which will grant me the power to trifle more effectively in the affairs of humans. They'll discover they need my blessing after all."

Lindsey mentally recoiled, but she wouldn't show that kind of weakness in front of Aphrodite. "That's despicable."

"You presented the opportunity. I'm simply taking advantage of it."

Dax had moved close enough that he could probably hear their conversation, but Lindsey didn't dare look behind her to try to spot him. Since he hadn't revealed himself— and Aphrodite clearly couldn't sense him—Lindsey accepted that he did, indeed, have a plan. Next time, they'd have to discuss the plan *before* confronting the callous goddess of love.

An image of working with Dax, sharing her life with him, clicked into place in her mind, and Lindsey stopped fighting the obvious. She wanted a next time. Enough to fight for it, even if it meant relinquishing control.

With a scowl, Lindsey released her magic, letting it

absorb back into her hands with a shudder. "Fine. Leave Dax alone, and I'll bring you the seal."

"Excellent. I'll be accompanying you to the house."

Lindsey turned and started picking her way toward the path out of the ravine. "Whatever."

A quick flash of light in Dax's location caught her attention, so Lindsey changed direction slightly to aim for his signal. She took her time choosing the least muddy spots to place her feet, waiting for him to move away before she approached.

As she stepped onto the slight incline that led to his former hiding spot, Lindsey shifted her weight and let her foot slide out from under her, sending her tumbling forward into the brush. One hand landed in a bed of pine straw and sharp pebbles, the other landed on the smooth glass of a mirror.

Aphrodite let out an annoyed sigh behind her, but Lindsey carefully wrapped her fingers around the golden mirror's handle. In hindsight, the magic smeared all over the outside hid the parts that reached deep inside the metal. And an ornate mirror made perfect sense as a sacred object for Aphrodite.

Lindsey located the magical seal and popped the artifact wide open. A deep well with dregs of Aphrodite's magic revealed itself, and Lindsey tightened her grip on the handle. *Here* was her choice. Dax had brought her the mirror, exactly when she needed it. He knew as much as she did about the sacred objects, and he could have taken any number of other paths in an attempt to protect her. But he hadn't. He'd trusted her to choose. Risk her life or risk his.

She pushed her fire magic into the mirror in a steady stream as she turned and held the artifact up where

Aphrodite had a clear view. The gold heated, turning pale orange where it touched her skin. "Your turn to make a choice."

Aphrodite's nostrils flared. "Traitor," she whispered through clenched teeth.

The word wasn't meant for Lindsey, but the fear she'd been waiting for finally flashed in Aphrodite's eyes.

"Sophie!" Her high-pitched shriek drew the young girl into the open, trembling, but holding the taser again.

Lindsey wasn't sure she could halt the stream fast enough to stop the girl, but then she didn't have to. Dax came out of the woods, swift and silent. He scooped Sophie up, keeping a hand over hers on the taser, and quickly carried her well out of Aphrodite's reach.

For a split second, Lindsey bobbled the magic stream as the reality that Dax had truly stayed crashed over her. Relief and joy made her giddy until a wave of fatigue nearly buckled her knees.

Another shriek brought Lindsey's focus back to Aphrodite as the goddess lifted a hand, ostensibly to throw another piece of the forest at her, but her gaze moved past Lindsey. Her Dax radar told her what had caught Aphrodite's attention—he'd come out of the trees behind her.

The goddess smiled, and Lindsey chanced a look over her shoulder. A vine trailing from the tree next to him had snaked along his shoulders and around his neck. Dax grimaced silently and yanked at the garrote, but it didn't budge. Her dream flashed across her mind, and rage nearly blinded Lindsey.

She mimicked the goddess' stance, raising her free hand, and a circle of fire roared up around him, roasting the vine to ash. The pine straw underneath him crackled and smoked, but the flames did nothing more than caress him. Lindsey said a silent thanks to whichever Fate had decided to make the guardians immune to demigod magic.

Aphrodite's hands clenched into fists, but then her shoulders slumped. About time. Lindsey wasn't sure how much more power she could pour into the mirror *and* a shield.

"Fill the mirror, or I will. You don't belong here."

"Neither do you, halfbreed." A scowl darkened her features as she reached for the mirror. She hissed when her fingers came in contact with the hot metal, but she didn't let go.

Aphrodite held her gaze, and Lindsey recognized the rage and impotence there. A twinge of pity tried to take hold, but she rooted it out. This goddess didn't deserve her pity. A rush of magic brushed against her as Aphrodite poured her essence into the artifact.

Excitement stole her breath. The plan had actually worked. Despite her own worst fears, she'd managed to trap a god. Lindsey tugged on her magic, trying not to touch Aphrodite's on the way in, but something held it fast.

She yanked harder, to no avail, and her pulse sped. Lindsey couldn't pull her magic out. Her mind calmed, easing the panic. If ensnaring Aphrodite cost Lindsey the power she'd worked so hard to control, so be it. She wouldn't hesitate to seal the artifact. The transfer happened in seconds, but a lifetime went by in Lindsey's mind.

Aphrodite's form faded to nothing, and a shadow formed in the mirror's reflection, roiling inside the glass. The seal locked closed again, and all at once, Lindsey's magic returned to her in the mother of all snap-backs. Like an elastic band, the force hit her in the chest and settled painfully inside her.

The circle of flames sputtered out as the world began to slowly spin. Lindsey reached out to steady herself against a tree, but missed entirely. Hadn't she just been standing in a forest?

Her thoughts muddled together, and her eyelids dropped closed. She fell in what felt like slow motion as her balance abandoned her. Instead of hitting the ground, something caught her weight. Her head lolled against a hard shoulder that smelled like home.

A soft touch caressed her cheek, leaving a trail of tingling fire behind. "Lindsey, open your eyes." The voice rumbled next to her ear and pulled her away from the heavy darkness where she floated.

She scowled and turned her face into the yummy smell. "No."

The uncomfortably full feeling receded, and Lindsay realized the weightless sensation was from being carried. Her head ached like a bitch, and every breath came with a jolt of stinging pain from two spots on her stomach. But underneath it all, serenity tempered the suffering.

Dax held her, and she didn't want to be anywhere else.

"Stop torturing me, Lindsey, and open your eyes." With a sigh, she peeked up at him. He nodded and hefted her slightly higher. "Good girl."

Dax found a dry rock big enough for both of them and sat with his back against the cliff wall, holding her tight in his lap. Lindsey didn't have the energy or the inclination to argue. She had enough trouble keeping her eyes open.

"Where's Sophie?" The words came out garbled, but Dax understood them.

"I took the taser from her and sent her back to Kora with

a warning. She looked genuinely surprised when I let her go, but I think it was the vine that really convinced her the truth might not be what Aphrodite told her. She took off when you created the fire shield. Hopefully, it's not too late to counter Aphrodite's conditioning."

With great effort, Lindsey curled her fingers in the fabric over his chest and nodded. "Where's the mirror?"

He jerked his chin the direction they'd come. "Back there next to the sword. Nice deflection, by the way, but we should probably up your combat training."

Lindsey sighed. "I thought the same thing."

Dax sat quietly for a moment, running his hand up and down her back. "Why not just give her the seal?"

She'd expected a rebuke for risking herself, but his tone only expressed curiosity. "That was never an option. I couldn't risk the damage she'd do with that kind of power. Look at what she did to Sophie."

Dax chuckled and nuzzled her hair. "You're wrong, you know. You *are* made for heroics."

Her eyes burned with the prickle of tears as warmth swept through her, followed immediately by exhaustion. "I may have been wrong, but you were right. I was scared, so I intended to run."

"I know." His quiet agreement told her nothing about his feelings, but Lindsey wouldn't give in to fear this time. She refused to believe it was too late.

"I should have known better, and I'm sorry for not trusting myself enough to take a chance. I'm not running anymore. I love you, and I want to stay right here."

Dax framed her face with his hands and kissed her, softly at first, building to scorching heat as she pulled him closer. "I don't care where we go as long as you're with me."

He whispered the words across her lips, then eased back to meet her gaze.

"I love you too, but I'm not carrying you out of the woods for a second time."

She laughed and finally let her eyes close again as weariness pulled her under. "I don't care. I'll stay in this cursed ravine forever if I'm with you."

# EPILOGUE

*Lindsey*

SHE WOKE up in the cave. Again. At least this time her head didn't feel like it was going to explode, and she'd been tucked under the blanket on the sleeping bag. The lantern illuminated most of the space, but a secondary light source shone near the entrance. Lindsey squinted and a man came into focus surrounded by a slight reddish glow.

He had an impressive beard of rich russet and shoulders for days. The last thing she remembered was falling asleep in Dax's arms, so if this guy—another god, if she had to guess from the fact that she could just barely see through him—planned to kill her, he'd had plenty of opportunity. That didn't mean she'd relax though.

"Where's Dax?"

"Your guardian agreed to allow me a few minutes alone

with you. A feisty pick, that one. I heartily approve." His deep voice struck a chord. She'd definitely heard it before.

Lindsey sat up gingerly. "It wasn't really my choice, but thanks."

He waved away her qualification. "There's always a choice."

The god smiled down at her and extended his hand. Lindsey took it and let him pull her up. His face looked vaguely familiar, but she was certain she'd never met him before. For someone who'd been non-corporeal not too long ago, he had a good grip.

"Well done, daughter of my daughter."

Lindsey's brows flew up. "Daughter?"

He laughed, a full sound drawn up from his belly. "You thought with fire magic you were perhaps descended from Poseidon?"

She smiled. "That joke would probably be funnier if I knew who you were."

"Hephaestus of the Forge." He inclined his head, and several key pieces of evidence fell into place. The most important of which was that she recognized the feel of his magic.

"That sword is yours, and that was you in my dream."

"I wished for my descendants to have a piece of me, and I was concerned by what Calliope told me."

Lindsey shook her head, trying to process. "Calliope? When did she—" Her mouth snapped shut as she remembered all of the cat's mysterious disappearances. "She was meeting with you."

A smile flitted across his face. "She tried her best to convince me that you would benefit from my intervention. I believed her too late." Hephaestus shook his head sadly. "Aphrodite and I loved each other once, but in time, we grew apart. You did well with her. And now you need to do the same with me."

Weirdly, Lindsey's first reaction was a violent denial. After all the trouble with Aphrodite, she should be doing backflips that Hephaestus would go willingly. Before she could come up with a viable excuse to keep him around, he pulled the sword from behind him and held it out to her.

The symbols glowed in the lantern light as Lindsey reached for the hilt. "What does it say?"

His arms dropped to his sides, and his bushy chin rose. "Family. To remember the purpose of the sword—strength to protect those you love."

"We couldn't find a translation," Lindsey murmured to herself.

"You wouldn't. This language is long gone, like most of my people. The time of the gods has passed. Maybe we'll have another, but for now—for you—I choose the sword."

She wanted to argue, but she understood. According to the Fates, his mere presence put his descendants in danger.

Lindsey changed her grip on the sword and presented it to him. "I would have liked more time together."

Hephaestus chuckled and placed a big hand over the blade. "I would have enjoyed that too, I think. I wish you a good life, daughter. You've already made our line proud, now make it happy." He disappeared, and the sword warmed in her hands.

Lindsey stared down at the tarnished blade. *Family.* Something she hadn't really had until now. Part of her—a larger part than she'd thought she was capable of—grieved for the connection she'd just lost.

She took a shaky breath and moved to the cave entrance. Dax waited just outside, leaning against the boulder with his arms crossed. His scowl transformed into a wide grin when he spotted her.

"All better?"

Lindsey nodded and hopped down to the muddy creek bed. "All better. I know I said I'd live in this ravine with you, but maybe we could find a nice apartment in town. I am *really* sick of this cave."

He wrapped his arms around her waist and pulled her against him. "I'm with you, wherever that is. My truck is packed, and I'm ready to go."

She cringed and dropped her head. "You weren't leaving because I drove you away."

Dax laughed. "I was going to chase you across the state, whether you wanted me to or not. I love you. I'm not letting you get away that easily."

"I'm an idiot," she muttered. "But at least I came to my senses. We should get back. Alex and Sabine will be home soon."

"Or..." He lifted her chin, and the fire she encountered in his eyes caused an answering heat to spread through her belly and pool between her legs. "Maybe we could stay out here, alone, a little longer."

*Unfortunately, you're not alone.*

Lindsey groaned and glanced over at the cat trotting out of the woods. "Why? Why couldn't you let me have this moment?"

Calliope ignored Lindsey's plea and picked her way closer across the mud. *I have troubling news that needs your immediate attention.*

Lindsey glared, but Dax squeezed her waist. "What is it?"

The cat jumped to a small ledge at eye level with them in the cliff wall and sat with her chin high. *The seal is gone.*

**Want to know Dax's real name?**
Click on the link below to snag an exclusive bonus scene
and sign up for Nicole's newsletter!
Goddess Forsaken Bonus Scene

For exclusive giveaways, sneak peeks of future books, and
behind the scenes secrets, check out Nicole's reader group
on Facebook: Muse Interrupted Romance. Or connect on
social media at Facebook, Instagram, or Pinterest.

**Next up in Rise of the Lost Gods...**

Divinity Bound

*Grab your copy of Divinity Bound and find out what happens
when unwitting demigods and their fated guardians try to stop
newly released gods from running amok in the human world.*

*Available on Amazon or FREE to read in Kindle Unlimited!*

*Turn the page for your sneak peek at the first chapter...*

# DIVINITY BOUND

*I*

---

*Ana*

SHE'D NEVER MADE out in a cop car before. Technically, the SUV that pulled up behind her was a sheriff's car, driven by none other than Sheriff Shane Garrett. Her mind went immediately to the gutter every time she saw his official vehicle.

Ana relaxed her hands on the wheel and tried to calm her racing heart. Failing to parallel park wasn't against the law, so the esteemed sheriff had no reason to question her. She watched in the side mirror as he got out of his vehicle and shaded his face as he peered toward her.

Worn jeans clung to his thighs, and an orange UT Austin shirt stretched across his broad chest. Off duty, then. He'd double-parked behind her, but she doubted the few people availing the services of downtown Deckard in the middle of the afternoon would care.

The two large boxes in the back seat blocked her view of him as he crossed behind the car, but she knew what Sheriff Garrett looked like when he walked. A smooth, graceful cadence that showed confidence in his body. She'd know. Her life up until the last few months had focused on squeezing every last drop of beauty from her movements.

And this man was beautiful without trying.

He appeared on her side of the car and ran a hand through short, dark hair as he approached. She reminded herself that according to the townspeople—and Kora—he didn't take advantage of his authority. Kora swore he was kind, and Ana tended to believe her boss' judgment calls. Still, her stomach trembled as she rolled down her window.

Humid air smacked her in the face, making a mockery of the air conditioner. "Sheriff Garrett. How can I help you today?" Ana adopted her customer service voice. A bland smile and limited interest could hide a surprisingly large amount of anxiety.

He tucked his thumbs in his front pockets and leaned down to meet her gaze. "I've asked you to call me Shane."

She didn't dare, at least not to his face. Using his name felt too intimate, especially while staring into dark eyes that saw too much. "Did you stop me just to remind me of your name? Because I assure you. I remember."

He chuckled. "You look like you're having trouble."

"I've never been great at parallel parking, and all the practice here seems to have made me worse instead of better."

"Want me to try?"

Ana stiffened. "Not particularly. Do I have a choice?"

A flicker of hurt crossed his face so fast she thought she

might have imagined it, but he straightened and shrugged. "You always have a choice."

Ana sighed at the prickle of guilt, knowing she'd give in. "If I can't get it this time, it's all yours."

He nodded and walked back to his SUV. Instead of getting in, he leaned against the front and crossed his arms. Apparently, she now had an audience. Fantastic. That would really help her perform better this time.

Sweat dampened her shirt, but she didn't bother rolling up the window. Why give the good sheriff a nice, cool car to sit in? Ana jerked her attention away from the mirror where she'd been staring and focused on the maneuver in front of her. Pull forward, back up at an angle, pull forward at the opposite angle.

Her brows flew up as she stopped the car neatly next to the curb equally spaced between the other two cars. The thrill of triumph raised goosebumps along her arms, but the tingling sensation didn't stop at her skin. Prickles raced down to the tips of her fingers, and a dull glow formed around the steering wheel.

Ana gasped and dropped her hands to her lap, clenching them tightly around each other. *This* was why she didn't go out much. The last thing she wanted was to draw attention to herself, and unpredictable magic hands would ruin any chance she had at blending in.

Her pulse raced as she willed the power to fade.

"Well done. I promise you'll get better with practice."

Ana jumped at the male voice next to her. The sheriff had returned.

He rested his arms over her open window and glanced at the two boxes in the backseat. "You need any help taking those up to your place?"

"What makes you assume I live here?"

He raised a brow. "Everyone knows you moved into the apartment above Kora's shop. Maribeth told me you were having trouble because your knee was still bothering you, and Reggie said I should stop by to make sure you used the locks since there aren't a lot of people around once the businesses close."

Small town gossip struck again. His gaze settled on her face, and Ana prayed her hands had stopped with the dramatics. She couldn't look down to check, but the telltale prickle had disappeared. "My knee is healing nicely, and I make sure to lock up whenever I'm home. I'm very cautious with my safety."

He tilted his head with a sardonic twist to his lips. "You're going to make me stand here and watch you struggle to carry both those boxes up the stairs with a bum leg?"

For a second, she considered the idea. Ana hated being the center of attention, but this man brought out a stubborn streak she hadn't known she possessed. He'd no doubt make good on his promise, and deep down, she *wanted* his attention on her. Not like that though. Not watching her fight with the unwieldy boxes and the tiny stairway.

Ana peeked at her hands, relived to see the glow had faded. With her magic safely dormant again, she didn't have any good excuses for denying him. At least, not any that wouldn't cause suspicion.

She smiled up at him with fake enthusiasm. "Thank you for your kind offer, Sheriff. I accept."

He leaned closer, and the façade melted into real heat she saw reflected in his eyes. "Please call me Shane."

Had she been worried about being too close?

Her nails dug into her palms, a reminder that she couldn't risk anyone finding out the truth. Especially him. She'd let him carry her boxes and help her park all he wanted, but that didn't mean Ana could afford to lower her guard.

"We'd better hurry before someone needs to use their car." She jerked her chin toward the vehicle behind her that his SUV blocked.

The charged moment passed. He opened the door for her to step out and moved away. "We'll get there one day."

Ana shook her head. She didn't understand his interest. They'd known each other for months—he'd stopped to introduce himself on her first day in town—and when she couldn't physically avoid him, she tried to put him off with polite small talk. Her reticence didn't seem to make a difference. He always smiled and tried to lure her into conversation.

She opened the back passenger door and wrestled one of the boxes out of the tight space while he did the same on the other side. His tee-shirt strained against his biceps as he hefted the box, and Ana sighed. In other circumstances, she'd welcome notice from a nice, attractive guy, but the events of last December had shown her even nice guys couldn't be trusted.

They trudged up the short stairway to the second floor, and Ana counted time in her head. Had it been eight months already?

Sometimes, the pain in her knee zapped her right back to that night at the barre when her foot had slipped, and sometimes, she forgot that her life had been completely different before this year. Deckard, Texas felt like home more than Magnolia or Houston ever had.

Granted, the trees looked the same as the ones on their estate, but here, she had the freedom to explore in those trees whenever she wanted. No high stone walls, locked gates, guards—nothing but herself to hold her back.

Her doorway didn't boast much of a landing since it hadn't been built as a primary residence. Kora and David had renovated the storage space above their store last year into an efficiency apartment, and then Kora had strong-armed Ana into moving in rent-free.

The sheriff waited next to her door, taking up more than his fair share of the tiny space. She braced her box against the wall on the opposite side as she wiped sweat off her brow then dug out her keys.

He tilted his head and squinted at her. "The sun is brutal today. You should be wearing a hat."

"Where's *your* hat?" Ana cringed on the inside at her sassy tone. She didn't flirt, and she certainly didn't antagonize county officials with the power to detain her.

He grinned and leaned against the wall while she struggled to work the key in the old lock. "Got a thing for cowboys?"

She hadn't, until she'd met Shane—Sheriff Garrett. "I have a thing for men not telling me what to do with my fashion choices or my body."

The door finally opened and blasted them with a wave of frosty air. Ana nearly closed her eyes in relief. The thermostat had been acting up the last few days, so she never knew what temperature to expect.

She jumped at the touch of a hand against her back, then fixed a cool expression on her face. The sheriff held his box with one hand and urged her to go through first with the other. The motion reminded her strongly of the men she'd known in her youth. Good 'ol boys that never let a woman touch a door with her own dainty hands.

Ana shook him off and twisted the box's weight away from her hip. With the first step, a spike of pain burst out of her knee and up her thigh, and she hissed out a breath.

Only a few more steps to get into the apartment, but they might as well have been miles.

The sheriff leaned past her to set his box in the entry, then did the same with hers. Ana concentrated on the stained wood in front of her feet as the waves of agony slowly subsided. She should have known better than to let his hands distract her.

Before she could protest, he'd scooped her up and carried her into the sparse apartment. Ana couldn't fault him for his form, he didn't jostle her knee at all as he kicked the door closed. Unfortunately, she'd wrapped an arm around his neck to steady herself, which put her way too close to his mouth for comfort.

"Is the couch okay?" He turned his head to ask the question, and Ana realized his blue eyes were shot through with gold.

She nodded, and they maneuvered her to a sitting position with her knee resting on one of her two throw pillows. As glorious of a distraction as Shane turned out to be, the pain in her leg reared up for a second round.

After a second, the ache in her knee abated, but her thigh refused to relax. Ana pushed on the hard knot with the heel of her hand, but she couldn't get good leverage without her knee flaring up. She winced as the cramp went on and on while she tried to breathe through it.

Her self-appointed savior squatted in front of her, and she glanced up into his face.

"What's wrong?" His calm tone reminded her of the doctors after her surgery.

Ana licked her dry lips. "Muscle cramp."

His hands hovered over hers, but he stopped short of actually touching her. "Can I try?"

"I can handle it. I'm not weak," she gritted out.

"I never thought you were. Come on, Ana. I'm trying to help."

Her name on his lips in that honeyed voice sent hunger spiraling through her, a weird contrast to her throbbing leg. She grimaced and moved her hands to give him access. Instead of massaging as she'd done, he gently stretched her leg to lengthen the muscle, careful not to aggravate her knee.

When he did finally put pressure on her thigh in long, slow strokes, the cramp started to ease. Ana closed her eyes and let her head fall sideways against the couch. Her sweat had dried to a sticky film, so her hair adhered to the side of her face where she leaned. Despite the cold air, heat thrummed through her in rhythm with his touch.

"Since I'm getting up close and personal with your thigh, maybe you can finally start calling me by my given name."

Ana cracked her eyes open. "Why is this so important to you?"

"Because I want you to see me as a friend, not an authority figure." He concentrated on his movements, giving her the rare chance to look her fill.

Tousled dark hair and stubble along a strong jaw could have been any number of suitors she'd rejected, but his eyes always tripped her up. It wasn't the color—though she liked the dark blue—but the compassion he never tried to hide. As if he could read her thoughts, he glanced up to meet her gaze.

Ana didn't bother pretending not to stare. "What makes you think I don't see you as a friend?"

"I've noticed the way you are with Kora and David, even Dax. You let them in, at least a little bit. You've known me just as long, but with me, you're guarded. Why is that?"

Warning bells went off in her head. Those were the kind

of questions she needed to avoid, but she wasn't sure she could feign icy indifference with him trying ease her pain.

"I don't know you as well as I know them," she whispered.

"You would if you gave me a chance. Ask me anything you want. I'll give you an honest answer, and you'll know a little more."

She broke the staring contest to watch the motion of his hands—warm and calloused against her skin. Should she play his game? Curiosity ate at her. He hadn't demanded anything in return, so what harm could come from asking a question? Worst case scenario, he lied to her about something inconsequential.

Except, she didn't want to ask something inconsequential. She *wanted* to know if she could trust him. Her time in Deckard would come to an end at some point, and she'd better have more than spotty magic and an injured knee on her side.

"Why did you go into law enforcement?" Ana forced her gaze up to meet his, wanting to see his face when he answered.

"I wanted to help people. As simple and complicated as that. Unfortunately, law enforcement doesn't always succeed in that endeavor, but I try."

His sincerity never wavered, but Ana had proved in December that her judgement couldn't be trusted. Still, it was a nice answer. Now the real test began. He'd asked why she revealed more of herself to her friends, and the answer was that they never asked for more than she could give them. They accepted her mysterious past and her unwillingness to talk about anything before she'd moved to Deckard.

If he pushed her to open up, she'd know this whole conversation had been a ploy.

He flashed her a smile that caused her pulse to race. "Was that enough of an answer?"

Ana nodded. "For now."

"See, quick and easy. No harm done."

He had no idea. Shane—and he'd always be Shane now in her mind, he'd won that much—continued to rub until the knot in her thigh subsided completely. His fingers lingered even after the pain had ceased, stroking her skin, and Ana fought the urge to slide off the couch and into his lap.

Talk about mixed signals.

Instead, she scooted around him to stand. "Thanks for your help. Really."

He straightened next to her, and Ana hesitated as she stared up at him. One answered question didn't make someone trustworthy, but he was right that she'd taken a chance on a few of the others in town. She was under no obligation to answer if he asked something too personal.

"In the interest of fairness, I'll give you one question, but I make no promises to answer it."

Shane rubbed his chin. "Only one, huh? What's your middle name?"

The question surprised her enough that she answered without thinking. "Nicolaevna."

He cocked his head. "There's a story behind that name. Maybe you'll share it with me some time."

Unlikely, but then, she'd have thought the same thing about developing magical powers, meeting a god, and going into hiding. All of which turned out to be extremely likely.

"I suppose we'll see."

Shane smiled at her restrained response as if she'd just challenged him. Maybe she had. If his pursuit of friendship was any indication, he wasn't the type to give up easily. Ana moved past him to open the door.

He picked up the not-so-subtle hint and made his way to the exit, stopping next to her to search her face. "I have one more question."

Ana crossed her arms and leaned against the frame. "Now you're getting pushy."

"A simple yes or no, I promise. Are you going to the Lantern Festival tonight?"

"I hadn't planned on it." Why hadn't she just said no? She'd made it sound like all she needed was a good reason to attend.

"I'm meeting Kora and David at nine. Why don't you join us?"

Because she couldn't afford to like him any more than she already did. Not to mention, people would definitely notice magical glowing hands after nightfall. Unfortunately, she couldn't tell that to Shane. "That was two more questions, and I don't enjoy festivals."

He raised a brow. "You moved to a small town where there's a festival almost every weekend."

"That doesn't mean I enjoy them." Ana hated that she had to lie and stay hidden. Leaving her old life had given her the chance at freedom, but her current life squandered the opportunity.

Shane shoved his hands in his pockets and shrugged. "Maybe you haven't gone with the right people."

And was he the right people? She pressed her lips together to keep the words inside. Eight months, she'd been hiding. For what? To live the same lonely, sad existence she'd had before?

Ana wavered, staring across the room at the bland, grey couch which doubled as her bed. Almost nothing in this apartment was hers. She'd left Magnolia with a suitcase and a backpack to come to Deckard, where she'd lived for months in Moira's guest room.

Before the accident, she'd been plagued by restless energy, pushing her body to the limits on the practice floor again and again. Ana's injury had forced a change, but the twitchy feeling didn't go away, slowly building again until it clamored in her head, as if she needed to stretch and move. Taking over the apartment had been a big first step in claiming her life, but she wanted that forward motion to be a beginning not an end.

Shane watched her and waited. Hot air blew across her legs from the open door, reminding Ana of his quick actions when she'd hurt herself by forgetting to be cautious.

She tried to discourage him one more time. "Aren't the festivals just an excuse to get people to spend money?"

"Partly, but they're also an excuse to socialize and create a sense of community. They can be fun if you let them."

"I seriously doubt that," she muttered.

"Then give me a chance to prove your terrible opinion wrong. I promise you'll have fun."

Ana wanted to go. Not for the festival, she'd been mostly truthful there, but to spend time with people she enjoyed. Add Shane to the mix with his quiet confidence and undeniable charms? That cop car fantasy wasn't too far off.

He must have sensed her caving because he held his hands up in surrender. "You'll be with your boss and her husband in addition to me, and I promise to leave the hand-cuffs at home."

"Okay, I'll go, but don't be disappointed if I cling to the shadows and want to leave early."

A broad grin spread across his face. "I promised you fun.

If that means lurking and people watching, I'm with you, but you have to at least try the funnel cake."

Ana bit her cheek to keep from smiling back like a giddy child. "I can agree to that."

"And I'm paying."

She narrowed her eyes. "I can pay for myself."

"Nope. I refuse to allow you to use cost as an excuse to not have fun. Besides, what kind of a date would I be if I didn't?"

Ana tilted her head. "Since when is this a date?"

He reached out and pulled one of her hands free to kiss her knuckles. "Since I convinced you to spend time with me."

The touch of his lips sent heat rushing through her. "You and my boss and her husband and most of the town. Not very romantic."

Shane rubbed his thumb across her fingers then let go. "I like to start small and work my way up to grand gestures. I'll swing by around eight forty-five. Wear something comfortable."

"There you go again, dictating my clothes."

He waggled his eyebrows. "In that case, I'd like to put in a request for a unicorn onesie. The horn just does it for me."

Ana couldn't help it—she laughed at his antics. "Go away, Shane. I have things to do this afternoon."

He did a ridiculous, triumphant dance out of her apartment that involved wiggling arms and a hip maneuver she'd like to see again in different circumstances. "I knew we'd get there. I'll see you tonight, Ana Winters."

She shook her head and waved at him as he bounded down the stairs. A little thrill of excitement wouldn't let her hold back the smile anymore as she closed the door. In less than an hour, Shane had coaxed her into friendly banter and a sort-of date. Not to mention given her fodder for her fantasies with his touch.

The man was more dangerous than she'd given him credit for. She'd have to be careful at the festival. One night of fun could ruin all her careful planning, especially if his temptation proved too much to resist.

Ana ripped open the first box where Shane had set it and started unpacking new linens—yet another gift from Kora and David. She absently stacked them on the couch while she replayed the encounter in her head. Nothing stuck out at her as suspicious, but how would she know until it was too late?

What she *did* remember clearly was the silky promise in his voice.

*See you tonight, Ana Winters.* He was half right. She'd meet him tonight, but he wouldn't be seeing Ana Winters.

Technically, Ana Winters didn't exist.

---

Did you enjoy your first chapter? Snag your copy of Divinity Bound today!

DIVINITY BOUND

# A NOTE FROM NICOLE

I *love* Greek gods. Can you tell? This series will have a lot of twists and turns, but it'll be rooted in all that juicy mythology we can't get enough of. Personally, my favorite has always been Hades, and I'm making sure each of the major gods gets some book time. Which are you most excited to see? Send me an email at nicolehallbooks@ gmail.com and let me know.

Special thanks to Joel R. Williams III, SSgt, USAF for his knowledge of the Armed Forces. Any mistakes made are my own. As always, I would be nowhere without my editing gurus: Nicole Schneider, Liz Gallegos, and Jo Perry.

Curious about Kora's magic and Ana's secrets? You'll find out more in Ana and Shane's book, Divinity Bound. Want to know Dax's real name? See if he tells in the Goddess Forsaken Bonus Scene, click here or find it on my website (www.nicolehallbooks.com).

Join Muse Interrupted Romance, my Facebook group, for daily shenanigans and sexy man chest pictures. Sign up for my newsletter, for first access to new releases plus extra content, giveaways, sneak peeks, and first looks at new covers.

If you have time, would you mind leaving a review on Amazon, Goodreads, or Bookbub? Reviews help other readers like you find books they love.

~Nicole

## ALSO BY NICOLE HALL

Modern Magic series

Modern Magic

Accidental Magic

Insidious Magic

Treacherous Magic

Impulsive Magic

Rebellious Magic

Chaotic Magic

Rise of the Old Gods series

Muse Interrupted

Goddess Forsaken

Divinity Bound

# ABOUT THE AUTHOR

Nicole Hall is a smart-ass with a Ph.D. and a potty mouth. She writes stories that have magic, sass, and romance because she believes that everyone deserves a little happiness. Coffee makes her happy, messes make her stabby, and she'd sell one of her children for a second season of Firefly.

Let Nicole know what you thought about her sassy, magical world because she really does love hearing from readers. Find her at www.nicolehallbooks.com or Muse Interrupted Romance on Facebook!

Want to find out when the newest Nicole Hall book hits the shelves? Sign up for the weekly Muse Interrupted newsletter. You'll get a welcome gift plus new release info, giveaways, exclusive content, and previews of the new books especially for fans.

Cover designed by Germancreative

Edited by Jolene Perry, Waypoint Author Academy